Only Fools and Horsepower

John Nevill

Michael Terence Publishing

First published in paperback by
Michael Terence Publishing in 2020
www.mtp.agency

ISBN 9781913653934

This book is dedicated to all the guys that never made it home; to all the long-suffering wives and girlfriends of TIR drivers; and to Micky Rogers, the bastard that got me hooked in the first place.

'The time has come,' the Walrus said, 'to talk of many things: of shoes, and ships, and sealing wax. Of cabbages and kings, and why the sea is boiling hot, and whether pigs have wings.'

One

Of belly tanks and dipsticks

Apart from a lone security guard sitting in a small plastic cabin with his feet on the desk, the rest of East India Docks seemed deserted when I arrived.

I could see the guy watching 'Match of the Day' on a fuzzy black and white portable. He looked relaxed and comfortable, and I was in two minds whether to disturb him… but it was raining and I was getting wet, so I thumped on the door anyway.

I obviously took him by surprise because he jumped involuntarily and his feet were airborne in an instant. It's as well he wasn't drinking anything because he went into a bit of a speed-wobble and nearly fell off his chair. Trying not to laugh I watched as he shoved a peaked cap on his head and made to open the door all in one urgent movement.

As we faced each other in the dripping doorway the guy tried to adopt an air of authority, which didn't work - and didn't quite suit the situation either: this was the East End of London on a wet Sunday morning - not high noon at Tombstone, Arizona.

I smiled, said hello, and told him why I was there. But he was obviously pissed off at being caught on the hop because, although his expression softened a bit, he continued to play the Sheriff. He shook his head slowly, knowingly, and said something like, 'Er, I don't think so, Chief.'

I took an instant dislike to him.

I told him again that I had to meet someone, but he wouldn't have it, and I began to wish I'd simply walked straight past his cabin in the first place. Jobsworth said he couldn't let me in for security reasons - but I began to suspect otherwise: I think the match must have been boring because it was becoming obvious that he just wanted some company and an ear-hole to bend.

That was all I needed. I was on a mission and had more important things on my mind than idle chit-chat, so I Insisted that I was going to be met by somebody.

'Who's that then?' he demanded as if he were testing me.

'Roy Bradford,' I answered. 'He's at…'

'Oh yes,' he interrupted. 'I know him. I'm sorry squire, but he's not in today.'

I assured him that he would be but he just laughed, a bit too smugly, I thought. He then proceeded to tell me that no one was at work anywhere in the docks that morning, nor, as far as he knew, would there be 'til the following day.

I knew he was lying.

He reminded me of the train-spotter type, with his silly self-satisfied grin and trousers that didn't reach his shoes. I guessed his name to be Malcolm and cringed at the thought of any kind of conversation with him - even though I was an hour early and had nothing else to do - so I kept insisting, saying Roy wouldn't be happy if I was late.

He seemed a bit put out by that and said, haughtily, that if I really wanted I was free to find out for myself - Matey!

So I did.

He was right.

As I walked between the crumbly old buildings I got the impression that the whole area had been abandoned ages ago and discovered what a depressing place the docks could be on a gloomy Sunday morning. The fact that it was now pissing down didn't help much, and I suddenly found it difficult to be excited at the prospect of starting a new job.

Because I didn't have a car to shelter in I had to take refuge in the doorway of an old warehouse. It was cold and the whole place stank of rotting vegetables and dead bonfires. The docks themselves hadn't been used as such for ages and the only ships in residence were half-sunken rusting hulks waiting to be salvaged for scrap.

The warehouses had been taken over by various small businesses as workshops, haulage yards, etc. and just about everywhere else was overgrown with weeds and strewn with litter. It reminded me in an odd way of the railway allotments we used to play on as kids, and I soon began to idly reminisce, thinking of a dozen things I'd rather have been doing than standing in a dank warehouse doorway waiting for someone to show up... but talking to a member of the blue anorak brigade wasn't one of them.

I'd changed location and was marking time under a staircase when my new boss eventually rolled up an hour and a half later. I had both hands in my pockets and was hunched up against the weather looking and feeling a bit sorry for myself, but I got no sympathy from Roy - very few people do. Instead he just squeezed his huge frame out of the van, nodded in my direction and ran up the stairs to open the portacabin with something like a smile on his bearded face.

For some reason he made me nervous. I think it was the fact that in appearance he reminded me of Geoff Capes, and his body language gave me the impression that he was about to rip the portacabin off its stilts and chuck it into the Thames. I gingerly followed him into the 'office' as he switched on the electric fire and glared at it, as if daring it not to work, then plonked himself down into a battered old swivel chair. It groaned as he spun round and opened a drawer in his desk. Without looking up from something important on the cluttered tabletop, he simply tossed a bunch of keys at me and said 'Here you go - DIP 334. It's out front.'

I think I'd expected more of a welcome than that, but all I did get was the impression that he didn't want me in his office. So, even though I was really gagging for a cuppa, I tactfully decided against asking if he was going to put the kettle on and retreated, preferring instead to show some enthusiasm for the job.

Back outside in the rain once again I fumbled with the doorlock of a rusty old Irish registered 111 Scania, trying one wrong key after another, and getting even colder and wetter in the process, until I realised that the bloody thing hadn't been locked in the first place...

I could sense Roy watching me from the comfort of his office, and could almost hear him laughing, but I didn't know whether to be embarrassed or angry. In frustration, I yanked the door open and let it bounce against the hinges, threw my wet bags in and climbed up after them growling at myself.

Once inside the truck I remembered something important and my mood quickly changed again as I clambered across the cab to the driver's seat on the left-hand side, trying to make it look like a pre-planned manoeuvre.

My stomach knotted as I settled behind the wheel of that truck for the first time, and I suddenly felt like a kid again on Christmas Day. There were so many things to play with I just didn't know where to start: The cab itself was huge, the driving position much higher up from the ground than I'd expected, and the steering wheel seemed oddly out of place. It was small in comparison to the size of the truck and looked like it belonged more to a Transit van. Having the gearstick in my right hand also felt strange - especially when it described a much larger circle in neutral than it ought to when I stirred it around. But it was pleasing in an odd way: this was a real international truck - a 'left-hooker'.

Apart from the windscreen wipers, everything else seemed just the same as it would in a right-hand drive, including the pedals - which my feet didn't reach. It then took a couple of minutes before I realised that to any outside spectators I must have looked like a ten-year-old kid playing in his dad's car as I bounced wildly up and down trying to adjust a drivers seat that refused to budge... So I decided I'd better try and contain myself. Being my first day on a new job I knew I couldn't afford to stuff things up by blundering around like the beginner that I was: I had to at least behave like I knew what I was doing. One false move, I figured, would surely give the game away then I'd not only be out on my ear, but probably cop a black eye into the bargain.

Or so I thought at the time.

I was to have a passenger with me that day, Tony Gillier, a stocky fair-haired man in his early thirties, with a mean expression, a bum-fluff beard and a wonderful, though thoroughly undeserved nickname - Naked Brain. Tony arrived unseen as I was playing with my new toy and had gone straight upstairs to the office for a cup of tea!

Tony, an Essex man and a regular subbie (sub-contractor), had arranged to get a lift with me because his own truck wasn't in the country that day. It was parked in the docks at Zeebrugge, Belgium, where he'd left it on return from his last trip rather than bringing it back into England - a common practise at the time for those without certain paperwork...

In consideration of this a loaded trailer had been shipped over to Belgium for him 'unaccompanied', where it now awaited his arrival. As we were both loaded for the same destination – Salimpaşari Customs, (pronounced Salim-pashar), Istanbul, Turkey - (not much of a delivery address I know, but Tony didn't seem bothered). I had been given the important task of chauffeuring him and all of his kit to Zeebrugge with instructions to 'stick with him, follow the arse-end of his trailer wherever it goes, and do whatever he tells you…'

Simple huh?

Well that, at any rate, was plan A…

Thankfully, Roy didn't hang around long once he'd given us our instructions for the trip, handed over a wad of 'run money', and a mountain of paperwork to each of us. He said his Sunday dinner was in the oven, but Tony reckoned he was probably hoping to get a couple of pints down his neck before he went home to face it. Then Roy's final words of 'encouragement' before we left consisted of: 'Get there, get back, and don't spend all my money on the piss – okay?'

I was stunned and thought, fuck me! What's he on about? But all I could do was nod my head nervously, not really knowing what else to do. I looked across to Tony for a clue, but he just laughed as he dropped his kit over the balcony at me, so I figured Roy had simply made a joke, picked myself up and left it at that.

That left Tony and me, a stack of incomprehensible paperwork you could have wallpapered a four-bedroomed house with, and a bloody great truck that I was about to aim in the general direction of Turkey! Shit, I thought, this is really it!

I suddenly wanted to go back home.

It was December 1985. I was all of twenty something, a bit naïve, full of pride and, if the truth be known, a little bit scared, but more than chuffed with myself at having landed such an exciting job. I was about to fulfil a dream by shipping out to an exotic overseas place on my very first overland trip as a TIR driver (TIR: Transports Internationale Routiers. Fr. - International Road Transport) - and this was it - there was no turning back!

The rules and regulations of the TIR Convention - the official gobbledegook governing the administration and movement of commercial goods between countries within the E.U. and those outside (and between those not connected with the E.U. at all) - were written up in French. I don't know why, perhaps because the acronyms are easier to pronounce. I mean, IRT driver doesn't have quite the same appeal, does it? But on the road TIR more commonly stands for 'This Is Ridiculous', which is much closer to the mark (as I was soon to discover). It was under such rules that I would now be expected to work. A set of rules completely different and much more complicated (and often ridiculous) than any I'd had to work under elsewhere and of which, I freely admit, I knew bugger all.

I was nervous. I was in the company of a professional TIR driver now and desperately wanted to do the right thing. It felt like the first day at a new school, but there were no other kids around to take my cues from, so I had to try and bluff it, to try and make an impression on my own instead of hiding in the crowd waiting for someone else to make the first move.

Age 9, 15th June 1966

The only drawback to me making a good impression in front of Tony was the small but important fact that I had only ever driven an articulated truck once before in my entire life. And, sadly for me, I was about to prove it.

The biggest thing I'd driven before with any regularity was a 2800 DAF furniture van - and that hadn't weighed in at close to forty tonnes, didn't have the steering wheel on the 'wrong' side, and didn't 'bend in the middle' as artics do.

Naturally I'd neglected to mention this at the job interview, but suddenly wondered if I should let Tony in on the secret or not. Stupidly, I decided not to. I figured it was a bit too late in the day to start making kerbside confessions and considered asking Tony if he wanted to drive instead - seeing as he knew the way and all that - but I realised that wouldn't do either. I could hardly expect my passenger to drive the truck simply because I didn't know how to, could I? Or because I was shitting bricks. My pride wouldn't allow it. And after all, I'd been clever enough to bullshit my way into the job in the first place, hadn't I? So why not this? I mean, at the end of the day, driving trucks is what the job's all about…

It was about two hundred yards to the exit gate - a bloody long way it seemed to me at the time - especially with all those broken palettes and abandoned cars in the way. So I took a lot longer than I really needed to get my kit sorted out, stow things away, check all the knobs and switches etc… but I knew I couldn't put it off forever. Tony was getting impatient with my dithering for one thing, and by hanging it out I was just making myself more nervous. So, with the engine already running and sufficiently 'warmed up' - something I'd been told was important - I sized things up in my mind, lit another fag and set off… in the wrong gear.

I quickly decided that trying to find the proper gear would be a waste of time because the truck soon stopped bouncing up and down. It put me off a bit though because I was suddenly wary of trying to find the next gear up: the gear stick was really sloppy - like the linkage had come adrift - and I was worried that I might crunch the gear, or miss it altogether… so I left it in third. And anyway, as far as I was concerned, I was already in the next gear up.

I managed to steer around all the obstacles successfully and really surprised myself when I reached Malcolm's hut without killing anything but, as I looked over at Tony to say something I saw a strange expression on his face. It immediately spoke volumes. It said: 'You wanker'.

I felt like a complete dipstick. Two minutes into the job and I'd given the game away already. It did nothing for my pride, and even less for my confidence, but there was worse to come: as I tried to get out of the dock and onto the busy main road I failed to give enough turning room for the 'forty foot' trailer in tow, and came very close to knocking down the old brick wall that ran the length of the docks. That was when I did what any sensible person in my position would have done - I panicked. Trying desperately to correct my mistake I promptly over-steered in the opposite direction and took us straight into the path of an oncoming bus.

My new friend wasn't very impressed - I could tell - but he was good enough not to say as much. In fact, I heard nothing more than a whimper really; no screaming, no hysterics… I was impressed. I put this commendable behaviour down to the stoicism of an experienced TIR driver, made a mental note of it for future reference, and nervously carried on. However, after zigzagging my way through the Blackwall Tunnel just half a mile or so from the docks - and which, believe me, looks impossibly small from the cab of a truck - I did hear some other, stranger noises that told me his resolve might have been crumbling a bit.

Considering the amount of adrenaline that was rushing about inside my veins it was a miracle I drove the next few miles without doing any serious damage, and when we eventually reached the M2 motorway, trembling, but thankfully in one piece, it was a sheer delight for both of us.

I remember the motorway seemed extra wide that afternoon especially after the confines of the tunnel, and because of it I began to relax a bit and started to get the 'feel' of the truck. The width I was pretty much okay with, but the length of it took some getting used to: fifty-feet-and-some is a big difference to the length of a furniture van, and it was off-putting to know that I couldn't judge exactly where the back end of the trailer was in relation to everything else. The biggest help here was that in England when one truck passes another, the guy on the inside will flash his lights to let the other driver know that it's okay to pull in. Without that, I reckon I would have sideswiped the first truck I tried to overtake.

Most surprising of all was the incredible amount of weight behind me. The load on board weighed in at twenty-one tonnes, I was carrying a tonne and a half of diesel (1500 litres), plus the truck and trailer itself which weighed in at fifteen tonnes empty! Couple that with the spare wheels, tools, and all the other bits and bobs that international trucks carry, and you come up with a gross weight of thirty-eight tonnes - and more! That weight coupled with the forces of gravity 'pushed' the truck down even the gentlest of slopes with an amazing ferocity, like it had a mind of its own, and I was constantly on the brakes to keep the speed below warp-factor. Uphill was the exact opposite, where the forces of nature intervened again to slow the truck to half its speed in a matter of seconds, which kept taking me by surprise, and I was up and down the gearbox like a racing driver just to stop the thing from stalling.

It felt so alien to me: watching the trailer in my huge wing-mirrors as it followed my every move; learning to change gear at the right time without crunching them, knowing when to brake - and when not to - and getting used to the size and weight of it all. No drive before or since has ever been the same. At the time I could hardly believe my luck: here I was behind the wheel of a fully freighted '38 Tonner' thundering down Her Majesty's Highways en-route to an exciting overseas destination, and I was buzzing!

However, just as I thought I was getting the hang of it all we came to the top of Jubilee Way, just outside Dover, when it was suggested that I might like to stay in a low gear (I had ten to choose from) and try to keep my foot on the exhaust-brake button (auxiliary brake system) as 'It's a long downhill run into the docks and we don't want to arrive too quickly, do we?'

I nodded, but having been a little unnerved by Tony's sudden concern, I forgot to ask if he knew where the exhaust-brake button was and, as a consequence, we went screaming down Jubilee Way like the 7th Cavalry in full charge, with the engine revving its bollocks off and threatening to explode at any moment and throw bits of itself all over Kent. By luck more than judgement I managed to steer her around the roundabout at the bottom of the hill instead of zooming straight across it, and eventually brought the whole lot to a shuddering halt twenty yards past the police box at the entrance gate, when I accidentally pulled the dead-man's handle on instead of the indicator.

The trailer creaked as it rocked from side to side and I realised I was still holding my breath. I let it out slowly, hoping not to show the fear I'd felt during our unceremonious entry, when it suddenly dawned on me. My ordeal was over, I was there - Dover docks – I'd made it! The shell shock disappeared rapidly and I felt a great surge of relief. I then looked across to say something big-headed to Tony just in time to see him leaping silently out of the cab...

I soon stopped trembling, regained control of my knees and began to feel really chuffed with myself: I had conquered the biggest hurdle and driven this monstrous truck all the way from London to the south coast of England without mishap - well, almost - and I felt like a hero! My confidence returned and suddenly I was ready for more: I was impatient. I wanted to book straight onto a ferry and get going - I knew I could do it, I'd just proved that - now I wanted to get across the channel and prove it to the rest of the world... I was invincible and thought that nothing could stop me!

Unfortunately, Her Majesty's Customs and Excise had other ideas, and it was a full two days later before Tony and I headed cautiously up the loading ramp of a Zeebrugge-bound Townsend Thorenson freight ferry, with severely amended paperwork and thumping hangovers.

During our two day 'rest' at Dover I learnt a valuable lesson. It was that this sort of thing happens all the time and that the job simply cannot be rushed. Problems of all sorts, I discovered, are common on TIR work, and hold-ups that run into days are the norm. I would have to learn how to be patient. This, I soon found out, is best achieved in the relaxed atmosphere of the nearest bar, and in that department Tony proved to be a very patient and helpful tutor.

Tony made no mention at all of my peculiar driving habits during this time, for which I was more than grateful. He'd probably seen it all before anyway. Because of that I was able to relax in his company and before long we got on quite well. Especially when it was my round.

Tony's trailer was out of action when he eventually went to collect it in Belgium. The belly tank - a reserve diesel tank slung under the chassis - had been damaged. Hundreds of litres of red diesel (rebated diesel - duty free - for use outside the E.U.) had spilled all over the loading deck of the ferry and, more obviously to us because of the yards of sand on the ground, all over the trailer park in the docks which, needless to say, had made a little bit of a mess.

It was their fault. One of the 'Tuggies', a shunter, whose job it is to take unaccompanied trailers on and off the ferries, had accidentally punctured the tank, so it was down to the ferry company to put things right. Yet another hold-up, but I was under instructions to stay with Tony so, hard as it was, we bit our lips and promptly did the grand tour of Zeebrugge – which we did our best to drink dry.

Then, because Christmas had crept up on us by the time we got rolling and crossed Germany in record time, the Austrians - lovely people that they are - decided to wait until we both entered 'no man's land' between the two borders before putting the barrier down across the road for three days.

We were then 'forced' to put up in a cute little hotel in Salzburg for the duration - one of those wonky, half-timbered jobs with coats of arms and mediaeval writing all over the place – where Tony got so out of it that he didn't even notice the huge great castle - the Hohensalzburg Fortress - a beautiful 1200-year-old edifice that dominates the city and which loomed right outside our bedroom window, until it was time to leave!

The rest of that trip continued in pretty much the same vein which, from start to finish, should have only taken two weeks or so. At the end of the day, it was closer to five! And we didn't even get a bollocking for it! It had been one of those great, traditional British cock-ups from the word go. I'd not only loved every moment of it, but it also meant I was 'in' – and proud of it!

I'd made some good friends in some low places, spent more money than I thought was possible, had some outrageous laughs on the strength of it, and still been paid for all my troubles!

I learnt other things on that trip too, not least of which were Roy's final words of 'encouragement': 'Get there, get back, and don't spend all my money on the piss.' We did – spend all his money on the piss that is, but at least now his enigmatic words made more sense to me. As for his money… well, that's the way it goes.

As I learnt, there are no official qualifications needed to become a TIR driver. Only unofficial ones. Unlike a tradesman who has to train for years to become qualified and is then presented with a piece of paper to prove it – lorry driving is not classed as a trade, so nobody gets issued with diplomas or certificates for doing it. You need not be a mechanic to drive a truck. Nor does the job rely on a driver's ability to speak German, Greek or Arabic, or be able to quote every road number between Barking and Baghdad.

It's just not like that.

I discovered it's very much a matter of a person's attitude with TIR work - not aptitude. And the apprenticeship, if there is such a thing, is done the hard way. First hand. Behind the wheel, and alone.

Where no-one can hear you scream…

Two

Of bandits and bullet holes

At the end of that first trip I really felt proud of myself and swaggered around a lot, acting like a conquering hero returned from war. I felt I'd achieved something great and unique, as if nobody else had done it before, simply because I'd driven a battered old truck across Europe and back.

And didn't everyone get to know about it.

I went back to the pub I was living at, the Malt and Hops in Kings Cross, and spent the best part of a week boring everyone shitless with stories of bandits and bullet-holes. I was so full of myself that I must have been a right pain in the arse to anyone within earshot of the bar. The regulars at that pub, including Dave the normally patient landlord, must have thought their prayers had been answered when I eventually had a phone call to tell me it was time to ship out again.

I was to leave England that time full of enthusiasm, but with a head far too big for my inexperienced shoulders, though it wouldn't be too long before I was brought down a peg. To date I had done just the one, not-very-successful trip to Istanbul, and I'd only achieved that by tagging along behind someone else. Even so, I really thought I knew it all, but I was to be taught a very valuable lesson: I was to learn that there is more to TIR work than I could have imagined; that there is a much more serious side to the job than fun and games and simply aiming a truck in the right direction. I was to be taught that lesson by my own ignorance and one other inescapable factor – Winter.

The winter of 1985-86 was pretty severe across mainland Europe – even by its normal standards – and I was totally unprepared for it. The only winters I'd experienced before were mostly tame English ones, those that descend on London, and the odd one or two in South Wales where our Nan lived – you know, the cold, damp and gloomy ones. And the only snow I'd really seen was one heavy fall in the Brecon

Beacons and the few flakes that sometimes fell down 'The Cally' – Caledonian Road – and I always remembered that as being fun.

I never knew that the snow that falls in Central and Eastern Europe wasn't just a few flakes, or that it wouldn't be quite as much fun. Well, I wouldn't have – I didn't spend a lot of time in Geography classes at school, and nobody else had bothered to tell me about it. Neither had anybody bothered to tell me that driving on the stuff in an articulated truck was bloody dangerous.

So off I went in blissful ignorance.

I was loaded for Istanbul again, which I thought was great because I reckoned I knew the way by now and didn't need to follow anyone. It was also my first real opportunity to show that I could do the job unassisted.

This time I had a different truck. The rusty old Scania had been handed back to its regular driver after the Christmas break and I'd been put in charge of an old Mack instead. The Mack, WZM 307, belonged to Ernie Samuels, an owner-driver from Southend. A quiet-spoken, accident-prone man with a permanent tan and long sideburns – a smashing bloke. Ernie knew what winter was all about – but he didn't bother telling me. Well, he wouldn't have – he wanted me to drive his lorry.

The Mack was a prehistoric animal. It was huge – much bigger than the Scania – and it was mean-looking. It had a dented chimney (exhaust stack); a monstrous sleeper cab with studded leather upholstery and was big enough to sleep three people. It had two bent gear-sticks, one for low and high range and the other for the gears; it had five reverse speeds and dozens of knobs and switches whose functions I never did figure out – probably because none of them worked. It had bits of chrome all over the place – mostly on the floor where they kept dropping off and, just to round it off, it had multi-coloured flames painted up both doors and a picture of Mickey Mouse on the front! If the truth were known, it was nothing more than a rusty old nail that had been driven into the ground, but it was Ernie's pride and joy, and I thought it was the dog's bollocks.

Or at least I did to start with.

The trip down to Turkey wasn't too bad. It took the regulation week or so to get there, what with cancellations, and drinking sessions, and the weather had been fine. It was cold but clear, so driving conditions were good and the three of us that ended up 'running' together kept stopping in lay-bys to have driving competitions in the Mack to see who could get most gear changes in reverse without jack-knifing or killing anything.

When I eventually got to Turkey, having gone via the 'tourist route', i.e. straight through Yugoslavia to Greece, and along the Northern Greek coastline, the Mack broke down halfway between the Turkish border and Istanbul.

It was nothing deadly serious at the time: the bolts that held the half shaft in, (the shafts that turn the wheels), had come loose and were shearing themselves off one by one, which meant I was in danger of losing my drive. Had the 'diff-lock' worked I could have locked the gearing together and driven on just the one shaft, at least to get me out of trouble – but this was the Mack and the only thing that worked on it was the ashtray.

Being short on spanners and spares – and know-how – the three of us put our heads together to bodge things up for running repairs, using just about everything bar sticky-backed paper. But it did the job and we managed to creep into Istanbul without having to call out the cavalry.

Our regular stopping place then was 'The Chefs' (chef is a commonly used word for boss, chief) at Avçilar – a rough and ready Caterpillar repair yard about fifteen kilometres west of down-town Istanbul itself. It had a muddy pot-holed car park the size of a tennis court, a small workshop, a drivers' room that needed an oil change, and an outside 'spread-axle' toilet (hole in the ground, no cistern, a bottle of water to wash the shit off your arse and a stick to poke everything down with)... But we liked it, mostly because it was cheap and convenient. For years it was always known as 'our' yard in Turkey, because it resembled the shit-hole at the East India Dock, and because very few other drivers from outside our company – Tanker International – bothered to use it.

In residence at the Chefs was 'our' mechanic – Kasim – a local lad the size and density of a brick spread-axle shit-house, who did most of our repair work – often on tick – and who used to get on well with the drivers because it was they who had taught him English over the years. Hence a driver would often be greeted with something like 'Ullo you cun', are you iz 'en? Izzy goot? Wassa proberlem kamyon? Gimme sossige sannerwidge, cuppa tea, gissa fag… Fuck off 'en!' Or words to that effect. A great bloke, Kasim – strong as an ox and would do anything for the drivers. He commanded a lot of respect.

Kasim did the necessary bodge job on my half shaft and gave it the usual Turkish guarantee, i.e. from the workshop to the main road, and I thought no more of it. When I'd finished tipping (unloading) and had a day or three on the beer with the rest of the lads, as you do, the weather was still quite reasonable, so I suspected nothing. All that talk I'd heard in the drivers' restaurant from the old hands on Middle East work about ridiculous temperatures, frozen brakes, methanol, snow-chains, paraffin mixed with diesel, and thermal undies, seemed nothing more than beer talk and hot air to me, so I just let it go in one ear and straight out of the other. I was more interested in drinking large quantities of Efes – the local beer – and having a crack with the lads… which turned out to be a mistake.

On the way back from Turkey the weather started to take a bit of a turn. I was sent up into the hills of Bulgaria to load twenty tonnes of wine for England and while I was there it started to snow. Not much to begin with, but enough to make the going uncomfortable. The roads in 'Bulgy' are bad enough anyway, what with pot-holes, cracked edges, crumbling surfaces, or surfaces worn to a dangerously smooth shine, but I hadn't realised just how dangerous those roads could be to an artic when there was a covering of snow on them. I'd always assumed that because articulated trucks are so heavy that they'd have no problem with a bit of snow on the ground; that they'd be able to plough on through and not even be bothered by it.

As I discovered it's quite the opposite: with no weight on board a truck can very easily lose traction. Wheel spinning, even on wet roads, is common, especially uphill, and even more so on that British favourite – the 'twin-steer'. Trailer wheels have no difficulty 'locking up' and skidding either. Air brakes (brakes operated by a compressed-air system) are *very* efficient and too much pressure applied to the foot-pedal – which is all too easily done on bumpy roads – will simply cause one or more wheels to 'lock', creating the risk of every drivers' nightmare – a jack-knife, miles from the nearest bar.

On snow and ice those risks are increased many-fold… and if I ever find the dickhead who came out with the saying 'New snow, driver go', I'm going to bury him in the Blue Peter garden with a snow-chain up his squeezy bottle!

It's obvious really, but I didn't know why I was wheel-spinning or why my brakes insisted on locking up every time I touched the brake pedal – I just continued to slip and slide my way across Bulgaria's hills looking for a winery until my trailer ended up in a ditch. Apart from scaring me shitless, it only cost a few packets of fags to get pulled back onto the road by one of the locals, but I was so embarrassed with myself I never told anyone about it afterwards.

Most English trucks were 'running' (transiting) through Yugoslavia at the time, as opposed to Romania and the other Commie Bloc countries, and that's where I made my way back to after I'd eventually got loaded. From the border at Gradina we would transit west-ish through Nis, Belgrade, Zagreb and Maribor up to Austria – and on into civilisation. But that time I only got as far as Slavonski Brod – between Belgrade and Zagreb (now Croatia) when the bolts that Kasim so generously replaced in Avçilar started popping again:

BANG! One went off like a gunshot and scared the living daylights out of me – then, BANG!... and another BANG! Until all of a sudden the bloody truck just didn't want to go any further. Panicking, I made what I considered a valiant attempt at free-wheeling into a petrol station before I got stranded on the roadside, but I even made a balls-up of that because I slid in there a bit too rapidly on the snow, hit the brakes, bent her double and ended up with my unit blocking off the pumps and the arse-end of my trailer sticking right out in the road.

As luck would have it, there was a small workshop next to the garage and a friendly 'Cloggie' – a Dutchman – parked on the snow-covered forecourt right next to that. The Cloggie – bless his wooden socks – ended up towing me backwards off the road so I was out of everyone's way, then courteously played the part by sharing my beer and indulging in the usual round of piss-taking, 'Fokking vell don English – yor modder vood be really proud of you... Does she know you are oud in dis ting?' And so on.

In the end it cost me a crate of beer and four hundred Deutschmarks.

The beer went to a worthwhile cause – two hangovers – and the Deutschmarks, the most commonly used currency in a lot of European countries, went to the 'Jughead' (Yugoslav) mechanics who very kindly bodged the repairs and ripped me off for the privilege.

That day the snow started to fall in earnest. But I didn't care at the time: I was mobile once again and all I wanted to do was get up to the border and try to get through it into Austria.

On the way to the border – which was a good few hours driving time from Slavonski Brod – the snow started to fall like leaves, millions of them, all to-ing and fro-ing as they floated down. It was weird to drive through. It had a hypnotising effect on me and I kept feeling as if it were the road itself that was moving under my wheels, instead of the truck actually moving forwards. Einstein would have had something to say about it.

I had to keep blinking and screwing up my eyes to try and keep everything in context. Opening the window helped, it kept me awake but it was bloody uncomfortable. It was also very slippery. I spent a lot of time in the middle of the road trying to stay on course because of the severe camber, and it was just as well that there was very little other traffic on the road, otherwise I'm sure I would have had an accident.

It wasn't long before I started to get pissed off with slipping all over the place and all I kept thinking about was the border. Once I was through it, I told myself, I could park up, go to bed and forget all about the snow and the driving, when suddenly there was another BANG! Yet another bolt had sheared off! I could hardly believe it! I'd only just had the bloody thing repaired – *a second time!* And here I was listening to the new bolts popping off again.

I was fuming, but what could I do? I couldn't turn around and take the truck back to Slavonski Brod – it was too far for one thing, it was snowing like a pig, and it was also in the wrong direction. No driver likes to go back over the miles he's already covered, it's self-defeating, time wasting and also a waste of precious diesel. And anyway, what would be the point? I'd already been ripped off once for a repair job that obviously wasn't any good.

BANG!... Another one went. Fuck it, I thought, I'm nearly at the border... BANG!... Bollocks – keep going. Every five or ten k's (kilometres) another bolt would pop. I'd stop, try to find it – or what was left of it – hammer it back into one of the least elongated holes and just carry on, hoping for the best.

By the time I got to Sentilj, the Yugoslav side of the border with Austria, the snow was about a foot or more deep. I was slipping and sliding all over the road and my heart was in my mouth. It's a hairy experience to have a loaded warehouse (trailer) trying to overtake the office (truck) when it's supposed to stay in place behind and do what it's told. And I really didn't want to come off the road twice in one trip.

I had only two or three knackered bolts left in place as I slid into the car park, and it was such a relief to be off the road again when, BA-BANG – PING – CLUNK!... The remaining bolts noisily disappeared and the half-shaft noisily parted company with the truck! And that was that... Goodnight Vienna.

I think I screamed then. I'd had enough. I was soaking wet and freezing cold from rummaging around in the snow looking for broken bolts, completely knackered and very pissed off with it all. But at least I'd made it to the border – even if I was still on the 'wrong' side of it. After I'd fully expected to get stranded on the roadside all night, I was now off the road and could at last breathe a sigh of relief.

Or so I thought.

I decided enough was enough for one day – I just wanted to sleep. It was still snowing, as cold as a witch's tit, and there was nothing I could do anyway – so I left the engine running, kicked off my boots, and went to bed fully clothed right where the truck had stopped itself.

It made no odds where I was 'parked' – the rest of the car park was deserted. A sheet of pure white, so I was in no danger of being in anyone's way, or of having drunken coppers banging on my cab at some ungodly hour telling me to move – as the bastards do. I was literally the only vehicle there. I'd not even seen another car or truck on the road for hours – the whole country had seemed deserted. So I thought sod it – tomorrow's another day.

But in that border I would stay.

I slept like a baby, which was bad news for me because at some time during the night the engine cut out. The temperature had dropped a fair bit overnight and the diesel had 'waxed', which basically meant that the bitch had frozen up with the cold. Had I known better I could have prevented it by giving the engine some stick to keep the diesel warm as it circulated and got returned to the tank. Or I should have at least set the throttle to a sensible tick-over speed before I crashed out. But I didn't know, and I was asleep and didn't notice a thing until morning.

At the time I knew bugger all about freezing points, or of the water content of diesel anyway, or that when that water content crystallised from the cold that it made the diesel turn gooey and thick, which meant that it wouldn't flow and wouldn't burn. Or that in winter-time I should have been using an additive with the diesel to lower that freezing point – an additive like petrol or paraffin, for instance... All I did know that morning was that the engine had stopped by itself, and that it was bloody cold.

I turned the key and pushed the starter button to fire her up again – I was shivering and wanted to get the heaters blowing – but all I got was a slow Er, Er, Er... So I tried again. And again and again. Nothing. The bitch wouldn't have it. I swore at her, punched the steering wheel, kicked things and kept turning the engine over until most of the life had gone from the batteries (the cold also affects a battery's performance) but all I got was a noise like a low growl from a sleeping dog, and I realised it was time to give up.

I remember being confused and angry. And cold. I couldn't understand why the engine wouldn't start. She'd been running alright when I limped into the border the night before, so why the hell wouldn't she fire up now? I knew I hadn't simply run out of diesel, I had rakes of the stuff. I just couldn't understand it.

I don't know when it had stopped snowing that night, but in the morning the snow on the ground looked a fair bit deeper than it had when I'd pulled in. I could see no tyre tracks behind me, so it must have snowed quite a bit. There were no other trucks in the car park either so I couldn't even get a jump-start. There was just a sheet of white. It was misty and hazy with no visible horizon, which I found intimidating, and I felt very alone.

I was stumped then. I just didn't know what to do, so I sat and stared, puffed away on my usual round of breakfast cigarettes, and brewed up some coffee.

Sometime during the morning I ventured out to look for help, though where I thought I'd get it from I had no idea. In the end all I did get was cold and wet. The uniformed arse-holes at the exit barrier just told me to sod off when I went down to talk to them, and got really annoyed when I asked about a telephone. So I got no joy there.

There was a Motorest – a motorists' restaurant – at the border, not that it deserved such a grand title. It was about a hundred metres from where I was 'parked'. From fifty metres it could only just be seen: it sat in a bit of a dip on the inward-bound side of the border, and with all that snow on its sloped roof, looking like a huge dollop of vanilla ice-cream about to slide off and cause an avalanche, it just blended in with the rest of the Arctic landscape.

I trudged over and spent an hour or so in there, where I shivered again because the heating didn't work, and drank lots of local coffee – black stuff, thick with sludge and powdery to the taste – a bit like Turkish coffee served at the temperature of lava. Really nice. The cheerful lass behind the counter looked at me like I was a criminal when I asked about a telephone – so I gave up on that one. The whereabouts of *the* telephone in Yugoslavia was obviously a state secret, and anyway, the girl must have been too busy to chat seeing as the place was empty, so I dropped it.

I then decided to try again at the barrier – to appeal to their better nature; explain that I had a problem; to make them understand and maybe have them take pity on me... But once again they just told me to sod off, so this time I did – straight past the barrier and down the road into Austria.

There's a small restaurant at Spielfeld, the Austrian side of the border, known as Mama's. The English drivers used it all the time, so I parked my bum in there, had a meal, drank loads of very expensive 'proper' coffee, felt really pleased with myself, then went to phone Roy.

He was not a happy bunny. After lots of effing and blinding and, 'have you done this, have you done that?' he gave me some simple instructions on how to get the engine re-started, along with 'stay with the truck, phone straight back if there's any more problems', etc. So off I went.

The Yugos went apeshit when they saw me tramping back through the border into their country, but they didn't actually stop me from entering. Before too long I would wish they had.

When I got back to my immobile home, wet and shivering after crunching across snow that was gradually freezing solid, I began to feel pretty pissed off with myself. I'd been going over the conversation with Roy and thinking how angry he'd sounded. It dented my ego to think that I'd let the side down. I'd been trusted enough to go out on a second trip and had almost convinced myself that I could do it standing on my head, but when it came to the crunch I found I couldn't even do a simple thing like start an engine. I'd fucked up, I'd upset Roy, and it hurt my pride.

Roy had gone on about filters and things, so I knew that I had to get the cab up in the air and try to change the fuel filters – that much at least I thought I could handle… Wrong again: I couldn't even get the cab to go over! I pumped and pumped with that lever but the bitch wouldn't move one single inch in the air, no matter how much I swore at it. Great, I thought, feeling even more defeated – what next?

I really didn't fancy another argument with the coppers at the exit barrier – even though Roy had told me to phone straight back if I had any more problems: they were already downing large Slibovich's and with their naturally cheerful dispositions it wouldn't have taken much for one of them to lose his rag and clump me with a stick. And anyway, it was getting dark, so I left it.

There was nothing else I could do right then except to try as best I could to keep warm, so it was two pairs of socks, two jumpers, a woolly hat and gloves. If anything else fitted, it got put on. I must have looked like Humpty Dumpty, but I wasn't in a fashion parade – I was fucking cold.

That evening the temperature dropped again and everything began to freeze up – even the ice-cream lid on the Motorest. I was making cup after cup of coffee on my Turkish bomb – a gas bottle that looks like a stunted World War Two aeroplane bomb – (they used to explode like one, too) – and trying to enjoy what warmth I could get from the feeble flame. But it was still freezing cold in the cab of that Mack so I figured the best way to keep warm was to curl up in the huge bed. So I did.

The next morning my bomb wouldn't light. It felt bitterly cold inside the truck, like there was an icy draught coming in from somewhere, and I couldn't even have a brew or warm my hands, which soon began to feel numb. It was ages before the gas lit, but it wasn't enough to boil a kettle. By this time I was shivering, so off I went to the Motorest for morning coffee and a friendly chat with the waitress about the weather.

The haze still hung in the sky giving the place a spooky atmosphere, which was made worse by the fact that the border was still deserted. There hadn't been another vehicle in or out since I'd arrived. It was obvious by now that all the roads were blocked as the snow that had fallen and drifted was frozen solid, like strange carvings, and the only sounds I could hear were the noise my boots made as I crunched across the car park, and of my own rapid swearing.

Eventually, after a bit of a one-sided conversation with the miserable cow in the Motorest, I plucked up enough courage to try and get through the border again and use the phones in Austria. There was another shift on at the barrier and surprisingly they didn't seem the slightest bit interested in me. They were also on the Slibovich – a good anti-freeze – so I just strode past, waving my passport in their general direction, and slid back into Austria.

It was less than a kilometre from the car park to Mama's and I thought the walk would have warmed me up a bit, but it hadn't. I felt chilled to the bone and it took ages for me to thaw out, even though the heating in the restaurant was up full. I drank lots more expensive coffee, had another meal – ham and eggs was my favourite – then phoned Roy and got shouted at again.

I was told that Ernie was on his way down in another truck – a Ford that he'd just bought from Paul Williams (Animal), that he was running with two others – Paul Wimhurst and Johnny Bradford (no relation to Roy), and that the three of them would be there soon to help. Like an idiot I believed it.

Roy was also worried about the load of wine I was carrying: under those temperatures the bottles were freezing up and popping their necks off, which was ruining the load – I knew that for a fact because there were already red stains running down the sideboards and marking the snow – almost like the trailer itself had been bleeding.

He also said that there had been some money transferred to me via one of the customs agents at the border, and I thought, that's handy – especially as I hadn't asked for money! So I wasted no time finding Hans' office to lay claim to it. I was a bit disappointed, but not really surprised, to be told that 'Nein zair iss no moneys for you now. You muss komm beck tomorrow mornink. Ja?'

I went back to the truck feeling pretty miserable and very cold. That night I took the bomb to bed with me – I figured the cold must have been affecting the gas somehow, without knowing why, but it worked because the next morning I got a flame strong enough to make coffee!

The money did arrive that next day and I wasted no time in drawing three hundred quid's-worth of Austrian schillings, whereupon I went off and had a huge meal, bought supplies of Marlboro cigarettes, some food, chocolate, a rake of beer and a bottle of whisky.

Ernie and the others still hadn't arrived by this time and I soon got fed up with staring out of the window at Mama's hour after hour hoping to see them pull up outside – because still nothing was moving. Virtually no traffic at all had passed through the border in either direction since I'd been there. The roads were still blocked in both countries and I wondered just how long a wait lay in store for me.

On my way back to the truck I was relieved of a few beers by an already drunken copper, then politely sent on my way with a smile! I could hardly believe it – I'd just learnt how to make a friend in Yugoslavia!

I had a bit of a job getting back to the truck across the ice with so many goodies in my arms, but slipping on my arse a few times was nothing compared to a full stomach and the prospect of a belly-warmer to go to bed with.

That night I got well pissed and forgot to take the bomb to bed with me. Needless to say I went without a hot drink in the morning.

Poor visibility at the NUR *Petrol Station*

Three

Of hot air and icicles

And so it went on for about another week as it steadily got colder and colder. On the rare occasions that the sun came out the exposed snow would begin to melt and run, then quickly chill off again until there were huge icicles hanging from everything – including the truck. The Motorest soon began to look like the wicked witch's castle: it looked like it had a great portcullis gate in front of it with icicles hanging from the roof almost to the ground, and it glistened like it was alive. It was a fascinating transformation. But I had never experienced such coldness in my life.

I'd wake up each morning shivering and spend the days just trying to keep warm. Before long almost everything in sight was frozen solid. Even the wheels of the truck itself were frozen into the ice! And still it got colder.

I staggered into Austria a few times, hung around Mama's, ate, spent Ernie's money, phoned Roy and got the same panicky message, 'Yes, they're definitely on their way, they should be there by now, just stay where you are.' Then I'd trudge back into Yugo, climb into the truck and crawl into bed with the bomb.

I'd lay there looking at the frozen interior of the cab, or stare at the bleak landscape of what was normally a busy border and I'd think of home – of the Malt and Hops – of what I'd have given to be standing by the gas fire with a pint of 6x in my hand... Then I'd wake up trembling, sometimes uncontrollably, until one day, when I'd had enough and I decided to plant myself in an Austrian hotel room for the duration, the Yugos refused point blank to let me across the border anymore.

That was when the shit hit the fan for me.

The temperature continued to drop, the Motorest closed its doors, there was still no traffic moving, no people about – except at the barrier – and I don't remember seeing any birds or other wildlife. It was like a barren arctic wilderness. Austria was now off-limits to me so I was quite literally stranded on the deserted Yugoslav side of the border with a knackered truck, no heating, no communications, a gas bomb that was getting harder and harder to light – and with nowhere to go. The roads were blocked – what could I do? Walk back into a deserted country and end up like Captain Oates?

I kept thinking of all the 'hot air' I'd heard, but not listened to back in Istanbul and cursed myself for being so stupid. Had I not been such a know-all I might have learnt something and maybe prevented the situation I was in. I could have possibly stopped the engine from freezing up on me in the first place. But no, I wouldn't listen, wouldn't heed the advice and now, as a consequence, I was in the shit. I didn't know what to do, and I was suffering for my stupidity.

Before long it got to the stage where I'd just stay in bed all day looking at crosswords or trying to play mind games to pass the time, like counting icicles. And even though I'd put on as much clothing as I physically could, I still couldn't keep warm.

I woke one morning, whichever morning it was, and the whole interior of my cab was covered in white furry stuff. My heart nearly skipped a beat when I opened my eyes and saw it.

My immediate reaction was one of panic and I thought fuck!

I thought I had snow-blindness or something. My heart was going ten to the dozen and it really put the shits up me. It was brilliantly white, not to mention weird, and my fuzzy brain couldn't figure it out. I even wondered if I was still asleep and dreaming. I'd never seen anything like it before. The windscreen was covered in it, the dashboard, the doors, the roof… If I'd seen it on a wildlife programme, I'd have said – oh, that's pretty – but when you wake up in the morning and the bloody stuff's all over the inside of the cab – it's a different story.

I lay there for ages in shock, just staring at it, my breath coming out in gasps, like cigarette smoke, until it dawned on me: my breath – it was the condensation from my breath! It had frozen into ice crystals during the night (nights?), layer upon layer of it, and had formed a kind of frost on the inside of the cab! Some of the crystals were nearly a quarter of an inch long and the whole thing looked like a white shag-pile carpet! It was incredible.

On the ninth or tenth day there – I can't remember which – the world just closed in on me: the haze grew denser and everything fell still and silent – I couldn't see ten feet in front, there wasn't a breath of wind and not a sound could be heard anywhere in my little world – and that night the temperature plummeted to minus thirty degrees centigrade.

That was the time I thought I might actually die in that truck. It scared me shitless and I don't think I have ever felt so lonely.

The cold really got to me after that. My senses became clogged, my reactions slowed. I couldn't think straight, couldn't move properly, couldn't even co-ordinate my actions – just trying to light a cigarette was a mission. I couldn't hold the fag properly, I'd fumble with the matches, drop them, try again… My fingers and toes were numb, my ears and nose hurt and breathing the bitterly cold air was painful. I slept a lot, or tried to, mostly with my head under the bedding, and when I'd wake, I'd be trembling and close to tears.

It got to the stage where I didn't know if it was night or day – and I didn't care. I just wanted to lie in bed with all my clothes on and try to keep warm. And that's just about all I did. I had nothing left to drink – my water had frozen. I couldn't find the will to eat – or the ability to do it – even though I knew I had to. All I wanted to do was sleep, wrapped in layers of clothing, swaddled in the quilt like a cocoon.

I laid like that for three more days and nights. By the time the roads were re-opened and the cavalry arrived on my doorstep, I was in a shit condition. I must have been close to hypothermia or dehydration, or something, I really don't know, but when Clive Osborne turned up two days ahead of Ernie himself, I was a frozen wreck.

I had been there for thirteen days.

Clive knew what to do. The first priority was to get my body temperature back up to normal, so I was manhandled into the cab of his 141 Scania for the thawing out process, with the engine running, the heaters blowing, and supplied with lots of tea.

It took a while but it had the desired effect, though it was pretty painful. My fingers and toes hurt like hell as the warmth was brought back to them. It felt like I'd dipped them in boiling water or held them over an open flame. My ears and nose stung so much that I thought they would crack up and fall off like on a Tom and Jerry cartoon.

As I sat there steaming and crackling, peeling off layers of clothing, Clive gave me the third degree. He then confidently set about the task of restarting the Mack. Alone!

He lit small fires under the fuel tank and the oil sump in whatever containers he could find. This was to warm up the diesel and the engine oil prior to starting. The diesel for obvious reasons, and the oil because under those temperatures it would have thickened to the consistency of treacle, and if left like that would have created unnecessary resistance when trying to turn the engine over - and it wouldn't have done much of a job at lubricating anything either.

The next task, while the fires were burning – the fires themselves consisting of old skiddies, socks and T-shirts soaked in diesel (his diesel – not mine) was to get the cab up, check for any obvious damage and change the fuel filters. That was easier said than done – everything was still frozen solid, and the cab wouldn't budge.

Sometime later – it may have been the following day, I can't remember – Ty Jarvis turned up en-route to Greece in his Transcontinental – and promptly got stuck in to help Clive. I remember being impressed by both of them. There had been no questions asked, no hint of not helping, no moaning or excuse making, the pair of them had simply assessed the situation and got stuck straight into it, conferring every now and again, then trying something different.

When something failed to work there was no – 'oh, fuck it, I can't help – ta-ta mate'… Far from it – the more difficult the problem, the more effort they put in. Neither was I made to feel any guilt at having landed myself in that position in the first place. The worst I got was from Clive, who said, 'You couldn't have broken down on the other side of the border, could you? You prick!'

I thought they were brilliant, and I didn't know either one of them from Adam. Here they were, two strangers, attacking my truck with spanners and biscuit tin fires while I sat in Clive's cab drinking tea! I couldn't fault it – these people and their attitudes are what it's all about at the end of the day.

They messed about with the Mack all day long and though tempers did begin to wear a bit thin there was no question of them giving up. I wasn't much use to either of them – I still felt weak and exhausted. I tried to fetch and carry as best I could, but all I managed to do was slide about on the ice, bump into things and generally get in the way. Ty, a bearded quiet-spoken feller from the Bristol area, would just look at me and say 'Woi doan you put the kettle back on ole mate, weez gagging for a noice cuppa'... It was his polite way of telling me to sod off, get back in the warm and keep out of their way.

Eventually the cab was raised, the filters changed and a pair of jump leads produced. My heart pounded. As I watched them I thought again of the conversation in Istanbul, and I cringed – it was guys like these that I had mentally accused of being full of wind... But I had learnt my lesson: in future, I told myself, I would listen. And I would respect. Clive and Ty had been at it all day, and they were almost blue with cold. I could have cried for them.

Soon, for the first time in two weeks, the engine was spun over. It was such a lovely sound at the time – even though the bitch wouldn't actually start. It took a bit more time and a lot more patience on their parts, but eventually they did manage to fire the engine up – and didn't she sound like a bag of shit. She was popping and farting, shuddering like an epileptic and chucking great clouds of smoke all over the place – but the smiles on all three faces spoke volumes: they said YES!... I have never felt so relieved as I did at that moment – nor so grateful. I could have kissed the pair of them.

After that, all manner of bolts were hammered into holes in a bid to get me mobile again to drive just one kilometre down the road, and into civilisation on the Austrian side of the border. So near, yet so far – could she do it...?

Could she bollocks... The bloody air pressure wouldn't build up to release the brakes.

I thought by the looks on their faces that they were ready to give up – but no – they just discussed what to do next and got stuck in again. I couldn't believe it! A fire was lit under the air tanks, the airlines to the trailer were disconnected, the brakes on the trailer were wound off and... nothing. The needles on the air gauges still wouldn't budge – and neither would the truck. The compressed air system was frozen solid from the frozen moisture content in the air itself, and that had to be unfrozen before the system could work. Again, had I listened I would have known to keep the air-tanks drained of water, and to use methanol in the system to stop it from freezing up in the first place.

It took an hour or so of warming the air tanks, valves and pipes, and revving the engine, to build up enough heat and air pressure to release the brakes. And eventually it worked. I was off! At last – after two whole weeks parked on the ice I was mobile once again, and as I moved off, heart in mouth, I heard Clive despairingly scream, 'Slow down, you silly bastard, you've got no trailer brakes!'

Clive, who had actually arrived to relieve me of my trailer and pull it back home, very politely allowed me to slide through both sides of the border – alone – with the now brake-less trailer that he was supposed to be pulling, and then let me part company with over a hundred pounds cash to pay for what was *his* Austrian transit tax! I couldn't fault it – Clive Osborne, the professional. Everyone had a good laugh about it afterwards though – except Ernie, of course, whose money it was.

Ernie and the rest of the gang, along with 'Buttons' (David Button), arrived the day after I got through the border, by which time I'd had lots more hot food and drink at Mama's, and in various trucks, and was thawing out nicely. The large coffee cognacs helped.

I didn't realise it at the time, but it was pointed out that a shower and a shave might be in order because I looked, and smelled, like the creature from the pit. I still had the same clothes on as I had two weeks previously – not all of them, obviously, just the basic three or four smelly layers – and I was honking. I was also a bit underweight. Weight that to this day I've never managed to fully put back on.

But I was happy. I'd made some friends and learnt a very valuable lesson: that in this job winter and ignorance can kill. And it could quite easily have killed me – another day or two under those conditions and who knows, I might never have woken up. All because of my own stupidity and pig-headedness. I realised then that this was not a job to be taken lightly, that there was a lot to learn and that I still had a long way to go.

A few people were surprised that I even wanted to carry on driving. Most seemed amazed that I'd even stayed with the truck and not left it there and buggered off. I had people say to me afterwards, 'Fuck that, I'd have dumped the truck where it was and come straight home',

(How, I'd like to know?); or 'You prick, you sat there for how long?'; or simply, 'You prick!'

I couldn't understand it at the time – it hadn't occurred to me to leave the truck – so it was never an option as far as I was concerned. Why would I want to do that? Sure, I wanted to go home – it obviously wasn't at the bottom of my list of priorities – but I never thought of going home *without* the truck! I mean, the Mack, shed that it was, was my job – a job I'd wanted for a long time – and it was also my temporary home. What would I do without it – walk back to England?

I'd also have been out of work – I'd certainly not have been paid – and I'd probably have copped a pasting from someone for good measure. Plus I'd have had a bloody hard time living it down and trying to find another job. And that goes for anyone who dumps a truck abroad: abandoning a truck overseas is a big no-no on this job, except under very exceptional circumstances.

Physically I was in a bit of a mess for many days after landing in Austria, but Ernie made sure I was well looked after – he had good reason to: after three or four days of fattening up and sleeping in the warm again, he popped the question:

'So, are you ready to go back down again, John?'

I looked at him in surprise, not believing my ears or knowing what to say. He just looked at me with a slight grin on his face and one eye closed, as he always did, from the cigarette smoke, and I asked, 'Er, back where?' sensing the answer.

'Turkey.' He said quietly.

I thought he was joking and politely asked, 'Are you fucking joking?'

'Nah. That's what I'm here for, to do a 'turn-around' with you. Didn't Roy tell you?'

'No, did he fuck. You're making this up.'

'I'm not. That's what I brought the other truck for – I'm going to scrap the Mack and you can take over the 'new' Transcon' (Ford Transcontinental). It's loaded for Turkey – it's outside.' Then, after a pause, he said, 'Sorry mate, I thought you knew.'

I was sure he was winding me up – but he really wasn't. He actually wanted me to change trucks with him, turn right round and drive all the way back to Turkey through the snow with another load! I could hardly believe my ears – the cheek of it – I wanted to say something, scream, to call him a bastard, to kick him in the nuts – but like an idiot, I simply said yes.

That was my next mistake. Having changed all my smelly kit from one truck to the other – which I'd named the Pink Panther because of the disgusting interior décor – and boldly set forth for all points East, I got just 300 kilometres into Yugoslavia and broke down…

I was out for about two and a half months on that trip – turn-round included. In total I'd spent the best part of three weeks broken down, two of those parked in sub-zero temperatures. I'd had another day and a night on the roadside trying to get the Pink Panther restarted, and a hairy twelve-hour hitch-hiking session with all manner of drunken locals in an effort to get back to Austria again for help. I must have needed my brains tested.

Ernie was still in Austria; drinking expensive beer in Mama's and more than a little surprised to see me casually walk back into the restaurant again.

I told him the sob story over a few beers and we gingerly laid new plans – I think it must have been plan Z by then. The following day we chucked some spanners in the Mack, which had been repaired yet again (properly this time), and bobtailed (drove without a trailer) back into Yugo to try and resuscitate the Panther.

The saga continued. The Yugos didn't want to let us in to start with, so after a bit of a heated discussion about parentage we had to search out another border. The 'Tranny' – when we got there – was still a non-starter. We couldn't figure out what was wrong with her, so after towing her down the hard shoulder, we left her in the nearest service station and promised the guy in the garage a bottle of whisky to keep an eye on it until we got back. We then hooked up the Mack to the trailer, sucked all the diesel out of the Panther's tanks and promptly set off to double-man it down to Istanbul!

By now it was turning into a farce. Ernie had dropped a gearbox on his toe at a scrapyard in England while buying a brand-new-second-hand half shaft and hub for the Mack, and his foot had swollen up to the size of a melon, so, needless to say, he ended up riding side-saddle and I was lucky enough to do most of the driving.

In Istanbul we picked up Ernie's son, Paul, who had been staying with Kasim on a sort of a holiday. Kasim got a severe bollocking from Ernie for bodging the first repair job and rewarded us with one of his usual lines, which went something like: 'Nah you, Issa Chon stoppy Kamyon proberlum, me come looky see, worky goot halluf-shaft, chef see him speaky no proberlum Chonnie a'go Yugo anner proberlum inner Yugo you, me no cun'!

Paul came back to England with us in the truck, so we had three people in one cab – an invalid, his extremely pissed-off son, and a novice – talk about the three stooges. Ernie had his manky foot on the dashboard (or under my nose) for most of the trip, from which he kept picking scabs and bits of flesh and tossing out of the window; the weather was atrocious all the way down and back; and because of my inexperience and our lack of snow-chains, it was a miracle that we didn't end up in a ditch somewhere.

We had little food between us and hardly any money; the cab stank of socks, sweat, cigarettes and putrid flesh; we got lost in the hills in Bulgaria trying to find the same winery I'd reloaded at only the previous trip – and we still had the cheering prospect of trying to rescue the Panther on the way back. The Mack even overheated at one stage, even though the outside temp was still sub-zero! The radiator grill got blocked with ice and completely stopped the air flow!

Tempers were short and we spent long periods in complete silence, not knowing what to say to each other, and constantly wondering if we'd get down the next hill without jack-knifing – or up the next one without losing traction. And in the backs of our minds all the time was the prospect of yet another breakdown miles off the beaten track. Poor Paul – who'd had a shit holiday anyway – spent most of the time staring through the windscreen in stunned silence, wondering why the fuck he hadn't just stayed in England in the first place.

And so it went on. And on…

***

About eleven weeks after leaving the UK on a simple mission I returned to Dover skint, tired and shell-shocked. Waiting on the dockside to greet me as I drove off the ferry was a small dapper man of middle age, dressed like he'd just come from the members' enclosure at Lords.

DC 'Tommy' Tucker, a plain-clothed policeman attached to Special Branch at the docks, held up a manicured hand to stop me. He then politely gave me the third degree – where had I been etc., what was I loaded with… He then asked to see my road permits – German, Austrian, Yugoslav and Turk.

Road permits were his favourite, knowing some outfits ran on Mickeys… but he had no joy with me. He only wanted to make an arrest, impound trucks and prosecute the 'cowboys' – bless him.

He gave me a wry grin and let me go, knowing full well that we'd meet again. I then made a beeline for Kings Cross and a pint of beer, but didn't do quite so much bragging that time at the Malt and Hops. There didn't seem much point. I had overdone it with the exaggerated stories weeks before, so who now would believe the truth? Few people bothered to ask anyway. I wasn't surprised and, to be honest, I really didn't care.

The realities of the job had brought me down to earth with a bump and put paid to all that nonsense. I had experienced something that few – if any – of my so-called friends could have imagined, let alone understood and it had changed me.

I soon found life in the pub pretty dull, even though a few weeks before I had dreamed of being there. The beer and the gas fire were okay, but I began to find the scene boring. It was the same routines and the same dreary conversations day in, day out. I got impatient with it all and began to wonder what the hell I was doing there. The pub and the people hadn't changed – I had. Life in jolly old England hadn't changed – it's just that I'd come to realise what a drag it all was.

It wasn't enough for me any longer. I wanted something more – wanted that little bit extra. I'd discovered that there was a whole new world to explore 'across the water', way outside of the nine to five bit, disasters notwithstanding, and when Ernie rang a week later and sheepishly asked me if I wanted to ship out again, I couldn't get to the East India Docks quick enough.

Clive 'Pikey' Osborne died suddenly of a heart attack in the middle of Bulgaria in June 1996. He was a good friend. He deserved better than that.

Four

Of border queues and barbecues

By April I'd actually managed to get another trip to Turkey in the bag without fucking up anywhere along the line, which really chuffed me to bits. I think it impressed one or two other people at the time too – my then six-year-old daughter being one of them – and totally gob-smacked everyone else.

Roy was simply suspicious and claimed that I'd either cheated or had help from somewhere so, to make sure that it hadn't just been a lucky fluke, he gave me the usual, 'Take your time, there's no rush – just get there…' etc., and promptly shipped me out to see if I could do it again.

That time, after not rushing to get there, I tipped at the Ford plant 'over the bridge' again (the Bosporous) and was then sent off to the enchanting little town of Radauti in Northern Romania – the mission being to pick up a full 'back-load' of cheap, self-destructing portable barbecues. (I had one – it fell to bits as soon as I threatened it with a match).

There was still a bit of snow and ice on the ground at that time of year – more so the further north I went – but at least the back of winter had been broken by then, so road conditions weren't as bad as they had been. Which was just as well because I still had no snow-chains with me.

For some reason, probably unjustified in view of the fact that I'd just knocked over a trouble-free trip, I had the feeling that I was on probation for my earlier cock-ups. Because, even though this would only be my third time ever into Romania, I'd already come to the conclusion that it wasn't my most favourite place – and Roy knew it – so it felt like I was being sent there as punishment.

Ernie told me to stop being paranoid, saying that whoever was available at the time got sent there – regardless of who was in the bad books. But I wasn't so sure. Anyway, as it was pointed out, it's all part of the job – like it or lump it. Nobody said it would all be peaches and cream. Ernie also tried to assure me I'd been forgiven for my earlier mistakes; that it had all been forgotten… but I also learnt that nothing *ever* gets forgotten on this job, it just doesn't get brought up in conversation as often.

Anyway, I was still in work, so I figured I wasn't doing too bad. All I had to do to keep it that way was knuckle down, learn the job, and hopefully have some fun.

Being sent to the frozen wilds of Romania in a clapped out old truck would certainly help towards the first two – and come about ten light-years from the third.

It's a fair old trot from Istanbul to the top of Rumo. 1,150k's to be slightly more precise (700 miles). And it wasn't exactly the easiest 'run' in the world at the time. What with two of the worst borders in that corner of the globe, and some equally bad roads to contend with, it wasn't the kind of return load that had me leaping about with joy – especially as Roy was fond of adding things like, 'can you be there tomorrow?' at the bottom of the telex (Remember them?)

Getting out of Turkey with an empty truck ought to have been a quick and straightforward job, but at 'Kapik' (Kapikule) it could be a real mission, lasting anywhere from a couple of hours to the best part of a day. Then, after queuing to enter 'Bulgy' (Bulgaria) at the imaginatively named border of 'Kapitan Andreevo' for an hour or three, there were the joys of a five to six-hour slog across a country with nasty roads, nasty coppers, and the equally nasty 'cobblestone mountain' to contend with – a mountain pass that was largely surfaced with cobblestones and with numerous craters where the rest of the cobblestones should have been.

But that was a breeze – all twelve to eighteen hours of it – compared with trying to get into Romania at the border crossing of Giurgiu.

The dented, rusting sign said something like 'Welcome to the People's Socialist Democratic Republic of Romania'. But whoever did the amateurish stencilling should have added: 'Abandon hope, cigarettes, beads, bangles and trinkets all ye who enter here…'

The queue to get through this border often 'began' where trucks came off the 2km long rusting iron bridge – the so-called 'Friendship Bridge' - that spans the Danube, the geographical border between the two countries. There was a faded white line halfway across the pot-holed bridge that marked the boundary, but it wasn't really needed because as soon as you crossed that line in a truck, Romanian soldiers would materialise from thin air, from huts and from behind girders to let you know without a doubt whose half of the bridge you were on.

They'd wave trucks down, trying to make it look official, like a passport control or something, but all they wanted was cigarettes or anything else they could ponce. I fell for it the first time over, but after that I learnt to drive straight past, returning the victory sign they'd be waving over their mouths.

The queue itself was never all that long. It was only half a kilometre or so from the bridge to the barrier, if that, but it was long enough because the bastard thing never seemed to move. The only thing that did move with any regularity was the swarms of flies and mosquitoes that bred in the swamps alongside the river.

Practically all trucks had to join this queue, whether they be loaded or empty, Romanian or otherwise. There were one or two exceptions, such as diplomatic cargoes, that were allowed to drive straight to the front. But as a general rule nobody else could jump this queue, and most that tried were severely bollocked, fined, and sent back again. Some drivers have told me that they regularly used to jump the queue here – but I think they must have meant jumping up and down with frustration.

Under 'normal' circumstances the rules state that certain loads, such as livestock, refrigerated goods, hazardous loads etc., are allowed to ignore border queues and go straight to the front, for obvious reasons. But this was Ceauşescu's Romania and nearly all loads of this nature were headed in the opposite direction – for export.

Very little of this nature went 'in', except for transit – and that mostly to Russia. The majority of British hauliers tried to avoid Rumo if they could, reload elsewhere and transit Yugo instead. So, any traffic going in was mostly their own fleet (F. Troop) making its way home, Russians in transit, or 'foreigners' like myself who were going in to pick up a load for export. Some companies did transit Rumo and the 'full Commie Bloc' regularly– as the rest of Eastern Europe was known. Falcongate was one of them, but in the '80s they were in the brave minority.

Just about anything of value – or of any use – that was produced in Rumo was sold abroad: furniture, textiles, tyres, beef, barbecues… The profits added more noughts to Ceauşescu's bank balance, and the rest of the population – over twenty million – were forced to live in misery.

This must have been one hell of a place to live – a country under a dictator's thumb, run by fear and poverty, with harsh punishments, *kontrolled* and enforced by an unwilling military full of spotty youths, and by an over-willing state secret police force – the 'Securitate' of which, it was rumoured, approximately thirty percent of the population had, at one time or another, been informers for: people – ordinary folk – that would willingly 'grass' on their friends or neighbours in return for 'favours', or to get a gold star on their communist party membership cards – or just to be left alone themselves.

Here everyone and everything was *kontrolled* and that meant all TIR traffic. But to be fair they used to give a harder time to their own than to any. I've seen Romanian drivers take severe slappings at this border, in full view of everyone. Probably for having an extra pack of coffee, or too many cigarettes, or something equally heinous stashed in the cab. It meant – and showed – that they were in control. And didn't they enjoy it.

It also meant that when these arseholes in unbuttoned, unpressed greeny-brown uniforms decided to clump a driver and take his truck to pieces as it sat on the weighbridge, they did just that. I've also seen them order another Rumo driver to open his toolbox and clean his own screwdrivers and spanners with a rag, before they used them to dismantle the poor sod's dash, his door panels, roof panels etc.

Never mind how long all this took, or how many trucks were in the queue waiting their turn to be *kontrolled*, nothing moved in that truck-lane until that vehicle was half-heartedly reassembled and allowed through the barrier - or sent back to Bulgaria in kit form.

There was room to squeeze another truck past the one on the weighbridge – just – where they could, if the fancy took them, *kontrol* the next truck in line before they finished with the first. But it was usually too much for them to cope with all at once, so it rarely happened. Or if that next truck in line was loaded and needed to use the weighbridge itself – forget it… Or if they were all pissed again…

Apart from dismantling cabs, opening up loads to see what they could nick, going through drivers' personal effects to do the same, breathing alcohol fumes all over the place, intimidating people and being generally obnoxious, these people were *always* on the scrounge. They would accept almost anything, but their favourite 'gift' was Kent cigarettes.

Kent were useful – much more so than 'Lei', their own currency. It was reputedly the brand smoked by Ceauşescu himself and, apart from being the obvious status symbol that these fags provided, a packet or three of Kent could pay for anything from a bag of groceries to a doctor's bill – which Lei could not.

But these arseholes were also on the scrounge for whisky, porno mags, pens, fag lighters, cassette tapes… just about anything 'western', or anything they couldn't get their hands on in their own country, they'd take. So the first time through I gave them some Kent and a 'Keep fit with…' cassette.

I never did find out if they saw the funny side of that one.

After that I made a habit of giving them all kinds of worthless cassettes each time I went in: 'Portuguese in six weeks' in a Pink Floyd cover; a blank posing as Kate Bush; 'How to give up smoking by hypnosis…' etc. Anything useless to them that I could lay my hands on, they got. They could never hear them played either because I only had a radio – not a radio-cassette, so they'd just grin, pocket it and let me go.

Officially they weren't allowed to be in possession of foreign currency. That was a big no-no in Romania, punishable by equally big slaps on the wrist – but it didn't stop them from taking it and calling it a 'souvenir'. Not that there was much danger of them getting caught with it – seeing as they'd have to catch themselves – and where better to dispose of 'illegal' hard currency, Deutschmarks and Dollars mostly, than with their confederates in the bank or small duty free shop at what is an international border which dealt with the stuff twenty-four hours a day? (When they weren't curled up in their cots fast asleep, that is).

It took anything from a few hours on a good day, to a day and a night to get through this border – and there was fuck all there: if a driver needed a shit then he went under his trailer. Or if he wasn't the bashful type, he stuck his arse over the low concrete wall and shit on the flood plains below – that were patrolled twenty-four hours a day by Kalashnikov-armed soldiers with fixed bayonets (the rumour was that they had no bullets).

There was nothing in the way of food to be had here either. All drivers had to take their own grub with them in the truck – or they simply went without. Nor was there much food to be bought once inside the country: unless you happened to be extremely fond of tinned fish, the shops were empty.

Opening 'the box' – the food locker common on most TIR trailers – or even daring to knock up a sandwich in the cab, could prove hazardous. Not so much from the clouds of obnoxious insects that would rapidly descend and invite themselves to lunch, but from the obnoxious young soldiers that did the same.

These guys could pick up the scent of a corned beef sandwich from five hundred metres, and were quicker off the mark than Linford Christie. They were annoying, persistent bastards who would stand right over you and whine, pull pained faces and make sawing actions across their stomachs to tell you they were hungry. Sometimes they got lucky as a driver took pity on them and gave them something to eat. I'd often give them something myself – after all, they didn't want to be in uniform patrolling a stinking border – and most of them were genuinely hungry, which is why they sometimes got a whole tin of dog-food to themselves.

Some drivers, myself included, used to take tins of food to feed the 'stray' dogs in Turkey. They were lovely creatures – dead friendly towards the English, but filthy, unfed and uncared-for by the Turks. The only attention they ever got from their lords and masters was a thrown rock or a toe up the arse. So we used to make friends with them, feed them, chuck sticks for them, and then put our caring relationships at risk by hosing them down every now and then – something that most of them hadn't experienced before, and weren't too impressed with.

In return they showed us great loyalty and affection. They'd make a beeline for all the English trucks that pulled into the car park, wide-eyed with lolloping tongues and wagging back ends. At night they'd religiously select their spots and sleep under our front bumpers – even if a particular truck or driver hadn't been there before they somehow *knew* it was English. It was weird, but strangely comforting.

They never seemed to go to 'foreign' trucks, and they'd follow us everywhere – even into the restaurant, which really pissed the Turks off. They also gave us enormous satisfaction by periodically attacking foreign drivers without warning.

The Turks hated the fact that these dogs 'adopted' English drivers. They rarely did or said anything in front of us, especially when Eric Owen was in town (Eric had a bit of a reputation for bringing out large bruises on anyone he found mistreating animals). But as soon as our backs were turned they didn't hesitate to lure them down to the other end of the car park and shoot them… Anyway, feeding label-less leftover tins of Pedigree Chum to Romanian border guards was an amusing way of making new friends.

Two days after leaving Istanbul I found myself in Romania, knackered, and with at least another ten hours of driving ahead of me to get to the factory. So I did the sensible thing, I drove one hundred metres from the barrier, parked up and went straight to bed.

What seemed like five minutes later, I was rudely woken up by the local Sheriff and told, in no uncertain terms, to clear off. I wasn't too impressed, but there's not much a guy can do when an irate copper has his hand on the butt of his gun, insisting that I'd done wrong just by being there Even though I was 'off' the road in a car park that I think belonged to the shabby motel next door, and which quite often had trucks in residence replacing dashboards and door-panels, the police, for some reason, obviously thought my absence would be a good thing. So I had to move – and it was a foretaste of things to come.

By law, ordinary members of the People's Republic weren't supposed to have any sort of contact with 'outsiders', such as myself. That meant talking to anyone, poncing a fag, asking the time or giving away state secrets over a beer. But the rules, enforced by the Securitate and its next door neighbour, didn't deter the hordes of scruffy, barefoot kids and petty thieves that religiously descended on TIR trucks whenever they came to a halt – whether that halt be at a crossroads, a level crossing, traffic lights (when they worked), lay-bys or whatever.

I could hardly believe it to start with – I thought, you cheeky little bastards – because wherever I stopped the truck, it got mobbed. If I pulled over for a brew, miles from anywhere, with not a soul to be seen – and absolutely convinced that I was alone – the little sods would materialise from thin air, like they'd just been 'beamed down' en-masse!

These kids, some as young as six or seven, others even younger in the arms of elder brothers and sisters, all wearing woollen skull-caps that covered the ears and laced under the chin, would descend like a swarm of insects, all babbling at once, all with outstretched arms, pleading eyes, grubby faces and non-stop mouths begging for 'Gummi-gummi' (bubble-gum), 'chocolata', or biscuits, bread, soap, Kent...

It was heartbreaking to look at the desperation on these kids' faces – many of them no more than babes. At first I felt really upset and sorry for them. I somehow felt responsible. I was a 'grown-up', and these were just children – orphans some of them. I had everything as far as they were concerned. They had nothing, and here they were mobbing foreign TIR drivers begging for food, trying to care for each other and generally living a shit life when they ought to have been playing on the swings, kicking balls around, cuddling up to mum or dad...

I used to buy large boxes of bubble gum in Turkey – about two hundred to a box – and if Tony Meddins was around I'd relieve him of some miniature chocolate bars (Milky Way, Mars Bars, etc.) before they got delivered to Kuwait, and try as best I could to give each kiddie a sweet. But that only made things worse, because the moment you gave them something all hell broke loose. They'd scream and shout even louder in excitement, press in closer, hanging on to wing mirrors, wipers – each other. A dozen or more arms, outstretched hands, wide, pleading eyes and nit-ridden heads would all try to force their way in through the open window at once. The noise was incredible. I found it upsetting and sometimes a bit scary, so I learnt that the easiest way out of it was to grab a large handful of gum and just chuck it to the ground away from the truck. As soon as they went scrabbling for it I'd fire up the engine and drive away. Often with a lump in my throat.

After that I'd simply chuck a load of gum or chocolate out of the window and bugger off before they got to the cab.

No matter where I stopped in Rumo someone always came up to the truck begging. And not just kids. It became annoying, frustrating and a bit of a strain on the nerves. They were demanding, persistent, and sometimes hostile. I was threatened more than once (though at the time – pre 1989 – the threats rarely came to anything), and I've lost count of the amount of gypsy curses I've had put on me for refusing to part company with something.

I had no chance of grabbing more than a couple of hours kip all the way up to Radauti, and I only achieved that by bunging some fags to the coppers at one of the many kontrol posts (Kent Kontrols) on the roadside.

When I eventually got to Radauti and found the factory I was relieved, but felt emotionally drained and knackered. I then went to the gateman, who was armed with an ancient bolt-action rifle, and introduced myself, but got nowhere. There was lots of jabbering, arm waving and tutting, but not much else, and I really wasn't in the mood for it. I mean, surely it was obvious what I wanted…? I'd just reversed an Irish registered artic 100 metres down the entrance road to their factory, with the back-end open to show the trailer was empty, for Christ's-sake – did I really look like a travelling tobacconist?

Half an hour later I got a response when an ugly woman knocked on my cab door and got told to fuck off. 'Hello Eenglish,' she screeched, standing back on the pot-holed pavement. 'No loading today – loading morning. Must telephon to Bucharest… is protocol.'

'What?' I asked, looking more surprised than I actually was.

'No possibill loading before telephon to Bucharest. Telephon no working today,' she said with a shrug. 'Sorree.'

So I shrugged, said ta, pulled the curtains and tried to get my head down, expecting a nice long sleep.

I say 'tried' because the moment my head hit the pillow I got hassled again. Not from kids this time – I'd already bunged the gateman to keep an eye on them – but from more adults. Men and women of all ages began tapping on the door asking for food, fags, blue jeans (blooge), nylons – even for bloody carrier bags! (Plastic bags with a logo were a status symbol). I couldn't believe it: my man at the gatehouse was doing a brilliant job of keeping the kids at bay, but obviously thought it was okay to let his woolly-hatted friends and family pester me.

In the end I just ignored the knocking and crashed out. I was pissed off, tired, and more than a bit disappointed - not one of the women there had knocked on my door offering sex, as I'd been led to believe they would! I'd heard so many campfire stories about the hordes of gorgeous Romanian women – which there were – who regularly threw themselves at drivers in exchange for beads and trinkets – which they didn't – that it just wasn't cricket! I'd had all the demands right enough, but none of the offers! Maybe it was me, I thought; maybe I was doing something wrong... Maybe I should have spoken more politely to the gateman.

I did get loaded the following day, along with one extra barbecue in the cab – and two 'Long Vehicle' plates stolen off the trailer. After clearing customs I set off heading south, towards Yugoslavia – over loads of bloody great mountains in a direction that would ultimately add more than three days onto the journey home. This was because Roy didn't want us transiting through Hungary – the most direct route home – and wouldn't give us the road permits we needed just to make sure that we couldn't go that way.

Roy had a thing about Hungary and the rest of the 'Commie Bloc' as it was, Czechoslovakia and DDR (East Germany). He said it was unsafe, that there were no communications, that they were all a bunch of commie bastards, and that he had no way of getting help to us if we needed it... which I found a bit strange seeing as he regularly sent us to two of the biggest shit-holes in the Commie Bloc: Bulgaria – a country that was a law unto itself, had shit communications, and only a handful of TIR workshop facilities who couldn't empty an ashtray without charging a fortune or fucking it up; and Romania – a country virtually disconnected from the rest of civilisation, with almost non-existent communications (four to eight hours to get a line – 'Must telephone to Bucharest first – is protocol'), no food, no proper tarmac, fuel that resembled chip fat and kerosene, a public transport system that worked on gas bottles and ran by the Julian calendar, and not a single workshop worth its name...

But ours was not to reason why.

So south it was, over the hills. And more hills. And more... According to the tourist map of Rumo that the kindly lady in the visa hut had given me at the border, in exchange for a scandalously overpriced entry visa made up of sticky stamps, and a luke-warm tin of coke, I was actually taking the most direct cross-country route, but the badly printed map didn't show contours, or road sizes, or conditions – and the mileage was way out. The signposting was shit, and that includes the absence of the one that should have read, 'Welcome to Transylvania – please turn your clocks back two hundred years'!

For two days I crept, slid and weaved my way over narrow, bumpy, twisting roads littered, not just with snow and ice, but with broken spring leaves and bits of exhaust systems; with nuts and bolts, number plates, rocks (Turkish handbrakes) that had been left in the middle of the road by someone that had broken down and used them as wheel chocks.

There were ruts, bumps, veritable craters, dead dogs and dead donkeys. Live donkeys pulling ramshackle, unlit wooden carts full of furniture, firewood, scrap metal and people. Sometimes the passenger of these carts would strike a match when they heard a truck coming up behind them, just to let us know they were there. Sometimes not. So I took to straddling the centre line (where it was marked or not worn away). I figured that if I rounded a bend in the dark and there was a mobile haystack or something on the road, unlit or stationary, that I'd be in with half a chance of missing it.

A man and his donkey, braving the cold

And there were people. The locals. Thousands of them, some literally miles from the nearest habitation, at night, in dark clothing and big black woolly hats that looked like chimney pots. They were wobbling around drunk, pushing things, pulling things, carrying things like geese, milk churns, bundles of twigs – each other... Or they'd simply be taking their oxen for a walk, or sitting in the open drainage system chatting. There was even a funeral procession at one stage – a not uncommon sight in Romania – led by dozens of trilby-clad, moustachioed mourners in front of a decorated donkey cart pulling a roughly made coffin with the deceased on full view.

There were so many weird and wonderful things trundling up and down these rough, unpainted and unlit roads that at times motorised vehicles seemed quite out of place. I found it all very strange at first, and a bit unnerving at times, but I also found it fascinating. It was so alien to me that I felt out of place – the odd man out – and I sometimes felt like I was on another planet altogether. But after a while you get used to it. If I'd seen a rusty spaceship parked in the middle of the road, unlit, its landing gear chocked with boulders, a pile of hay on its roof and six little green men in waistcoats and woolly hats changing dilithium crystals with a wok – I don't think it would have surprised me.

And if all that wasn't enough, an even funnier thing happened to me on the way home...

When I hit that and subsequent borders, and Customs saw 'Country of departure – Romania' on my paperwork – everyone got serious, got off their bums, ordered me to pull to one side of the compound then promptly *kontrolled* me! Though not with spanners, screwdrivers or dogs – but with a bloody Geiger counter!

At first I just couldn't understand what was happening. I mean, what the fuck were these guys up to, zapping my radiator, my water barrel – and me – with a Geiger counter, of all things? They kept asking me, over and over, exactly where I'd been, what I'd been doing there, why had I come back the long way round...?

It made no sense, and I got very little sense from anyone I spoke to either, apart from 'Problem. Big problem. Boom, boom!', with lots of head-shaking and windmill imitations as I was given the electronic once-over.

I thought *What?* What the fuck do they mean – boom boom? An explosion…? A bomb…? Where? When? And why the Geiger-counters…? And then it dawned on me as I brilliantly put two and two together: a bomb, machines for detecting radiation… It didn't take Einstein to figure it out, did it…? THE BOMB! *Shit…!* It was obvious now: some dickhead had finally pushed the button, there were nuclear warheads being chucked all over the place, millions of people were being microwaved and here I was in communist Eastern Europe, smack bang in the middle of the 'enemy' encampment at the kick-off to World War Three…! Fucking wonderful!

I was the best part of the way home before I bumped into any other Brits and found out what had happened. Apparently, while I'd been up at a village by the Ukrainian border picking up a full load of barbecues and fighting off the women, the reactor in a nuclear power plant in the small Ukrainian town of Chernobyl had thrown a bit of an unexpected wobbler and decided to have a barbecue of its own.

I really didn't know what it all meant at the time, what the implications were, and it was weeks before any of us could get the full story about it. People kept talking about radioactive fallout and clouds of contaminated shit floating about in the atmosphere – but it meant nothing to me. I felt okay, and so did my mates. And I couldn't see anything out of place in the heavens. I think perhaps I expected to see something physical up there, or feel something, or maybe a smell. I wanted a solid sign, proof of what was up there, like tartan coloured clouds or a blazing barnyard falling out of the sky like a meteor… But there was nothing visible, nothing tangible.

But the more we learnt the more it concerned us. This was turning out to be a real threat – not an imaginary one. Even though it was invisible.

We all got to hear about this radioactive fall out being blown in one direction or another by the winds, but nobody seemed to know which way those winds had blown. There had been drivers all over Eastern Europe at the time – tipping, loading, drinking. Any one of us could quite easily have been contaminated. We all feared the worst about the radiation sickness and hair dropping out in chunks, so we set about religiously checking down our trouser fronts ten times a day to make sure that nothing had started to glow in the dark.

Water contamination was the big scare, apparently, which explained why radiators and water barrels were getting the once over. The blokes with the Geiger counters didn't do such a bad job week after week, and some of them even proved to have a sense of humour as they waved their magic wands and threatened to put hazardous stickers on our dicks.

It turned out that the winds had blown everything northwards over great swathes of Russia, up to the Gulf of Finland and on to Sweden, so I'd been in the clear, by a few hundred k's. But the fallout caused untold problems that are still surfacing today. There were fears of the food chain spreading the contamination over a wider area, and I remember farmers across large areas of Eastern Europe being told to destroy whatever crops they had in, for safety's sake. But I don't think many did – and we were convinced that the farmers in Yugoslavia hadn't, so we avoided eating anything there for a while… it gave red cabbage a whole new meaning!

The radioactive fallout of Chernobyl had lots of people jumping through hoops for a while – myself included. Incidents like that directly affect TIR drivers, whether it's because they actually get caught up in whatever it is or have to suffer the after effects, like border closures or witty immigration officials with Geiger counters. Some people are put off by it, or things like it, but if anything I reckon episodes like that make the job more of a challenge and at the time the thought of chucking it in or going back to anything else horrified me.

Five

Of Turks in Mercs and summer breaks

By April of that year I was beginning to get the hang of the work and soon settled into the swing of things. I quickly learned that because the odds are nearly always unfairly stacked against a driver and his simple quest to go from A to B, that the easiest way to get the job done without too much grief wasn't to be patient or abide by the rules, but to do what everybody else did and cheat. It was brilliant – I found I could bullshit and bend the rules as well as the next man, and I have to admit that I thoroughly enjoyed it. As a result I actually managed to get a couple of decent trips in before the summer began.

I soon became a lot more confident and really took advantage of the fact that there was no-one breathing over my shoulder and watching my every move, or telling me what to do all the time. It was so unlike any other job I'd had before where the rules had to be obeyed and time limits adhered to. Here it was the complete opposite where I could do pretty much as I pleased… and did.

I was learning all the time too. My outlook had already changed; the cockiness and know-it-all attitude were now things of the past – I'd already learnt one lesson the hard way and didn't want another. I discovered that I wasn't dealing with gods after all, that these people with the big names and reputations were just ordinary folk and that it wasn't such a great sin to approach them and ask for advice.

This seemed to be appreciated and most of the people I met were really open and forthcoming. Even 'The Animal', who had a fearsome reputation for biting off the heads of the new boys turned out to be nothing more intimidating that the cuddly Bob Hedley, a monster of a man with a ZZ Top beard and the temperament of Baloo the Bear.

I was making friends and even though there were a few arseholes who seemed to resent the likes of me and who insisted on putting themselves on pedestals, I soon learnt to recognise them and, more importantly, how to give them a wide berth.

I felt like I was becoming part of the gang and the whole thing – the people, the job, the way of life, began to weave its spell on me. Before long, I began to spend less and less time in England after each trip, and a lot less time and money at the pub. I felt as if I'd been missing out on something for years, that this was the way to go and I was determined to make up for what I considered was lost time.

I was getting to know my way around certain parts of Europe pretty well by now, the Balkans in particular, and mostly by memory or luck because the sign-posting in that part of the world left a lot to be desired. I kept trying out different routes and borders for the hell of it – and because I could. It wasn't long before I got to know Istanbul itself as well as I knew my own manor in Islington. I even learnt to speak a bit of Turkish which was great for impressing the locals and even better for impressing one or two of the friendlier backpackers that hang around Sultan Ahmet and the Pudding Shop each summer.

At the family home in Islington, North London

For TIR drivers, the 'world famous' Pudding Shop was a godsend and because we were regular customers there, they used to look after us. A guy called Sammy used to run the place, when it was well known and popular because of the film 'Midnight Express'. He had a big mop of black curly hair and got on really well with the drivers. To us it was a good base, a place where we could get a beer or a breakfast before legging it to the Grand Bazaar just up the road to hunt for cheap gold and leather, and a place to head back to afterwards for another beer and a hunt for the lonesome tourist. The place stank to high heaven because of the ever present smell of the blocked spread-axle bogs – but we liked it. We even used to take the odd staff member out drinking or nightclubbing sometimes, but I think one of them got into a bit of trouble with his missus, so that kind of died its own death.

Sammy left after a while and went to run a carpet shop by the Blue Mosque – and still does as far as I know. Then they did the place up after that, and to a lot of us it seemed to lose its atmosphere. The smell had gone (almost), so too had the dirty walls and the makeshift notice board where 'travellers' would leave messages for each other, or advertise for rides in trucks, which was replaced with a proper notice board. But it wasn't the same. We still put up Micky ads for lifts by "single Norwegian 25 yr old girl to England, please" just to wind the other drivers up though.

I had the Mack for a good part of that time and even though the bitch kept breaking down on me, I actually became quite attached to her. She'd kind of grown on me, like a knackered pair of boots.

I felt a certain pride in her too because I was one of the few British TIR drivers running around in an American 'twin-sticker' (two gearsticks). She stood out from other trucks, I got noticed (stared at mostly) and it made me feel good. I also learnt that it was common for drivers to become attached to seven or eight tonnes of rusting metal for equally daft reasons.

She also provided the butt for endless piss-taking. I had drivers approach me all the time asking, 'Iz it possibil for me to zit inzide und heff a look? I don't zee a truck zo olt before!' or, 'Me Grandad drove these fings in the war, mate! Can I 'ave a go?'

When Ernie finally admitted that her working days were numbered, and that she'd have to go, I almost took it personally. But it was when he told me to clear the cab out one day, because the poor old girl was being towed off to her final resting place – a scrapyard near the Blackwall Tunnel – that I almost shed a tear.

I knew I'd miss her. I felt lost already but, more to the point, I was concerned about my job prospects.

As it turned out my fears were unfounded because Ernie, bless his rancid socks, quickly made up for my bereavement by investing in another rusty old beast —an F89 Volvo.

By now, at the ripe old age of thirty-something, Ernie had decided that his driving career was over. Said he'd 'had enough of all that shit!' – that he never wanted to see Iraq again, that he now preferred the home life, fish and chips and a sit-down toilet… but he hadn't bothered to inform me! I'd been under the impression that my services were only required for as long as it suited him to stay home. That was fine by me, it meant that I got to keep a job. But it also meant a small break with tradition as it would be the first English registered truck I'd driven, as opposed to most of the others in the company which were on 'Paddy Plates' – Irish registered.

Roy had split with his business partner and Tanker International by this time and moved on to form a new company, in league with an ex-employee of the police force – a Mr Fred Topham.

Fred, a well-dressed, quietly spoken man of indeterminate age, with lots of well-placed contacts and a tidy seven-series BMW that he never did sell to me, was given the privilege of naming this new outfit.

This new company was imaginatively named 'Lawrabian International Freight Services', LIFS for short, which nobody liked, so it came to be known by all and sundry as simply 'Lawrabian'.

According to Fred 'Law' came from 'the letter of…' due to his connections with Plod. The rest came from 'Arabian' due to the fact that Fred had spent part of his working life as an insurance investigator, roaming the wastes of Arabia looking for 'missing' T.I.P. semi-trailers (the correct term for a trailer: semi articulated). The trailers in question had been hired from T.I.P. at various locations, and loaded for destinations all over the Middle East… where a fair number remained and ended up as Bedouin tents.

Lawrabian was one of the names under which Fred operated on his often fruitless expeditions to the Gulf and elsewhere, so he obviously thought it an appropriate title for 'our' new venture.

Ernie had decided to chuck his lot in with Roy and Fred after the split, offering to help with the move (in case anything needed 'moving'), and by volunteering to drive the brand-new-second-hand forklift.

With all things agreed the new company moved from the grime of the East India Docks to a shared scrap-metal yard on the A13 at Ripple Road, Barking. But, old habits being hard to kill, nobody bothered to tell me! It wasn't until I came back off a trip one day that I found I'd quite innocently driven into the wrong yard. I was greeted by a few regular faces, informed that I no longer worked for Tanker International – and promptly told to fuck off!

Anyway, after finding my 'new' employer a couple of miles away, I gratefully acknowledged the fact that I was still employed, and settled in to make the best of it.

I had more or less been given the green card (apart from the iffy Turkish insurance) to get on and do the job in any way I saw fit. My only orders were 'standing orders' which were more of an unwritten rule in effect, the same as those issued on my first trip, simply: "Get there – and get back!"

Perfect!

Or so I thought until I laid eyes on the 89, that is.

Although it meant I could now drop the Irish accent if I was stopped by the sheriff or the Ministry (Min. of Transport), I took an instant dislike to that Volvo as soon as I saw it. Everyone had been ranting on about how good the 89s – and its smaller sister the 88 – were, but to me it was just an ugly old heap and I was not impressed. There she was – OVB 736S – sat in one corner of the yard in full sunshine, refusing to sparkle. My first thought was, shit! What have I let myself in for? That's a museum piece, a fossil, even more so than the Mack! Something that wouldn't look out of place in a black and white war film, like the ambulance in 'Ice Cold From Alex'.

The cab was small and cramped, like a 'day cab' (one without a bunk), the bed itself being tiny, even for me – and I'm only 5'7". It had a small, split windscreen; one wiper that refused to work ('you only need to see out of one side!'); seemed comically undersized for the wheels it ran on, and had a 'faded with age' paint job that made her look like a paid-up, card-carrying member of 'F-Troop'.

OVB 736S (right) in all her glory

'F-Troop' was the not-undeserved nickname for Romtrans, the Romanian State fleet, whose colours were varying shades of blue – the same as my new mount.

F-Troop, bless their home-made socks, used to roam heroically across two continents at a slow canter, causing traffic chaos wherever they went, and would regularly break down at the drop of a hat because of their hopelessly underpowered and poorly maintained 'Roman-Diesel' trucks – a Romanian spec truck with an M.A.N. cab plonked on it. These ran on industrial heating oil, old sump oil, kerosene and anything else that burned – or converted into smoke. They were also allowed to enter the EEC with more than the regulation two hundred litre limit for fuel that applied to the rest of us. They always seemed to run in minimum convoys of three, presumably so that when one of them broke down his two komrades could form a circle and fight off the Indians… or at least stop one of them from doing a runner.

Though most of F-Troop consisted of these gerry-built monstrosities, they actually ran a few highly prized 89s of their own, and I had horrible visions of Ernie's new pride and joy being one of them. But I was wrong again: In fact that old Volvo really surprised everyone and did me and Ernie proud because at the end of the day she turned out to be the most reliable old workhorse I've ever driven. All Ernie ever said about her, with a fag in his mouth, one eye closed and a slight grin on his face was 'Told ya so'. I personally think it was a shame they stopped making them when they did because they were a lot more reliable than some of the crap that's been produced since, and because I became more attached to that truck in nine months than I have to any other before or since. Bless her.

To me, the job was a godsend. After a very shaky start I was now being allowed to roam around vast areas of the continent alone and almost at will. I'd also been given a green card (apart from the dodgy Turkish insurance) to get on and do the job in any way I saw fit. That meant taking as long as I cared and being able to spend whatever money I'd been given to go with! If I ever ran short of money (which was often) all I had to do was phone in or send a Telex asking for a 'draw', and money would be transferred to me via an agent somewhere along the line. Few questions asked and receipts not required. Thank you very much! My only orders were standing orders, which were more like an unwritten rule really, and were the same ones that had been issued on my first trip with Tony, simply 'Get there and get back…' It was like a schoolboy's dream come true. I couldn't fault it. And now, with the 89, I wasn't breaking down every day either.

So, I loaded up in mid-summer, jumped into the saddle of 736S, shipped out for old Constantinople – and drove straight into chaos.

In August of 1986, two things happened that shocked and surprised me: First was the 'August break', Europe's month off, and the start of the annual Turkish migration; the regular stampede of Turks leaving their homes and workplaces in the west to head back home to Asia Minor for a month. Gastarbeiters (guest workers) as they're known are basically a temporary Turkish import with a work visa. Herds of them. And second, the August shutdown started, which is when just about every factory, winery and warehouse across vast areas of Europe close their doors for the summer break.

The Turkish migration from Germany was a drivers nightmare that I thought would never end, and the shutdown of business across Europe was a dream that I didn't want to end.

I'd been warned about the 'Turks in Mercs' as they were called, but I was still in for a rude wake-up call when I landed on Belgian soil at the start of Europe's holiday period.

I'd expected the roads to be busy, but I didn't even get as far as the German border before seeing half a dozen accidents. It seemed as if every Turk in the lowlands had packed up work, crammed loads of presents and all their worldly possessions – including Granny and the zimmer frame - jumped into old Transit vans or a knackered old Merc saloon, with the sole intention of heading east to cause mayhem. It was their month off, their once-in-a-year chance to go home and show off to their friends and rellies and brag about how well they're doing in the Fatherland; to shower everyone with cheap tacky gifts and give it 'The big one' before they had to re-pack and head back, en-masse, to the Bundesrepublik and start driving their forklifts again in September.

The mayhem this migration caused was, and still is to some extent, bloody outrageous.

Even running on Belgian or Dutch plates they couldn't be mistaken for anything other than 'Turks in Mercs', and once into the Bundesrepublik their German-registered kinsfolk, the largest contingent of all, joined in the Wacky Races. 'Turks in Mercs' usually meant a minimum of six people in a dangerously unroadworthy Mercedes car – the sort favoured by the baddies in crap spy films – with the roofrack overloaded, the boot overloaded, the bonnet sitting up and begging and the boot bumper scraping the floor. Behind the wheel sat Mustafa with his moustache sandwiched between each hand at the wheel, or quite often, the fourteen-year-old son would be in charge as the car rocketed down the narrow, pot-holed roads at stupid speeds because was too tired to drive any more and the boy wanted to impress the rest of the family with his driving skills by reaching the Turkish border in record time. The accidents caused by this sort of behaviour were predictable and horrific.

There were streams of these German registered cars – some hired, some bought as bangers – hurtling eastwards through Germany,

Austria, Yugoslavia and Bulgaria twenty-four hours a day. All the parking areas and laybys would be choc-a-bloc with whole families camped out either in their vehicles, on the grass verges or simply on the tarmac. Or they'd be sat around in groups, enjoying a picnic in a ditch, or sleeping – and shitting – next to Ahmet and his tribe in the sunflower crops.

It quietened down a bit at night because, for some reason, a lot of them wouldn't drive in the dark hours. But these guys (the women rarely drove) didn't park up sensibly, they simply 'abandoned' and camped out wherever they could find a space, usually in total disorder and blocking something off. Some motorway services looked more like refugee camps: the women scarved and robed, belting the kids and cooking on gas bombs; the men flaked out on the grass smoking Marlboros and giving orders. The litter and mess left behind was a fire hazard, smelly and not to mention an eyesore.

The queues at peages (toll booths on the motorways) and at borders were farcical, with the arrival of each new convoy of cars trying to form its own lane where one wouldn't normally exist, and each 'new' lane claiming a noisy right of way over the next. Extra staff always had to be laid on and the police, fire and ambulance services were stretched to their limits.

By the time I reached Yugoslavia the situation had become downright dangerous. Their numbers seemed to have increased five-fold as they arrived from all areas of Germany and Austria to converge on Sentilj, and the main transit route through Yugoslavia on what was largely single lane 'national' roads, to the Bulgarian border at Gradina.

At Slavonski Brod – not my most favourite place – an accident involving Turks in Mercs and a local bus had slowed everything to a crawl. At least half a dozen Turk cars and vans (a lot of them ran in convoy) were scattered in fields and hedgerows; the bus was half-on half-off the road on its side, and bodies lay everywhere.

I was waved through to keep access clear for smaller vehicles, and had to zigzag past the carnage. It looked like a bomb had gone off. I pulled off the road soon after at a large motel-camping ground. It was a known stopping place for trucks, and as several were already in the cobble-stoned car park I wheeled alongside one and decided to call it a day.

Moments later a score of policemen arrived in tiny 'Zastavas' (about the size of Noddy's car) and closed off the sliproads. I had a momentary panic attack imagining they were about to come across and try to implicate me in the accident – a not-uncommon event in some parts of the world if the prospect of hard currency rears its head.

The reason, my adrenaline levels were glad to know, was that a fleet of ambulances and commandeered vehicles began to arrive ferrying the wounded to each other and to the motel.

It was like a scene from M.A.S.H. but without the laughs. The ambulances took who they could; bodies were carried into the motel and laid out in the foyer, uncovered. Some were left on the steps, others on the dusty driveway. Helpers moved about the injured, bandaging, comforting. Some cried and screamed. The rest lay in silence.

Having done their job of directing a few more ambulances the Yugo coppers stood around smoking, looking totally unconcerned. We had already been told to stay put – so we did just that.

Fatal accidents were all too common for obvious reasons and most, sadly, involved children. Nobody has any statistics that I know of, but it was rumoured that up to ten percent of Turks that joined this annual lemming run to the Orient never made it to their destinations in one piece. One in ten may sound a lot, but I reckon it's not too far from the truth.

The authorities of these countries hated the migration and most had little time for the Turks, especially the Yugoslavs. Many of those that were killed in accidents were just left where they died, sometimes for days on end, or their cars and vans, or what was left of them, were simply bulldozed off the side of the road because the services couldn't cope and, more to the point, couldn't give a shit. Any personal belongings were considered fair game by the police and locals alike, and were simply stolen or scattered in fields and ditches.

To experience this chaos and bloodshed first-hand and for the first time was horrifying, and it really hit me. It brought home to me just how fragile a persons life is out on the road, and how little that life is valued in certain parts of the world. Though I'd been forewarned it still came as a huge shock and even today, over a decade on, I still find it hard to accept that people can behave the way they do.

The other effect of the August shutdown on us, the drivers, was a lot less hazardous. Some may even say beneficial, because so many workers went on the missing list in August it was common practice for businesses to simply wind down to tickover for the duration. It meant that when a driver gets tipped in Greece or Turkey or somewhere in that part of the world, there's little chance of finding a decent back-load to England for a week or two, so at some stage of the month hundreds, if not thousands of trucks of all nationalities, would be parked up empty all over Europe – with almost as many drivers' bums parked in bars, or on beaches soaking up the sun!

A lot of drivers took their wives or girlfriends (or somebody else's) with them at this time of year, and made a holiday of it by swanning around the Greek islands for a week or two, or by doing the tourist bit in Istanbul and elsewhere. Leaving the truck for long periods wasn't a problem, there were, and still are, plenty of safe parking places in Greece and Turkey, so slipping away for a fortnight and leaving an expensive truck and trailer miles behind wasn't a worry.

There were always the odd one or two drivers that sat around and whinged about the money they were losing by being parked up (or 'square-wheeled' as the dickheads on the C.B. – Citizens Band Radio - like to say) or what they'd lose if they decided to run home empty. But they were in a minority, the rest of us just went out and had fun.

I thought it was fantastic that we could all just park up, bugger off and party for as long as it took and really made the best of it. Well, why wouldn't I? I had a wallet full of someone else's money!

I managed to avoid further mayhem by giving Bulgaria a miss and taking the more relaxing 'tourist route' through Greece. Greece was my favourite at this time of year, partly for the beaches, partly because everything is so laid back, and partly because we don't have to pay for parking – which of course means extra beer vouchers.

Twelve kilometres into Greece from the border with Turkey is the small village of Ardanio, situated around a crossroads – a Y junction actually, but everyone calls it a crossroads. Right on the junction is a BP station with a restaurant attached to it – as they often are in Greece. They call this place 'Ardanio Truck Stop'. We call it 'Maria's'. It is also known as the 'Piston Broke Club' amongst other things, and it's where a lot of Brits head for if they just want to get out of Turkey and park up for the duration.

It's a real international meeting place: the French (Kermits) use it – it was called the Frenchmans for years; the Vikings use it (Swedes and Danes), the Cloggies, Krauts, Alpine Turks (Austrians) and all sorts. Many a good piss-up has been had here, not to mention punch-ups (and not just during the August break). It's a good place to use as a base too because we'd often drop the trailers here and bobtail down to the beaches around Alexandropoulis, to top up the tan and see what's about.

Maria's ought to be included on every map of the area I reckon, or at least given a mention in one of those 'How to see the universe on a tuppence' books. Even the customs men and police at the border know it and use it, and will often say to us as we come into the country:

'How many days stay at Maria's?' with a smile.

But it should also come with a warning, or at least a hazardous sticker because it's a damn fine place to pay homage to the great god 'Metaxa' (Greek cognac) and collect the world's worst hangover. But I found that paying due homage each visit had its spiritual rewards because if you drank enough of it, it fended off the evil spirit known as 'mozzie'.

During this time I got to meet a lot more of the guys simply because we were all parked up together. Not that there are thousands of Brits driving trucks to Turkey and the Middle East – at the time I don't suppose there were more than seventy or eighty regulars at most, if that, and although most of them knew each other, or knew one another by name, they would, because of the nature of the beast, rarely get to meet or spend time together. More often than not, they'd pass each other on the road somewhere, or drive off on a ferry in Dover just as another was waiting to drive on, so, when they did get the chance to get together and party, they'd make the best of it. And Maria's is one hell of a good meeting place.

This was when I got to meet a few of the Middle East drivers themselves, a couple of whom I'd met before, but most of whose names I'd only heard. It was great – I was fascinated and awed by some of these people and would sit for hours at their table – the 'English Table' – and listen wide-mouthed to their stories of sun, sand and heroism. I lapped it all up. I was chomping at the bit and wanted to go to these places myself, to Baghdad, to Teheran and Jeddah, to Muscat and Damascus – I wanted to cross the Tigris and the Euphrates, to drive down the Trans Arabian pipeline (The Tap Line). I wanted to be Lawrence of Arabia and travel thousands of miles across scorching deserts and bandit country. I wanted to talk Arabic, wear a gingham tea-towel around my head and impress lots of people. I wanted to be able to sit with these guys – my heroes – and say, 'Been there, yawn – done that' and, just like all the other new boys and 'halfwayers' (those that only went to Turkey) who sat at the same table as wide-mouthed as myself, I actually believed most of the bullshit that was being said for our benefit…

It made no difference at the time, because even though I'd made some new friends and contacts and was fired up with enthusiasm about driving a truck all the way to the Middle East and back, it would still be a while before anyone was daft enough to send me any further East than Turkey.

My only real involvement at the time, and probably my most useful, was in my ability to order another round of beer in fluent gibberish. In Turkey this was easily done because rounds were ordered by the crate – usually Efes beer – and it was just a simple matter of fetching one, whereupon everybody just helped themselves until the crate was empty, and so on. Payment of the round was often deferred until one of the waiters came round and counted the empties – minus the ones we'd hidden or air mailed into the flower beds, of course.

My only other contribution at the time, was in giving whatever advice I could to the few drivers that had been 'lucky' enough to secure a return load to the UK from Italy – one of the few countries that seemed to keep its warehouse doors open a bit longer than most during the August break.

Most of the full time Middle East drivers and halfwayers actually knew bugger all about Western Europe, apart from where it was and how to get across it from one end to the other. It's fair comment though, seeing as most of their work was done within the world of Islan, and simply because I'd done a few loads to and from Italy in the furniture van before starting this work, I apparently was the man to ask.

I was chuffed to bits with that – it made me feel really useful and important, even though I couldn't really tell them much because I'd actually only done a handful of trips to Milan and Pisa. But it seemed to be good enough for them, so I really made the best of it and gave it the 'big one'. Here I was, still a relative novice, being asked questions and directions by men that had covered more miles in reverse than most of us do in a lifetime, and I was loving it.

So, I drove the twelve k's to the border at Ipsala with a hangover, and then took a steady four hour run to Istanbul.

Twenty-four hours later, having cleared customs and tipped the load, I headed back over the Bosporus Bridge from Asia into mainland Europe. I then made straight for Kasim's yard at Avçilar to park for the night, and to interview a well-earned tin of beer. Job done.

Most of 'Tankers' drivers, now 'Lawrabian', used to park at Kasim's, as I've said. It was expected of us. It was cheaper than elsewhere, and convenient for repairs, etc. though at this stage of the game the 89 needed nothing more than a good wash. She hadn't missed a beat or shed a bolt all the way down!

The majority of drivers though, Brit or otherwise, used to park elsewhere. Not least because the yard at Avçilar only had one hole in the ground to shit in, but also had no shower, no bar or restaurant – and no communications. So the next day I dropped the trailer at Kasim's and bob-tailed the ten k's or so to the 'Mocamp' to telex mission control in Barking for instructions.

The 'Mocamp', a motel and camping ground right under the flight path to Atatürk Airport, went by the title of 'Londra Camping'. It had a no-star motel next to a lichen-green swimming pool, a camping ground for backpackers and overland adventure buses, a restaurant, and a huge dusty, mosquito-infested truck park with resident pot-holes and an assortment of large trees growing in awkward places.

'Mocamp' was a term generally used by the older hands to the job who drove to, and through, Turkey in the early days of TIR and Middle East work, back in the late '60s and early '70s. In those days, I'm told, Turkey was 'bandit country'. Loads, wheels, diesel, side windows and drivers' wallets – even whole rigs – were fair game. Secure parking was a necessity rather than a luxury, and these Mocamps provided safe havens for overnight or longer-term parking.

The term Mocamp is pretty much consigned to history now, and even then, in the mid '80s, most of us just called it 'The Londra'.

Having snuck into the Londra without declaring my intention to the 'Abi' (used in the context of 'mate') at the entrance, to avoid paying for the parking, I bumped down to the bottom end of the carpark to the unofficial 'English parking', right beneath a row of oil-stained workshops.

The place was filled with trucks; Falcongates, Dow Freight, C.V.H., Whittles. Some sat alone or in small groups by their trailer boxes brewing up, cooking breakfast and fighting off the flies. Others still had their curtains closed, but with open doors or windows to allow free movement of air and dust. It was hot.

Having made my apologies for creating a minor duststorm, I headed towards reception on foot, past the spot where the Iranians parked nose into the wall so they could peek over at the female tourists in the camping grounds. I then lodged my hand-written telex message with the 'Abi' on the front desk to send at his leisure, and headed into the restaurant for a nosebag.

Sat in a corner alone was one of 'ours' – Lawrabian – so I went over to join him. 'Dirty Dick' hadn't seen me. He had one hand wrapped around a bottle of Efes, and his nose buried in a paperback book.

A bit of a loner in many ways, Dick was one of the gentlemen on the job. Truly gentle. His only failing being his inability to find a pair of jeans that stayed in place. We'd joke about his 'hydraulic' jeans that had a habit of forming in a bunch below waist level. He was always tugging at them.

His head popped up in surprise as I sat down, engrossed as he was in Anna Karenina or something. He smiled and made a very polite and generous show of greeting me.

'Hello, Dick. What's happening?' I asked.

'Not a lot, mate. There's no backloads at the moment. I've been empty all week. Have you, er, spoken to Roy?'

'No. Abi's sending a telex for me. Don't want to waste money on the phone, do I?'

'Quite right. I was up at Kasim's but I came down for the same reason – and a bit of, er, grub, of course.' He said, nodding towards his beer with a grin. 'You might as well have one, there's nothing moving.'

'I'll wait a bit,' I said, '- see what Roy has to say first.' So I went to grab some food instead.

It was a typical Londra Camp meal - bean soup, mutton with green things in oily red sauce, cold rice, etc., all of which must have tasted exquisite earlier that week. I grabbed a glass of black çay (pronounced chy) tea to go with it and another bottle of beer for Dick.

'Sounds like the lads are starting early again,' Dick said, cocking an ear at the laughter coming from the outside seating area, and I wondered if they'd eaten the same breakfast.

Picking up his book he added, 'I'll, er, leave you lot to it John, if you don't mind. Not getting involved again today.' His partly bloodshot eyes told the rest of the story.

Dick actually preferred the quiet life for the most part, so I gave him his second 'hair of the dog' (which rarely worked with Efes – it just got you steaming drunk again), scoffed the edible portion of my meal, bid him happy reading, and went to join the rest of the tribe outside.

Sure enough a gaggle of drivers were seated at the dusty tables, supping beer and holding a pow-wow about the 'Slut Bus' (overland adventure bus) that was due back that evening – and, of course, how many women were on board.

The fact that I'd invited myself to sit at a table full of strangers meant nothing. It was common practice for Brit drivers, and others, to congregate. It would be deemed 'snobbish' to do otherwise. After all, as the saying goes 'We're all in the same boat'. And anyway, this was Istanbul, not Isleworth.

The day grew hotter and busier. And the beer flowed. Drivers appeared in ever-increasing numbers – Turks, Poles, Hungarians, Austrians… and more Brits. The outside seating was soon full and we had for company a rake of Vikings and Cloggies, all yelling 'skol' and such-like as they piled into the communal beer crates.

Some of these guys had just returned from Baghdad or Riyadh, Kuwait City or Muscat. They were tired, dirty, unshaven and running short of money. Most had been away from homes and families for a month or two – but it wasn't going to spoil their fun.

There was talk of visiting the Grand Bazaar in town. Others wanted to go to the Pudding Shop (not the Pudding Club as some call it) down at Sultan Ahmet, to carry on drinking and have a go at pulling a tourist or two. Some just wanted to go straight down to 'Pig Alley' – the red light area – and simply get their rocks off!

This was an eye-opener for me. Being 'weekended' somewhere was one thing, i.e. being unable to load, clear customs or tip 'til a Monday, or not being able to 'run' during a Sunday ban. But here were these guys quite happily making holiday plans for the next fortnight!

Mind you, most drivers present were closer to their friends on the road than they were to homelives and families. To them this wasn't just a job, it was a way of life.

After what seemed a lifetime of drinking çay and staring at beer crates, I was summoned on the Londra's crackly, over-loud tannoy system:

'Ingiliss d-river Mister Chon, pliz kom to re-sepsyon… Ingiliss d-river…'

The Abi at re-sepsyon aimed me towards a vacant phone on the desk. The line, as always, was atrocious, but it didn't prevent me from hearing Roy scream at the top of his voice. 'Right Nevill, there's fuck all about so you might as well make the best of it. Okay? Contact me next week!'

Next week! Yes! Party time!

En route through the restaurant I grabbed a crate of Efes and passed Dirty Dick, who'd given up on his book, and was now entertaining a tableful of Turks with his famous rendition of, 'Kailinka, Kailinka, Kailinka-la-la!'

I'd soon have to prove myself though, because Roy decided to send us – Lawrabian – for our own return loads during August - to Italy…!

Resting up at Londra Camping

Six

Of dodgy permits and Rolex watches

The first time Roy ever sent me over to Italy for a backload should really have been the last, because it was a complete comedy of errors right from the word go.

To start with I got captured at the border on my way into the country for trying to pass a dodgy permit – an authorisation for a commercial vehicle.

This upset them a bit, so as punishment, I was given a full 'control', which consisted of a body search – luckily without the finger up the bum – and a complete cab control, which is when the bastards take the cab to bits by removing door panels, dashboards, roof lining and all sorts, and don't bother to replace any of it properly because half of the screws 'accidentally' go missing. Then they went through *all* my personal baggage and belongings – including dirty laundry, and *everything* was given the once over by sniffer dogs.

I then had the empty trailer taken apart, and that meant pulling up the floorboards and unscrewing the plywood that covered the headboard; emptying the trailer boxes, bashing the belly tank, shining torches through the filler cap, and letting air out of the spare wheels. Then I had to jack the cab over so the sniffer dogs could clamber over the hot engine, piss on the exhaust manifold and generally get covered in oil (Alsations if I remember – dead friendly, but thick) and yet another control from the large nose of a very serious-looking Inspector Cleauseau lookalike.

When they couldn't find anything else wrong and they got bored, I was given a serious but unwarranted bollocking from Cleauseau, which had me nodding my head and biting my tongue with mirth.

It turned out the reason for all this time-wasting nonsense was not so much because of the dodgy permit – they never really were a problem in Italy - but because I had Kasim with me and as they'd held us up to start with he insisted on doing lots of arm waving and shouting – in Turkish. This did not impress Plod very much and, because I'd said very little – due to the fact that I couldn't get a word in edgeways – the Italians accused me of being a Turk and of trying to run drugs through their border on a Turkish truck with a micky GB permit!

It was only when they realised that I wasn't Turkish and that the truck was actually from England (the British passport and expensive flip-flops gave it away – which was when I found out that being British and having the full weight of our diplomatic services and a fearsome reputation behind us, actually meant fuck all to an angry, embarrassed, senior Italian policeman. That embarrassment coupled with a vicious desire to 'get-even' took over – hence the full control.

Every other truck that arrived at the border that day must have loved us because every single one of them was waved straight through.

The 'damage' at the end of the day, believe it or not, was a carton of fags for the permit, which they were actually good enough to 'ramp up' (stamp) for me, and a wagging finger which said, 'Nexta time, Inglisi, use a deeferen' border – or this *will* go uppa you backside…'

Welcome to Italy, John.

The reason I had Kasim with me in the first place was because Ernie – always on the sniff to save a few bob - wanted to employ him as a driver. This is something Kasim wanted only too much because to be a 'TIR şoför' – pronounced shoffer (chauffer-driver) is a big macho thing in Turkey. The fact that he is the sort of bloke who will willingly graft twenty-four hours a day, is reasonably handy with the spanners and doesn't mind working for half wages, had nothing to do with Ernie's choice, of course.

The only real problem with this was the fact that Kasim knew bugger all about the job, and I'd been given the privileged task of teaching him what little I knew. Talk about the blind leading the blind! We'd already been arrested, locked up and fined in Germany on the way down because Kasim's German visa had expired and Ernie, in all his wisdom, had tried to change the date on it – with a felt tip pen! The Germans weren't too impressed so they decided to bang both of us up for the day and fine Kasim the best part of two hundred pounds, which came straight out of Ernie's run-money, so it hadn't been the best of trips to start with.

And the farce continued.

After we eventually entered the country and got loaded at Reggio Amelia I think it was – and then spent God knows how long running up the 'old roads' to avoid the Autostrada tolls because we were short of money, we eventually got into France and I put Kasim behind the wheel. I then wrote out a list of place names he had to follow, stuck it to the windscreen right in front of his eyes, went to bed and left him to it.

Mistake.

Consequently, Kasim got us so lost going up through France that I thought I'd never see home again. Not only did we end up on an autoroute that we couldn't afford, but I woke at one point in the early hours of the morning, to see Kasim merrily driving along in the dark *wearing sunglasses!* 'Issa stoppy headlighty a' shiny eyes, inni?!' So I buried my head in the sand and left him to it.

Then after going through the *same* peage booth *three times* and totally confusing the lady who took the money, he finally woke me up to announce that we were now hopelessly lost, desperately skint and 'Ar dunno me, issa proberlum chon. Where issa we go nah 'en?' I looked up blurry eyed only to discover that he'd landed us right in the middle of some poor sods farmyard a *kilometre* from the nearest main road!

What really took the biscuit, after we'd visited a local hauliers yard to try and raise some cash by selling Ernie's spare wheel (they laughed) was when he got us nicked, or rather 'apprehended' at St. Omer peage, which is only a stone's throw away from the ferry boat at Calais. Obviously we had no money left to pay the toll so, instead of trying to do a deal with whatever we had (which wasn't much), Kasim being Kasim went into one and decided to argue the toss… in Turkish.

Needless to say, when the police eventually let us go six hours later, having taken the cab to bits (it came apart easier this time), rummaged through the load on the trailer, and marvelled at the fact that an entire artic could actually run on a tank full of diesel fumes – I was not very impressed. And if I remember, we actually ran out of diesel trying to drive up the ramp onto the ferry, and were that skint that we couldn't afford one subsidised sealink-drivers-dinner between the two of us!

To get into Italy on that trip, I'd run up through Yugoslavia and entered, not through the main border near Trieste, but through a smaller, out of the way border further North, called Pesse, or Pessi, simply because I'd been told 'Nah, you won' 'ave any problems, don' worry, they're all fick up there…'

The Italians aren't thick, believe me. Overdressed and fond of Brylcreem and micky aftershave maybe, but not thick. For sure, Italy can be a wonderful place. I mean, they gave us open sewers, fizzy wine, the Fiat trucks (more commonly called the 'Vatican Mack'). They gave us spaghetti westerns, expensive shoes, suspect architecture – and the Mafia… which makes Italy a dangerous place. Especially for truck drivers.

Crime is rife in Italy and truck drivers, or more importantly, the loads they carry, are prime targets, because just about everyone a driver comes into contact with here will be bent – in more ways than one. It's actually one of the most dangerous countries in Europe for trucks and has just about the highest insurance premium for commercial goods.

Though there is always the risk of being robbed in Italy, it has to be said that most of the horror stories that have originated here will have been exaggerated. Tales always get stretched a bit by drivers, especially when there's nobody else around at the time of the event to challenge their story. But it's not difficult to sift through the lies. The danger is very real in Italy and most can tell if a driver is just gobbing off or if he's had a genuine experience.

To be held at gunpoint, bound and gagged, and told to sit still while someone drives off with your truck isn't something to brag about over a beer. I've met quite a few drivers who've been hijacked, and the fear in their eyes has told the whole story.

At first I used to take most of the stories with a pinch of salt. I'd done a fair few trips to Italy before, in the furniture van, and never once had a problem – even though I used to carry high-value loads of silverware and antiques. But I was just lucky. Over the years I would learn to appreciate the dangers of Italy, by virtue of being chased, robbed, gassed in my sleep and being approached by some individuals with hairy chests and a face full of make-up.

It's reckoned that a large percentage of it is Mafia controlled – which would make sense – whereby it's known in advance what loads are being brought into or taken out of the country because of bent shipping agents, importers, etc. and of course, customs officials, all of whom would be on the payroll somewhere along the line. It's then a simple matter of a phone call when the 'right' load is on its way somewhere, and Roberto's your uncle.

It's common knowledge in Italy, and simply accepted as the norm. And though being tied up and having a gun shoved under your hooter with the threat of being shot must be a terrifying experience, I've never known personally of any drivers actually being harmed – though I'm sure many have – and let's face it, psychological damage can be just as permanent as a stab wound or a bullet hole.

I once met a Dutchman wandering around a service area car park in a daze – his truck and trailer had just been taken from him at gunpoint, in front of several people who didn't even bat an eyelid! He was in such a state that the poor sod didn't know whether to laugh or cry.

Generally speaking a driver will be left with his life intact and the clothes he's wearing. If it's just the load they want, that's all they'll take. They'll leave your wallet alone and leave off with the serious violence. I think perhaps there may be some code of honour that forbids ABH (Actual Bodily Harm) against a driver, though I wouldn't like to put any money on it. It's probably more a case of a terrified working man doing the sensible thing when he's got the barrel of a gun pressed under his chin.

I had the shits put up me once when I was followed by a car for more than an hour. I was trying to find a warehouse where I was to pick up my second collection. It was late at night and I wanted to get to the place so that I'd be right on their doorstep and ready to load first thing in the morning. I was driving around and noticed a pair of headlamps in my wing mirrors. I suspected that they were following me and not just taking the same route, but I couldn't be sure, so I drove around in circles from one end of this industrial estate to the other and sure enough, the headlights copied every move I made.

After a while when the car refused to go away I got scared. I didn't want to stop the truck anywhere in case they jumped me – I'd already assumed there was a gang of them in the car – and I really didn't know what to do. I could hardly drive around all night and hope that they'd go away, or run out of petrol. I did consider ramming the car against a tree or a wall, but my instincts wouldn't allow it: if the car had purposely been trying to stop me or make me go somewhere I didn't want to go then it would have been a different story, but all it did was stay behind me.

There was nobody else about – not a soul. All of the buildings were shuttered and locked, the street lights were off and I thought 'Fucking typical – where's the local sheriff when you want one', so I couldn't even stop to round up a posse. I could only guess at how many were actually in the car because all I could see was the glare from the headlights, and it would have been obvious to them that I was alone – most drivers are and anyway, wing mirrors are a foot tall and eight inches wide – they'd see if anyone was in the passengers side.

Neither could I know if 'they' were after my load, my wallet or my arse, and I was getting more than a little bit worried when this car hadn't gone away after nearly an hour. Obviously I wasn't game enough to stop and ask their intentions, so I considered my options – both of them: Run away or run away, when the car suddenly tried to come by me and I reacted instinctively. I swung the wheel over to the left and stood on the brakes. Without thinking I grabbed the pickaxe handle I kept in the cab and leapt out to confront them.

The car was only a few feet away from the drivers door and very close to the out-turned trailer. I was suddenly really pissed off with this car and went straight for the left-hand side – the drivers side. I wanted to get it all over and done with – the adrenalin was really pumping and I was terrified.

As I moved forwards I could only see one person in the car and this suddenly gave me the extra courage I needed to keep my legs moving forward instead of into reverse where they really wanted to go.

As I ran I screamed 'Come here you bastard' while hoping he wouldn't, just as he slipped into reverse and backed away. My legs wobbled a bit as I quickly put the brakes on, and as I watched him back further and further away I began to tremble and thought to myself 'Thank fuck for that…' Twenty minutes later I was parked up under the street lamps of a motorway service area, still trembling, and that's where I stayed 'til daylight.

That may not sound like much of an incident to some people, but it put the wind up me. When a driver is on his own – which is most of the time – and in an unpredictable situation, I won't listen to all those 'heroes' who say, 'I'd have done this' or 'I'd have done that'… nobody knows what they'd do until something happens, and most people will take the easiest way out. I probably should have gone up to the motorway at the start, but it simply didn't occur to me at the time. It's so easy to say something after the event. Had there been more people in the car, or even if 'they' had been really determined, I would most certainly have lost either my load, my wallet or my virginity… or all three.

That was in Northern Italy, but Southern Italy seems to be the worst. To confirm this you only have to pull into a service area after dark – it's not often you'll see a truck parked up for the night unless they're mob handed, or loaded with animal waste or something equally useless.

Bari in S.E. Italy is a nice place. It's a port town and is fairly typical of anywhere in this part of the world that sees lots of drivers coming and going. Stand still for more than a few minutes and some little bastard on a motor scooter will scream past and snatch the wallet or passport from your hand – or even back pocket – and zoom straight off without stopping. Another bike is likely to turn up and 'accidentally' block the path of anyone who wants to give chase. Bari is a warren of alleyways and dead-ends down by the docks.

I was told that there's a person especially employed full time at the local cop shop whose job it is just to take reports and type up details of all street robberies in the town. He's said to be constantly busy.

Luckily for me, I never had to 'do' too much in Italy. It's not a country that's on the TIR list. TIR work is mostly carried out in Eastern Europe and other non-EU countries. European work, such as Italy, belongs to another group of drivers altogether. Drivers that only 'do' Europe and who have little or nothing to do with TIR work.

This is a different world from TIR. These drivers work under different rules and regulations and different paperwork. Their customs documents are – or were – called T. Forms (T = Transit). Not for them the reams of senseless red tape, road taxes, complicated procedures, communism, Island, manifests, religious niceties and greasy kebabs. These drivers carried paperwork that could be folded and put into a purse. They largely enjoy the benefit of good roads, good food and weekends at home. Their earnings are probably higher than the TIR earnings, and they mostly pay for everything with plastic. They don't have the worry of going home skint, breaking down every day or trying to reach a ferry boat in neutral because they're out of fuel.

These guys have always affectionately been known as 'T. Formers' or 'T. Form Charlies' – and I wouldn't have their jobs for all the tea in China.

They work hard – a lot harder than I care to, that's for sure. They load, ship out, go like fuck to get somewhere, often without proper sleep, then, when they tip, they're under pressure to tear arse to get reloaded and then chase the clock to get back again! Where's the fun in that?

These guys have all my respect and I reckon they're entitled to wear furry clogs with white socks, peaked caps, outrageous Bermuda shorts and tight-fitting shirts. They've every right to adopt macho C.B. 'handles' (nicknames) and then advertise those names on a 'number plate' in the windscreen. They're allowed to talk like transport managers on the airwaves, then drive straight past other Brits when they're broken down on the side of the road.

I can understand and accept all that because I don't have to work eighteen hours a day to keep the boss happy; I don't have to valet the cab every five minutes; I don't have to wolf my food down because I'm in a hurry to get rolling again before the engine stops crackling; and I don't have to worry too much about 'tachos' (tachographs).

A tachograph is the 'spy in the cab' as the media coined the phrase. The only people to ever use that phrase, surprise surprise. Everyone else just calls it a tacho. It's a disc of paper that slots into the speedo. The tacho head records everything from speed, driving time, mileage, etc. It's a real pain in the arse and if foreign police don't use it to nick a driver for the slightest infringement of what are quite complicated rules of driving, the authorities back home will, with relish. And bosses will use it to say 'Didn't do a lot on that day, did you?' or 'What happened there, get stuck in second gear, did you?' and so on.

In Eastern Europe, Turkey, or basically most countries outside the EU, tacho problems, like doing 73 in a 70 limit, or only taking 44 minutes break instead of 45, aren't really a problem. If it is, then it's usually a packet of fags, a bottle of beer or a dirty book. In 'civilised'

Europe, and especially in the UK, tachos are used to persecute and prosecute, because truck drivers – English that is, not foreign drivers- are easy targets. And T. Formers, more than most, have to bear the brunt of it.

I raise my glass to them. Partly because they deserve it, partly because I don't have to put up with too much of that nonsense, but mostly because I've got time to enjoy that beer – and they don't.

Fuck T. Forming, give me TIR any day.

Apart from the dangers of being robbed or hijacked, Italy can be an expensive experience anyway. At the time, it had the most expensive fuel prices anywhere in Europe, and road tolls were extortionate – which is why most T. Formers used to 'knock' them, by handing over a passport (for details to be written down, instead of handing over cash) by smiling, and by a shrug of the shoulders.

But one of the dearest cuts of all is the con-men. Italy's full of them and 'foreign' truck drivers are an easy target. When these guys turn over a driver, he'll lose more than the price of a meal. These guys can force gullible drivers to part company with their money as easily as taking sweets off a bambino.

They're the men who operate mostly in motorway service areas selling 'genuine' Rolex watches, or offering to change money at a better than normal rate. Their Rolex's are micky and the exchange rate is usually a wad of newspaper clippings.

These people are good – just ask Jem Cockerill.

Jem, a school teacher come TIR driver from Whitby near the Arctic Circle, and a man with possibly the bushiest eyebrows in the Northern Hemisphere, was done like a kipper by these guys one day.

He was on his way South to Ancona to catch a ferry to Greece – the tourist route to Turkey. He'd parked up on the motorway somewhere to have a brew (Y'cant buy a proper coopa Yarkshire tea in Italy tha nose) when in came this car and pulled up alongside him. Two guys hopped out and came over to introduce themselves. They said they had some camcorders and twenty-four volt truck TVs for sale, which they hinted were 'hot'. Was he interested?

Like an idiot, he said, 'Aye.'

For the giveaway price of *only* 800 Deutschmarks, they said Jem could have one of each because they just wanted to get rid of them – and, of course, there weren't many left. The goodies were in black bin liners in the boot of their car and were shown to Jem in almost comical secrecy. The cloak and dagger nonsense is standard practice and is only performed to help convince gullible buyers that the stuff is not only genuine, but an opportunity not to be missed.

Jem bit. He was interested because it was something he actually wanted, so common sense went straight out of the window and he asked for a closer look. The boxes were pulled out of the bin liners and he gave it all the once over with his beady Northern eye. It was genuine stuff, no doubt about that. He was impressed and thought, 'Hm… ar'll 'ave soom 'o that.'

After some 'oohming and aaring' the price for both items was haggled down to only 600 Deutschmarks – an offer he just couldn't refuse – his Yorkshire nature getting the better of him. Before he knew it he'd broken the seal on his wallet, paid the money, taken his purchase and the two guys had vamoosed, no doubt impressed by this astute Englishman with an eyebrow for a bargain.

Jem was then left holding the baby. He took his new toys out of the bag to have a play and suddenly thought it felt a bit light – a lot lighter than it did just a moment before. The boxes were the same, with their polystyrene foam and little plastic windows, and the goods looked okay, but… *Bingo!* – the penny dropped…

Yes, he'd been had. Well and truly. The camcorder and TV proved not to be that at all – they were something completely different. For 600 DMs – close on three hundred quid at the time – Jem found he was now the proud owner of two very intricately carved and artistically painted lumps of wood!

The bin liners had been switched right in front of his eyes and the original goods were now flying up the motorway at 100mph, still in the boot of the car… Nice 'deal'.

When he arrived in Istanbul a few days later, he walked into the drivers restaurant at Oktay's Transport Yard to borrow some money and scrounge a beer, and was greeted with a spontaneous standing ovation and a lengthy round of piss-taking.

News travels quickly on the grapevine.

Welcome to Italy, Jem.

Seven

Of groupage loads and G.V.60's

It was when I was driving the 89 for Ernie that I was sent on my first ever mission to Ankara, the Turkish capital. I saw it as a huge leap of faith on Roy's part at the time – and I was chuffed to bits. Ernie, being Ernie, just winced.

Mr Samuels himself didn't get much say in the matter: He was more or less obliged to let his truck – and me – go wherever Roy decided to send it. He didn't seem *too* bothered about it at the time though; I think he figured that if I could now get to Istanbul in one piece then I could surely manage that extra bit to Ankara without causing a major disaster. And anyway, it all meant extra pennies in his pocket at the end of the day, so for all he cared Roy could send me off to Tibet if he wanted (and I'm pretty sure he could have got the permits).

To date I hadn't been any further East than Hyderpasha – a mere stone's throw across the Bosporus Strait – and even though I could already puff my chest out and say that I'd driven a truck all the way to Asia – which I had simply by virtue of crossing the Bosporus bridge – to be now going *all* the way to Ankara itself, a further five hundred kms into the continent, instead of just tip-toeing in and out again was really a big event for me. It meant that I'd be taking one more step towards my ultimate goal, the place that, by now, I wanted to drive to more than anywhere else in the world – the Middle East.

I'd been given a 'groupage' load for this trip, which is basically a trailer load of mixed cargoes for more than one customer – a 'part load' for each one. Sometimes a groupage load will all come off at one place. Other times it means multiple customs clearances and as many deliveries. I'd been given three – Sofia, Istanbul and of course Ankara In that order.

I was excited at the prospect of going so far, but didn't dare show it: I was now supposed to be a 'professional' TIR driver and new challenges were to be expected and treated like water off a duck's back. But I thought, bollocks to all that macho nonsense. I just wanted to get rolling.

Going to the nation's capital also meant that I'd get to see some of the things I kept hearing other drivers talking about. Of the shitty roads and the traffic chaos, which were reputed to be much worse than the run of the mill shitty roads and chaotic traffic I'd experienced so far; of Bolu – a fearsome climb whose road surface was deeply rutted and dangerously slick from oil and rubber deposits left behind by ancient rigids – Tonkas – ranging from T.K. Bedfords to Dodges, and even old Commers because their tanks either leaked or had been overfilled.

Of the hill itself which goes – as it does – from dot to a thousand metres in a series of twists and turns and deceptively steep climbs. And of 'Death Valley' – a steep, treacherous six-kilometre downhill run that has witnessed many 'runaways' and claimed more than a few drivers' lives and which, sensibly enough for Turkey, has a peage situated right at the very bottom of it.

It was reckoned that the guy who manned the toll booth must have been a bit of an athlete, because whenever an artic, or an overloaded Tonka, lost the use of its brakes from overheating them on the way down and came screaming towards the peage at warp factor nine in a cloud of smoke, the guy only had a few seconds' grace to get out of his chair and leg it.

I'd also get to park in the Telex Motel at Ankara itself – a regular stop-off for Middle East drivers, and the last rendezvous for 'the boys that turned right, and the men that turned left' – a reference to those headed for Iraq or Syria and beyond, and those en-route to Iran, Afghanistan and Pakistan.

But I'd not actually stay in the Motel, of course – Allah forbid – no, I'd stay in the truck in the dusty, pot-holed car park where all the other drivers used to camp out, often for up to a week at a time while they waited for passports to be flown out with newly acquired visas (most drivers have more than one passport. At the time of writing I have three) or for Arabic manifests to be drawn up (for Iraq) – or even while they waited for a friend to catch up who they could run with. But most inviting of all, I'd get to enjoy the mystic delights of the evening's entertainment in the bar upstairs: The Belly Dancer – YEEESS! I could hardly wait!

To ease my pre-trip nerves I set about cleaning the truck – inside and out, and from top to bottom. I even tidied away all the junk – spanners, jump-leads, biscuit tins etc. – to make room for the extra supplies. It was the first time I'd been trusted with multiple deliveries and what with all the extra mileage and added time involved, I figured I'd need lots of rations – so I went out and spent a fortune on Pot Noodles.

None of Roy's trailers had boxes on them – the metal lockers usually on the right-hand side (kerb-side on the continent) where most 'proper' lorry drivers kept a tool box and a scrapyard in one and a double-ringed cooker with a hundred quids-worth of Tesco's best in the other – so all of our food supplies and spares had to be kept in the cab. Needless to say, fresh milk and veggies weren't on the shopping list, but it was no great hardship – a carton of long-life milk did just as well – and goes down nicely with a tin of mushy peas…

The reorganisation of all my worldly belongings turned out to be a waste of time anyway because almost everything I bought ended up in a cardboard box on the passenger's floor. But it gave me something to do at the time, and at least the inside of the cab smelled nice for a change. So anyway, there I was, loaded down with enough kit to do the South Pole and back, including a leaking bottle of coconut oil for the tan, and I set off from Ripple Road, Barking, feeling ten feet tall and bullet-proof, convinced that nothing could go wrong…

Boy, was I in for a shock.

The trip actually went quite well to start with. After the usual cancellations on the way down I eventually got to Bulgaria in one piece, found Central Customs in Sofia and parked up right outside the gates. I paid the copper a dirty book and a packet of fags to keep both eyes open during the night and to give me a knock in the morning – which he actually did! By mid-afternoon of that day I'd been cleared by customs, unloaded, stamped up, re-sealed, and was ready to roll again – job done!

The only hassle I got was from the fat woman who worked for Despred – the Bulgarian customs 'spedition' (agent) who kept pestering me to change money with her, for fear that 'her' computer would break down again and not be able to print out the goods manifest, in Cyrillic, which I needed to get tipped. So I obliged by changing ten Deutschmarks.

It turned out that the money change was a regular thing between her and English drivers. It was harmless stuff – ten marks was only about three quid at the time, or less, but it was a lot to her, especially being such a strong currency in a country whose money was only good for wiping your arse with – and best of all it got our paperwork processed in front of everyone else – or at least until the computer 'accidentally' threw another wobbler.

It also got us a fistful of Bulgarian Leva in return which, even at the black market rate, was about as useful to a TIR driver as a roll of fluffy wallpaper – But, at the small 'Bufe' bar inside the main customs building, it provided me with the means to enjoy a couple of gristly, sausage-shaped things that looked like dog turds, and umpteen cups of very nice but *very* strong Turkish style coffee.

Sofia Central Customs is not the most salubrious of places to visit – in fact it's a shitty old railway terminal with some equally shitty warehouses or 'magazins' attached. The whole place stank of damp and piss and had a thriving rat population, so I felt pretty relieved and very pleased with myself when I drove out of there with one empty bay on the step-frame trailer and eyes as wide as saucers.

***

By the following day I was in Turkey and parked up at the Chefs at Avçilar (a lot of drivers called it Kasim's, or Kasim's yard). After I'd said my hellos and downed a few glasses of compulsory sweet black çay that everyone drinks in Turkey, (men that is – I've never seen a woman drinking it), I grabbed my passport and all of my paperwork, jumped into a yellow cab – Taksi – and went straight down to the Noter office near Taksim Square.

A 'Noter' is a public notary. Here a driver had to get a statement typed up each trip – for a price of course – which said that his designated customs agent, in my case Alfa Shipping, was legally authorised to act on behalf of that driver's company or agent back in the UK. A load of bollocks really, but it had to be done. So, armed with my 'Noter Paper' I then went to Alfa's office itself, just a short walk up the street – not far from where Istanbul's first McDonalds opened. I then nodded and salaamed a lot, drank çay, handed over all the relevant paperwork they needed to clear the load at Customs – and sat back to wait.

Alfa's were also my intermediary agent for the part-load that was to come off in Ankara so I was in their office – and the 'Kebap' shop next door – for a good few hours as they read everything, wrote out a Turkish manifest in long-hand, covered it with sticky stamps, then signed it and rubber-stamped it, photocopied everything three times, stamped and signed the photocopies, photocopied them… and so on, until there was a stack of paperwork that would have had Greenpeace screaming.

This was then unfairly divvied up between me, them and the poor sod that would ultimately have to do most of the legwork. I was then told that I could leave and made to promise that I'd be parked outside the gates of Salimpaşari Customs (pronounced Salim-pashar) in downtown Istanbul before six a.m. the following morning – Imshalla (God willing). And off I went, as happy as Larry.

I then jumped into another cab and went straight back to Kasim's. I had two tins of beer, booked a 4 a.m. call with the old boy who pretended to be night watchman – and went to bed. It was not yet 8 p.m.

The reason for the early start was not because it's the sort of thing lorry drivers enjoy doing, but because there used to be – and still is as far as I know – a driving ban on trucks in certain parts of Istanbul that started at 6 a.m. Anybody who tried to get past the copper on point duty on the main road after that time was automatically fined a packet of Marlboro cigarettes and promptly made to turn off and park at the 'Stadium' for the duration – the sports stadium where England beat Turkey 8-1 at football and where Michael Jackson failed to turn up for his own concert a few years back and nearly caused a revolution (a few of the tribe were driving the stage trucks and were warned by the 'Polis' not to venture out until the natives were less hostile).

The rest of Istanbul is a no-go area for TIR trucks full stop – as I found out the hard way on my first trip when I lost Tony in the traffic and caused a rather large hold-up in front of the Galata Bridge – the floating bridge.

That morning I was up on time for a change and went haring off to customs down by the waterfront. I was 20 to 30 trucks from the main gates well before the ban started, and sat there waiting for the kick-off.

Even at that time of the day Istanbul is a hive of activity: The traffic was already in noisy full flow, there were people pushing handcarts up and down selling all sorts of goodies from çay to bread rings covered in sesame seeds and sticky stuff – even footballs, cassette tapes… and they all seemed to be in competition to see who could shout the loudest.

There were loads of shoe-shine boys punting for business who wouldn't take no for an answer – even if they saw a driver wearing flip-flops. They were lovely kids – most no older than ten or eleven. There was always one or two of the old boys there too, grizzled old things with tanned leather faces. They worked with ancient boxes that carried beautiful, highly shined brass vases and urns, which held their polish and waxes. There were water sellers too with huge, highly decorated silver water containers strapped to their backs who walked up and down in fezzes and brightly coloured traditional costumes shouting "Su, Su…" When somebody bought a glass of 'Su', or sometimes fruit juices, it was expertly poured as the guy opened a tap and bent forwards at a strange angle to let the liquid run from a funnel. It was always ice cold.

There were beggars too, one of them without legs who used to push himself around on a little home-made trolley, like a skateboard. And there were always packs of stray dogs, some with eyes or legs missing, all were manky and covered in shit. They'd prowl around nervously, tails between legs, hoping for a free feed, but all they ever got from the Turks was the usual kick up the arse or something chucked at them. There was always lots of rubble lying around, like a building site waiting for someone to start work, and there were piles of litter, clouds of dust, a strange smell and always *lots* of noise – and all at 5:30 in the morning!

To get through the gates when they opened was a feat of daring because one line of trucks suddenly became three, and it was a mission just to squeeze in without bashing into something – or someone! Once there, a man with the regulation moustache, an armband, a silly hat and a whistle would demand a piece of paper which had serial numbers, plus the usual amount of rubber stamps and signatures on, which authorised entry to the customs area. This was when my problems began because when I'd got past the gates and he put his hand out for mine, I couldn't find it.

The guy wasn't impressed. He started ranting and raving – as they do – and began to holler the word *'problem'*. So I smiled and politely told him to shut up. (It doesn't do to swear, they've heard all the

English swear words before and think they know what they mean). I then reached for my folder assuming I must have put the entry card with the rest of my papers when I left Alfa's office… But the folder wasn't where it should have been. In fact my folder wasn't anywhere in the cab at all – it had gone!

I then panicked. My chest felt like it was going to explode and I went straight into overdrive. The traffic behind me suddenly became chaotic and noisy – air horns were blaring off non-stop and the man with the silly hat was going ape-shit.

I rapidly turned the cab upside down trying to find the folder, but got nowhere. There was bedding, books, clothing and Pot Noodles all over the place – but not a sign of my plastic folder.

Before long, probably a couple of minutes in reality, but it felt longer, I thought I was going to get lynched as people began to tug at the door, bang on the cab or stand on the bumper yelling through the windscreen at me. Arms were going up and down all over the place and coppers, drivers, passers-by, street vendors and howling dogs all seemed to join in the condemnation at once.

I knew I had to do something quickly before the situation got dangerous, so I tossed some fags at the gateman, shoved the truck into gear, hit the horn and went for it…

Eight

Of aerials and pterodactyls

I'd solved one problem by getting into customs without an entry card, and earned a severe case of the shakes because of it, but that wasn't all. I'd lost my folder. All of my paperwork, except the carnet TIR and the rest of the bits Alfa's had kept, had gone with it.

All my invoices, my trip-tiks (from the word tryptych – temporary import licence), my green card insurance, log books, even a photograph of my daughter! All gone. Everything I needed to do the job and get back to England with was lost!

I couldn't understand it. I *knew* I had that folder when I left Alfa's office, and I *knew* I had it when I got out of the taxi at Kasim's yard – so where had it gone? It couldn't have been stolen, because I hadn't been anywhere else, just to the agent's office, the kebab shop and then back to the truck. It didn't make sense – it had simply vanished into thin air.

As I waited for a miracle to happen I went walkabout and saw another English truck being unloaded further down the dockside. Richie Thorne was in the back of his trailer, stripped to shorts and a string vest, chucking things around and shouting at the Teds (Turks). Richie, six feet something, covered in home-made tattoos, and with hands the size of shovels looked an intimidating sight. A Forester born and bred (Forest of Dean), calls everyone 'Bub' or 'Bubby' if he likes them, and tends to punch those he doesn't. I'd met Richie once or twice before and he'd always been the perfect gentleman. Well, at least he hadn't clumped me yet, so I went over and said hello.

'Allo moi bubby' he said, (I was safe) 'where you parked 'en?' So I pointed. 'Oh. Oi never seen y'come in.'

'No – had a bit of a hold-up at the gate.'

'Aah. Allroit now is it 'en?' he asked, dripping with sweat.

'Er – no. Not really.' I tried to figure out how to put the next bit: I knew Richie could have a short fuse – especially where work was concerned. He didn't suffer fools gladly and I fully expected him to launch into me and call me all the wankers under the sun. But he didn't, he just asked, 'Wassa matter 'en bub?'

'My paperwork's gone missing.'

'Yeah – they do that sometoims. Don' worry, 'e'll turn up.'

He'd misunderstood. 'No – the agents haven't lost it, I have.'

'Oh… You got a bit of a problem there you 'ave 'en boy. 'Ow d'you lose it?'

'Wish I knew. I only just found out myself.'

'Aah, that's not a problem, oi 'spect your agent can run up some micky's for you – they'll sort 'im out.'

He'd misunderstood again. 'No, I've already put my papers in – they've got my carnet and stuff. It's everything else that's gone missing.'

'*What?*' I thought he was going into one, so I quickly explained. He listened quietly and seemed genuinely concerned by the time I'd finished. 'Fuck me, you got a problem an' 'alf there boy! You'll never get out the country, not without y'trip-tiks an' y'permit… And don't forget, if the truck can't leave noither can you – it's all stamped on y'passport, remember?'

It was the last thing I wanted to hear, even though it was true. When a driver takes a truck into Turkey all the details, registration numbers etc. are stamped into that driver's passport – much the same as the person himself is stamped in. And just the same, those details have to be stamped out again on leaving the country. Without all the relevant paperwork at hand to prove that it was the same truck and trailer that I came into the country with there was, in theory, no way that I could get it taken off my passport.

At the time the Turks were sticklers for paperwork. They still are for the most part, but it wouldn't present the same problem today as it did then. It meant that I was in really deep shit and the truth was only just beginning to sink in.

Richie said, 'Talk me through it all again, boy, tell me exactly what you done yesterday, and don' you go missin' nothin' out. Let's see if we can't figure out what you done with 'im.'

So I went through it all again, step by step, and Richie listened. At the end he said, 'You sure you ain't missed nothin' out? Come on now boy, 'ow many beers d'you really 'ave, eh?' I'd only had the two – I wasn't likely to indulge in a private session when I had to be up at four in the morning – so I told him.

'Hmm – Allroit, oi believe y'.' Then, 'Y'din go in the chef's office for a çay or something an' leave it there?'

'No. They'd all gone home, there was only the old boy left. All I did was get out of the taxi, take a piss and climb into the truck.'

'Oh, roit... Where you 'ave a piss 'en?'

'Er, don't know, by the wheel probably. Why?'

'So where d'you put the folder woil you 'ad a piss?'

That got me, and my head spun as I tried to think back again. Taking a piss by the wheel isn't the sort of thing I'd log in a diary, and for a minute or two it just wouldn't come to me – Then, bingo! The penny dropped – *'On the fucking diesel tank – Shit!'*

With that I was off. I legged it back to the truck which was about 100 metres away, praying against all hope that my folder would still be there, or wedged in between the tank and the chassis... but it wasn't. I crawled under the truck and I crawled all over it, but there was no sign of it at all. Deep down I knew it wouldn't be there – I didn't really expect to find it still laid on top of the diesel tank – but I still felt gutted.

I went over the events again in my mind. I still couldn't be a hundred percent sure that I'd put the folder on the tank as I took a leak, but it was the only explanation that seemed to make any sense. Something could then have distracted me – like talking to the night-watchman, for instance – after all I did ask for a wake-up call from him and, apart from pissing on my boots I could quite easily have forgotten to pick the folder back up.

When I walked over to Richie's truck the result of my search must have been obvious – he said: 'I'm sorry bub. There's not much oi can do to 'elp you. Oi can lend you a permit but if 'e's not bin stamped in they won't accept 'im at the border. An' you'll prob'ly 'ave t'use the same border you come in at, y'know that, don' you?' I nodded, then, 'Which one was it?'

'Guess.' I said. Richie shook his head, and his voice softened.

'Oi'm sorry boy – oi can' see you getting' out, 'specially not at Kapik, you knows what they d'be loik up there.'

I did. Kapik was – and still can be – a real bastard of a border to get through even when everything was in order, and I wasn't too chuffed at the idea of trying to get out of there with hardly any paperwork at all. It turned my stomach over just thinking about it.

There was a compound at the back of Kapik – a muddy field actually, surrounded by a high chain-link fence topped with barbed wire. This was *the* compound; the condemned trucks' graveyard. Once a truck or trailer – usually both – had been impounded by the Turks for whatever reason, and consigned to the 'compound', that's usually where it stayed until it rotted and fell to bits, and practically no amount of pleading or bribing would get it released. By the time a truck got here the situation had gone beyond a mere 'backshish' (bribe or 'tip') problem anyway.

There even used to be people living in some of the tidier models. They were peasants and gypsies, not the actual drivers of the trucks – Most of them, we were told, were in prison. Some of these people used to sneak through a hole in the fence at night and mosey around the border begging off drivers, or sometimes, if they'd managed to scrounge enough money they'd ask one of us to get them something from the duty free. They were pathetic creatures and didn't really deserve to be told to fuck off time after time, but in Turkey, as in other countries in Eastern Europe and the Middle East, drivers become hardened to such things. Beggars, thieves and dropouts are an everyday sight and most of them would shit on you for tuppence – so it's dog eat dog.

Sure, we've all felt sorry for them at one time or another and tossed them a packet of fags or a loaf of bread, but I wondered what sort of charity I'd have got if the 89 were impounded and I ended up as their neighbour. Every now and again the police and customs guys at Kapik would have a purge and turf all these poor bastards out in the cold... But the trucks *always* stayed put.

Richie said, 'Oi think it's toim to get in touch with your agent, ole butt, an' 'en see if you can' tell Roy what's 'appened. There's not much you can do on yer own an' 'ey've gotta be told y'know.'

Again, I cringed. In the '80s there wasn't exactly a phone box on every street corner in Istanbul. There were 'jeton' phones, phones that took tokens instead of money, but they rarely worked properly – the lines were so bad on some of them that it would have been more effective to stand on the pavement and shout in the general direction of where you wanted to make the call. And for International calls a pile of jetons the size of a pyramid was needed.

Going to the local P.T.T. (Post Telegraph Telephone) didn't really appeal to me either. They're chaotic places at the best of times and making a simple phone call could be bloody hard work. Bloody annoying too when half a dozen locals moved within inches of your face to listen wide-mouthed to a conversation they couldn't understand a word of.

'I'll wait,' I said. 'Alfa's bloke should be here soon to organise the unloading – I'll tell him what's happened and take it from there. I'll see if I can swipe his car for an hour or two – there's half a chance my folder's still lying on the roadside somewhere, or maybe in the chef's car park. I'll drive up and have a look around. You never know.'

Richie looked at me as if to say, 'Don't be a prat!' – but it was a hope; something to hold on to – so I waited.

Before long my agent's runner arrived sweating and out of breath – he'd just run from the bus stop! He informed me that I'd be tipped soon, Imshalla. I told him that was the least of my problems. When he queried that I tried to explain via a bit of Turkish, a bit of 'TIR speak' – a drivers' language consisting of words from umpteen tongues, all of which have common meanings – and with lots of arm waving, hand signals and body language, which the Turks use a lot of.

When I eventually got through to him I thought he was going to have a heart attack. He held one hand to his chest, the other to his forehead, his eyes rolled backwards and he started wailing. I honestly thought he was going to cry. Then I had to go through it all again – in triplicate – and this just made him worse – they're great over-reactors, the Turks. But it was still a bit disconcerting.

I was then dragged off to a phone. He rang Alfa's, then he rang the yard at Avçilar to find out if my folder was still lying in the car park. It wasn't, but they promised to send someone out in a car to look for it. Then he phoned the office back and started wailing again. And so it went on.

By now, word of the Englishman's problem was getting around.

I was then hauled out of customs, thrown into a taxi and whisked off at crazy speeds through the busy streets of Istanbul.

Alfa's office was in total chaos when we got there. Arms were going up and down, everybody was shouting and running from one desk to another, phone calls were being made to Ankara, to Avçilar, to Roy and to Uncle Tom Cobley. Everyone kept staring at the ceiling talking to Allah and I was getting lots of very dirty looks. The Turks are past masters at turning a problem into a major disaster, and by now I just wanted to crawl into a matchbox and hide – I felt terrible.

I was rudely handed a telephone – it was Roy. *Shit!* The conversation was a bit one-sided, surprise surprise, and if I remember he hung up on me – Oh well, I thought at the time, at least he knows now.

It all seemed to be out of my hands then: things were being organised on my behalf and I wasn't even being talked to - so I buggered off next door to the Kebab shop.

I sat in a corner alone like a condemned man having his last meal. It was awful. I had no-one to talk to and no-one to blame but myself, but at the time it didn't help much to know that. I felt very lonely, a bit scared, and I just didn't know what to do.

After a while another runner came and found me. I forget his name, but he had a scar on his face, a wonky eye, and he spoke a bit more English than the first guy I'd dealt with (perhaps he'd been carted off on a stretcher).

'Chonnie,' he said, with one wide eye. 'Istanbul baggage (load) yok peroblem (no problem) – dokooments okay. Maybe doday, maybe doomorrow. Ankara baggage (pronounced baggaj) maybe peroblem. Maybe yok peroblem. Imshalla.' He shrugged. What this means in Turkey is – 'we know fuck all, but be ready for the worst.' Which was pretty much what I expected at this stage of the game. He then started waving his arms and pointed at his watch, which meant that nothing was going to happen very soon. I was then whisked off in another cab back to customs, escorted back to my truck and told to wait one hour. So wait I did. But for a bit more than an hour.

Off-loading the trailer that day turned out to be impossible. Word of my problem had gone about faster than a bushfire and customs had got wind of it. Even though it had sod all to do with the Istanbul part-load the Gümrük (customs) had money signs rolling around their eyeballs, and when that occurs, nothing else does... until palms are greased. This was going to cost, and it was going to be a slow, painful process.

Soon everyone had gone home, and by about 8 p.m. the customs area was pretty much deserted. The silence was delicious. The only company I had was rats, stray dogs, mangy cats and the smell – most of which came from the toilets near to where I'd parked, part of which came from the piles of rotting debris, and the rest from the Bosporus itself, which lapped at the quayside 50 feet away.

***

At some ungodly hour the next morning bedlam opened its doors again. Forklifts zoomed about in total disorder blasting their horns at everyone and everything; Tonkas (the small trucks that actually do all the doorstep deliveries of groupage loads deposited in customs by TIR trucks) were noisily causing traffic chaos as they each tried to collect loads from warehouses; that morning's influx of new TIR traffic began to arrive; whistles were being blown; dogs were barking and *everybody* was shouting. My final wake-up call was when the tape recorder at the local mosque announced first prayers of the day over the loudspeakers (a kind of air-raid siren in Turkish sing-song). So I lit a fag, struggled out of bed and put the kettle on. I didn't even bother to open the curtains – I figured I was in for a long wait anyway, so what the fuck – I didn't need to get up and dash about with rest of them.

Richie had gone by this time. The second part of his groupage load was also for Ankara and I remember feeling jealous of the fact that he was probably just waking up at the same time, but 500kms further east – where I should have been. There had been no need for him to wait because there was nothing he could do to help anyway. He'd given me directions and a few do's and don'ts (and some tea-bags) – and wished me luck – so that was good enough for me… But it meant I was on my own again.

At sometime, I can't remember when, the nameless one arrived, out of breath and sweating. 'Oh Chon, büyük peroblem (big problem) choc para, choc para, Gümrük (much money, customs), Alfa büyük peroblem – choc para.' I thought here we go, this is where I get stung – but he never asked for a penny, he just kept saying 'choc para, choc, choc…'

'How much para?' I asked. He just shrugged, 'Choc.'

Then he grabbed my arm, 'Chonnie – burrink kamyon – shimdi (now) burrink…' Then he ran off! I thought, 'Fuck me, slow down – I'll never be able to find you in this lot!' And he disappeared! So I fired up and crept forwards to look for him. When I found him, he had risked his life to save me another parking spot, valiantly facing up to a Tonka and a forklift that were willing to run him down to get him out of the way. I was impressed, but the Tonka driver wasn't when I slipped in behind him.

'Bir saat, bir saat,' (one hour) my friend said holding up a finger then making circles with it over his 'original' Rolex watch. 'Kamyon boş (bosh – empty) bir saat!' And then he buggered off again!

I was now parked alongside the wall of one warehouse facing the waterfront and all I could see through the windscreen was the arse-end of a Russian cruiseliner (there always seemed to be one moored in the same place).

I didn't get too excited at being told I'd be unloaded in one hour, I'd heard it said so many times in Turkey and it usually meant anything from three hours to a week. Time just doesn't have the same meaning here – so I put the kettle on again. By now just about everyone in the world knew of my problem and, Turks being Turks, began to crowd around to gawk, point, tut and wobble their heads. I soon began to feel like the two-headed man at a circus.

The weather was warm that day but very windy – I know, I have every reason in the world to remember it. Soon a gang of men arrived on the scene. All the Teds that had been so noisy – and nosy – suddenly fell quiet. They looked down at their feet, began to mutter, and became very humble in a matter of seconds – like someone had thrown a switch.

These new arrivals were important people, that much was obvious. They must have been – they all held bits of paper and wore suits that weren't too baggy and which actually matched top and bottom. They conversed quietly, nodding at everything one of them said. They held their Marlboro's delicately, almost effeminately, between manicured fingers, but they looked very sure of themselves and totally in charge. They looked bloody stupid too, with mud and dog shit all over their wedge-heeled shoes.

Before I could say boo, and without being consulted, someone had broken the customs seal on the back of the trailer and handed it to one of the newcomers. Then, half a dozen or more of the dockers began to tug the tilt cord out, unlace the flaps and drop the side gates, all in a hurry so they could look efficient and helpful in front of the 'sirs'. I stared in disbelief and horror. I couldn't believe it! The silly bastards were about to open up the side of my trailer in gale conditions!

I screamed and jumped out of the cab to stop them but was promptly leapt upon from behind by the nameless one who'd returned unnoticed. 'Chon – stop pliz,' he pleaded. 'Dis büyük chef. No peroblem Chonny – pliz.' Everyone was staring at me, but I was adamant: Opening a tilt trailer in strong winds is madness – the plastic sheet becomes uncontrollable and all kinds of damage can be done – especially if it whips up and takes someone's eye out. Which the driver would get the blame for…

'No – leave it alone!' I tried to grab the tilt cord from someone – the plastic-covered wire that laces up all the way around the trailer – but I was held back by three or four people, all shouting 'Yok, yok' (No). One of the suited bods came over then looking concerned and said to me in perfect English, 'Excuse me, but what seems to be the problem?'

'The problem, mate, is the wind – it's blowing a gale!' I said.

'So what has our weather got to do with this?' he asked, holding an arm out towards the trailer.

'It's bloody dangerous, don't you understand? Please, let me move the truck around the corner out of the wind. It'll be safer.'

He turned and said something to his mates in Turkish and they all began to laugh, which pissed me right off. 'I'M BLOODY SERIOUS!' I screamed and was promptly dragged away with a hand over my mouth. 'Chonnie – NO!' the nameless one pleaded. I tried to say, 'Hava – hava (wind) problem,' but it came out like, 'Ha'a, ha'a ho'em.'

Soon all the planks had been taken out of one side – the wooden planks that slot horizontally between each metal upright – and the Teds were struggling in vain to hold the sheet aloft with them so that the important ones could inspect the 'baggage'. Suddenly there was a loud THWOOMP! as the wind got under the sheet and tried to lift the trailer off the ground. It settled back into place seconds later but the Turks had already lost their holds on the planks – which were now on the floor – and the whole side-sheet of the trailer began to whip up and down like a huge plastic handkerchief.

Ropes were then produced from somewhere and tied through several of the eyelets which lined the bottom edge of the sheet – the idea being to heave at it from the other side until – in theory – it rested on the roof and exposed one whole side of the now violently rocking trailer.

Mistake.

I stood back, sensing what was going to happen next and could only groan in my helplessness. The suited ones had retreated a bit by this time too, knowing full well that what I'd said about the danger was correct, but being too proud and pig-headed to give new orders. So they slid back into the shadows and let the farce continue.

The wind continued to play havoc with all attempts to secure the sheet until – THWACK! The whole lot puffed out and tried to rise like a hot-air balloon - the only thing that held it down being one flimsy strap at the front and the remaining cord that was still threaded through the eyelets on the other side.

Then it settled, then rose again - THWACK! The Teds pulling on the ropes were almost physically being lifted off the ground by the force of each inflation – so, in the face of such fierce enemy action they promptly abandoned their posts and ran! Then the whole sheet – all 1200 sq.ft. of it (approx.) – took on a life of its own. It continued to puff its cheeks out to its full extent and then settle noisily back down again until there was one last almighty – THWUUMP!!! Seconds later there was a loud ripping sound followed by a rapid series of bangs as the strap at the front finally gave up the ghost, the eyelets on the other side were ripped from the plastic one by one and the sheet tore itself away from the trailer.

Everybody screamed and legged it. The sheet lifted violently off and went sailing into the air trailing ropes and tilt cord, like an out of control parachute. It scraped the side wall of the warehouse, destroyed an old floodlamp in the process, then made a beeline for the Russian cruiseliner, flapping like a Pterodactyl.

I saw people running away from the blunt end towards the nearest doors, yelling in fear and trying to protect their heads. The sheet scraped the railings at the back of the ship and the cord and ropes whiplashed whatever was in their way before the whole lot nose-dived unceremoniously into the waters of the Bosporus.

The trailer itself was now naked and fully exposed – just the basic skeleton of framework with torn and sad-looking remnants of the sheet flapping in the wind. The remaining load on its back being the Istanbul part-load, which was crated goods near the arse-end of the trailer, and the Ankara part-load at the front.

There were, if I remember, six thousand loose boxes for Ankara, a bit smaller than shoe-boxes, each containing one television aerial and weighing less than half a kilogram each. TIR loads are rarely palletised – especially groupage loads. The use of palettes reduces the amount of cargo space on a trailer (plus nobody ever wants to pay for the palettes) – so if the goods aren't in boxes or crates, they get 'hand-balled' on and off, i.e. crammed in by hand until the trailer is full to the gunnels.

The six thousand TV aerials had been loosely hand-balled on. The wind decided it was going to chuck them all off again – which it did. Within seconds of the Russian liner coming under attack, hundreds of little white boxes went sailing into the air like confetti and headed off in all directions, bouncing against walls, forklifts and people.

It was pandemonium. The Teds ran around in circles like headless chickens, shouting and screaming at each other as they ducked, bumped into things or tried to catch the googlies; the important ones rapidly did a disappearing act; the nameless one just stood against a wall with his head bowed, crying; and the tilt sheet along with half the intended load for Ankara went bobbing up and down on the Bosporus, slowly making its way towards Asia Minor…

A couple of strays looking for a feed

Nine

Of Tonkas and TIR kontrols

It took the best part of two days to get that little mess under control. The tilt sheet was eventually fished out of the water by a gang of Russian sailors using hooked poles, who thought the whole thing was hilarious, and was then shoddily patched together by a local tilt repair man, who'd been summoned to customs for the purpose, and who charged *me* a fortune for the privilege!

The load for Istanbul had been taken off soon after the sheet's flying performance – but Ankara's much needed TV aerials continued to disappear. That was my next problem – The Ankara load. Part of it was still at sea en-route to either the Crimea, in the north, or the Dardanelles to the south, and more of it now sat on top of television sets in various parts of Istanbul.

Copies of everything had been sent across from the UK but were about as useful to the Teds as a bacon sandwich. They were insisting I'd need originals, ones that bore an original customs' stamp from England… Another C.M.R. was typed up for me to be going on with, which in itself shouldn't *really* have been a problem. After all, it's only a delivery note at the end of the day, not the deeds to Constantinople – but the Turks make a problem if there's a dot missing off an 'i'.

Anyway, it wasn't much, but it was all I had – apart from my passport, a partially completed carnet TIR and a useless pile of photocopies – so it would have to do.

In the meantime Kasim's men, I was told, had been up and down the chaotically busy main roads from Avçilar to customs umpteen times looking for a squashed folder, but had found nothing. My mood should have been a bit grim by then, but I was so relieved to have been unloaded and ready to roll on to Ankara that I actually didn't give a toss. I figured that if I was in the shit anyway I might just as well go off to Ankara and make the best of it. So on Friday afternoon I pulled out of customs with a patchwork quilt trailer containing about two tonnes of TV aerials (instead of nearly three that there should have been), fought my way through the traffic chaos along the waterfront and went steaming up towards the Bosporus bridge – during the driving ban.

Normally the guy on the exit gate at customs was under strict instructions not to let any TIR trucks out onto the road until the driving ban lifted in the evening. But for some reason that ruling didn't seem to apply to me on the day that I left. I think they were just glad to see the back of me and I was allowed to leave without explanation, an exit card – or even a packet of Marlboro!

The Bosporus bridge during Istanbul's rush hour used to be a nightmare. It's a four-lane highway leading up to the old bridge but the Turks regularly turned it into at least seven. Nobody but *nobody* gives way to anyone – particularly during the rush hour and especially not to British TIR trucks trying to run the gauntlet.

The slip road brought me right out in front of the bridge and was the last road to join the motorway just a couple of hundred metres from the actual start of the bridge itself. Parallel to the slip road was always a cop car and a couple of 'chips' on motorbikes, whose job it was to control the traffic. I knew they'd be there, sitting in the gap in the central reservation. Normally they'd be sat around chatting for the most part, and would yell at someone through their loudspeakers every now and then as a token gesture of their presence.

Naïvely, I thought I was in with a chance of outrunning them by catching them unawares, so I came up the slip road like a bat out of hell with my headlights on full beam and my hazards flashing hoping to confuse everyone and make the traffic in front give way. In Turkey lights and horns are all important – the bigger, the noisier – the better. Anyone, be it car, bus or truck can command right of way simply by virtue of having lots of lights and making lots of noise – people just assume that the vehicle concerned is important, or on an important mission at least, and will often let it by.

That was plan A at any rate – to belt up onto the bridge like I was on an emergency call and force all the other traffic to move out of my way...

Wrong move. I only got about twenty feet onto the motorway before I realised my mistake and had to do an emergency stop.

It turned out that the 'Polis' had bigger, brighter and much noisier accessories than I had on the 89 and within seconds of coming to a halt I was hemmed in by flashing blue lights, angry faces and a stream of abuse over their loudspeakers. It was like a scene from a cops and robbers film. There I was surrounded by armed police with strobe lights and wailing sirens, causing untold traffic chaos at the entrance to the Bosporus bridge in the middle of Istanbul's rush hour – and all I could do was laugh.

Three or four coppers came banging on the door yelling all kinds of horrible curses and waving their arms around as if they were about to do a vertical take-off, and it was all too much for me – I just snorted and got a fit of the giggles. I couldn't stop myself. I think it was a release of tension more than anything, after the cock-ups of the previous few days, but the coppers didn't see the funny side of it to start with. They just continued to rant and rave – and I had snot and dribble rolling down my chin.

I couldn't have thought of an excuse then if my life had depended on it, so I simply put my hands up like they do on cowboy films and shrugged, as if to say – okay sheriff, it's a fair cop.

They seemed to calm down a bit then and, being Turks, I think they saw the funny side of it. Then, unbelievably, after questioning me and thumbing through my passport to make sure I wasn't an Israeli saboteur or something, about to blow up the bridge, I was given a mild wrist-slapping, a ten thousand lira 'fine', (sod all at the time), I parted company with a few packets of fags and, amazingly, I was allowed to carry on! So I did – laughing all the way, and as I came off the other side onto Asian soil I punched the air and gave a great whoop of delight.

As I went past the Hyderpasha turn-off I gave another little cheer. From here on in I was on new ground.

According to Richie's directions I had to turn off at the first Ankara sign and join a rough old stretch of dual carriageway as the motorway didn't go any further.

He wasn't wrong about it being rough. The camber on the road was so severe I thought the truck was going to pull itself off the road. The tramlines (ruts) and the mud didn't help much either, and some of the pot-holes were deep enough to swim in or rip off a bumper. I then had to go to war with an incessant stream of traffic which again formed more lanes than there were supposed to be and insisted on travelling at full pelt, swerving pot-holes – and other traffic – like dodgem cars, blasting horns and flashing lights at everything. It made overtaking bloody difficult – not to mention hair-raising and to make things worse there were loads of donkey carts and rusty old farm tractors adding their bit to the mayhem by trundling up the slow lane – *in the wrong direction!*

I then had to keep my eyes open for a 'TIR Kontrol' Post on the side of the main road at Tuzla, about 40k's up from Istanbul. It was just a small shed plonked in the middle of some waste ground that was manned by one or two coppers, and was where all TIR traffic had to stop and check in to get a time stamp on their police paper.

This 'Kontrol' system harks back to the days when Turkey was under military rule and everyone and everything was kept under strict supervision by the authorities – and that included keeping a record of all TIR trucks' movements. The system was – and still is to a certain extent – a pain in the arse because all the coppers wanted were fags or dirty books. These they could get by demanding to see a driver's tacho disc which they knew they'd always find a problem with, so, to avoid the hassle – and sometimes fines – it was easier just to go straight to the window with a packet of fags wrapped in the police paper. With my photocopy I knew I'd probably have to take inflation into account.

When I found the place I was glad of the chance to park-up for half an hour and get away from all the traffic – I'd only done 40 odd k's from the kick-off, but it felt more like 400. As soon as I stopped I was approached by 'No Bullshit' – an aggravating bastard that used to hang around the pot-holed car park selling dodgy watches and seconds T-shirts. His opening line was always 'Ah, Johnny (no matter what a driver's name was) I remember you – fife years before – you buy [from] me, no bullshit…' He said it to everyone – even first trippers like myself. He was still at my side jabbering on when I went to the window with two packets of fags.

The 'Polis' ignored him, as they always did, but they weren't very impressed with my photocopied police paper, especially as the reverse side – the side they put the rubber stamps on – was blank. There should have been one other stamp on it from Silivri TIR Kontrol, 60k's before Istanbul, and when he saw it wasn't there I was politely ordered into his office. I thought I was in for a wrist-slapping and a fine – but I was actually in for a shock. I was offered a seat at his desk and handed a glass of çay. The hatch over the window was closed to shut out the noise from No Bullshit – and any other drivers that appeared – then the copper promptly launched into a one-sided conversation about 'Muggarit Tatchair' and 'Manjastair Oonaitid'! It was great, even though I knew fuck all about politics or football!

***

Fifteen minutes and several çays later I left his office with a handshake and a stamp on my police paper! So civilised… even though he kept the fags.

As soon as I got outside I was assaulted by No Bullshit again. He was a persistent sod and just wouldn't go away, until I fired up and aimed the truck at him, and that was when I heard his other often-repeated line – 'Fuck you!…'

From there to Düzce, the next TIR kontrol at about the halfway mark was murder. I'd never seen so many overloaded Tonkas – some with loads five metres high and weighing up to twenty tonnes – about the same weight as carried by artics – and Kamikaze buses (the name speaks for itself) all going in the same direction at once. The trucks, mostly bonneted 'four wheelers' (two axles), all with multi-coloured paint jobs, eyes painted on the front, and 'Maşallah' written everywhere, screamed along nose to tail trailing thick clouds of black smoke.

When they came to a hill the average 'convoy' speed dropped from painfully slow to walking pace as nobody had the wellie or the roadspace to pass the guy in front. When one did have the acceleration to pass it was usually done up the nearside, with airhorns blasting, on the dirtstrip that commonly lines most Turkish roads. All this ever did was add to the chaos because huge clouds of dust were thrown into the air to mingle with the clouds of smoke, and nobody behind could see where they were going.

When a stream of these trucks reached the top of a hill, with all their straight-through exhausts (no silencers) creating some deafening harmonics, there would then be a free-for-all on the other side. They'd spread out like the Red Arrows aerobatics team trailing smoke in all directions and go hell for leather to pass each other two and three at a time. It was total madness, and bloody slow going. To cover just two hundred-odd kilometres from Istanbul to Düzce took well over four hours of driving time and was extremely hard work.

When I eventually turned into the 'Bulgy Camp', as Düzce TIR Kontrol was known, I felt completely knackered. It was late by then anyway, the weekend had crept up and, as it was, the coppers didn't like to let trucks go any further at night because of Bolu. So I called it a day… Time to park up and interview a beer. I would tackle the hill in daylight.

Saturday morning saw me in the huge car park of Düzce TIR Kontrol surrounded by Wombles (Bulgarians). The place was always swarming with them, and I felt a bit outnumbered being the only 'white man' there – so I made a cuppa, paid the going price at the window to get my photocopy stamped, and buggered off.

As I pulled onto the main road I felt nervous, but excited. The sign said 'Ankara 240 km' – a few hours and I'd be there! Just past Düzce is Bolu – the town situated nearly 1000 metres above sea level at the top of this hill I'd heard so much about. I wasn't worried about pulling a load up the hill because I only had a cup-full of cargo left on the trailer, but after all the stories I'd heard I was bound to be a bit nervous.

As it turned out Bolu – as the hill itself is commonly known – wasn't a disappointment – even though I was halfway up it before I realised I was there! The first two k's or so is in a straight line and even though it is deceptively steep, I was so 'light' that I went steaming up the middle lane – the 'overtaking' lane – like I was on the M6 in England. It wasn't until I'd taken the first three or four bends that I thought I'd better slow down a bit. Again, the cambers were a bit severe on some of the bends, and I wouldn't have been the first idiot to roll a truck going uphill – or bash into something that was coming down.

At every turn I expected to find myself at the top, but there always seemed to be another bend up ahead, or another steep climb and I began to think it would never end. The Tonkas and especially the Kamikaze buses, both driving with their usual brand of insanity, made it bloody hair-raising work too. It was a slippery, rutted, pot-holed three-lane stretch of road from top to bottom, but the Turks ignored that because most of the white lines had worn away and it was just the excuse they needed to turn it into four or five lanes. They insisted on using the up lane in the middle to come down on – regardless of what was in the way – and I was constantly on the brakes or swerving to avoid a head-on crash as the Kamikazes, in particular, just flashed their headlights and kept coming! (Kamikazes had right of way at the time – but they used to abuse the privilege). When I eventually reached the top of the hill I was shaking and out of breath.

After Bolu the scenery changed a bit. It seemed hillier, dustier, somewhat browner and less populated. It wasn't a drastic change, but it was noticeable – it was much more how I'd originally pictured Turkey to be, and I was fascinated by it. By the ruggedness of it all. By the primitive lifestyle of the farmers and young goatherders tending their flocks; the scarved and robed women; the men in woolly hats, dirty waistcoats and 'seven-day-shitters' – the baggy-arsed trousers worn by a lot of Muslims. There were towns and villages that sat on nothing more than dirt roads, all of which bustled with life, with overcrowded 'pavements' lined with goodies, street cafés, and packs of dogs.

I thought it was brilliant, but found it a bit difficult – not to mention dangerous – to hang on to the steering wheel and try to take photos of everything while on the move.

From there on in it was a busy but straightforward run and I was able to stoke the boiler a bit – until I came upon Death Valley a bit too fast, that is. I didn't know exactly where it started anyway, so it kind of crept up on me – at 90-odd kph – (the limit is 70 for trucks) and I had to throw the anchor out a bit rapidly. Luckily it's a dual carriageway, and with so little weight on board I was able to swerve around all the overloaded Teds that were creeping down in bottom gear.

It's actually quite a decent stretch of road and I began to think that all the stories I'd heard about it were exaggerated – but I was light and it had made me overconfident. Halfway down I was brought back to my senses when I saw evidence of just how dangerous the hill could be.

There's a deep 'V'-shaped gully that runs down the central reservation. Lying on its side in this gully, and surrounded by bits of broken crash barrier was a German-registered draw-bar outfit (roadtrain). There were no skid marks – he'd obviously 'lost' his brakes by coming down too fast and overheating them (when that happens the brake drums overheat and expand – away from the brake shoes). There were an awful lot of scrape marks in the concrete gully though where he'd crashed through the barrier and travelled on his side before coming to rest. There was no sign of the driver.

If that wasn't enough to slow me down, there was more evidence near the bottom. A Turkish-registered artic was buried nose first in the hillside – but on the opposite lane! He'd been going that fast out of control that he'd crashed the barrier and managed to completely jump the deep gully and cross the up-bound lane before smashing into the hill! The cab was crushed flat against the trailer... Amen. Then the peage appeared a bit suddenly – even though I'd been warned and was expecting it, it still took me by surprise. Sadly, the operator stood his ground and politely relieved me of the toll.

I missed the last TIR Kontrol Post at Kizilchammam simply because I didn't know where it was and went sailing straight past it. And I thought, 'oh fuck it, two out of four's not bad', as I flew past a line of trucks that had stopped to get their stamps. Then before I knew it I was approaching the outskirts of Ankara.

The Telex Motel is on the left going in, and I very nearly missed that too. It's a pretty non-descript place, much the same as a million other motels and restaurants I'd passed en-route, and I'd been looking out for the tell-tale signs of an English presence, i.e. scabby old units and unwashed trailers, with long-vehicle plates at one end and roof racks loaded down with beer crates at the other. But all I saw were more Wombles – So-Mat trucks (the Bulgarian State Transport Co.) were parked all over the place, but there wasn't a single English soul to be seen anywhere.

Even as I wheeled into the dirty carpark I felt disappointed. I'd expected the place to be full of Middle East drivers camped out for the duration, all enjoying an Efes kontrol and eyeing up the belly dancer, but the only people there were a couple of Bulgy's drinking çay.

At the reception desk the guy spoke a bit of English. He told me that he hadn't seen another English truck for a week. As if to confirm this he pointed to the notice board where drivers messages were always pinned up. 'Please pass to English driver so and so...' the messages read, 'reload from...' or 'Mike, your passport sent a.m. today' and so on. The dates on the Telex messages confirmed his story.

'Maybe one English come today' he said with a shrug – 'Maybe no'...I asked if Richie had been in, seeing as he had been due to tip in Ankara before me, and was surprised when he said 'No, Mr Richard no come. I know when Mr Richard come to Telex.' He smiled and made a drinking gesture by hitch-hiking his thumb towards his open mouth. Richie was obviously well known here.

As it turned out nobody, apart from more Bulgarians, showed up at all for the rest of the weekend and, to rub salt into the wound, even the belly dancer didn't arrive! So I sat around, nodded to the Bulgy's every now and then, read my book and got drunk on my own.

***

Getting back across the dual carriageway to go to customs during Monday morning's rush hour should have been made illegal. There were streams of traffic going at full bore in both directions and I must have sat there for at least ten minutes waiting for my chance. In the end I decided that the only way I'd ever get across this stretch of road was to do it Turkish style – like it or lump it – so I psyched myself up, put all my lights on, hit the horn and went for it...

I was still shaking ten minutes later when I pulled into the carpark at customs.

As I pulled in the guy at the gate yelled and chased me for something, but I was more interested in what I'd seen parked in the middle of the compound – Mr Richie Thorne! I was really pleased to see him but a bit surprised. I assumed he'd have been tipped and on his way home by this time, so as soon as I'd got rid of the gate man I went straight across and parked up next to him.

Even at eight o'clock in the morning the compound was already hot. I remember Richie was sat in a pair of shorts and a vest, sweating, even with both doors open and the electric fan blowing on him. He wasn't too impressed when I pulled up a bit too quickly and kicked up a great cloud of dust. But when he'd spat it out he smiled and said casually 'Alroit moi bub?' as if meeting another Englishman in Ankara customs was an everyday event.

'Yeah, but what are you still doing here – have you got a problem?' I asked.

'No. No problem bub. Oi din' get moi paperwork back 'til Froiday, so oi 'ad a beer an' came up 'ere las' noit.'

'Oh – I've been over at the Telex.' I said, trying to sound blasé about it. 'Why didn't you park there?' I asked.

'You must be joking,' he said knowingly – 'It's fuckin' murder troin t'get across that road in the morning...'

Then he said, 'You got 'im sorted 'en – found y'folder did you?'

'Er... Nope.'

'Oh. Well 'ow come's you's 'ere 'en?...An' what th'fuck's 'appened to your trailer?' he asked when he saw the miles of repair work. So I told him everything that had happened since he'd left customs in Istanbul...

***

'Problem,' my agent said when I dropped everything on his desk at 9 a.m.

'I know.'

He began tutting. A single tut, usually with raised eyebrows or an upward movement of the head means 'no'. This guy tutted and nodded so much he could have been Skippy the Bush Kangaroo. 'Tut – dis no good.' He held up the C.M.R. first (bastard). 'Tut – dis problem.' He held up something else then tossed it to one side. 'Tut...' And so on, until he'd tossed all my efforts to one side and I was forced to take an intense dislike to him.

'Big problem,' he said when he'd finished discarding everything. 'You must speak Alfa,' he said rudely. So I did – on the public payphone across the compound because the arsehole (Ipna) wouldn't let me use the phone in his office.

Erdoğan (pronounced Air-doe-ann) – our man at Alfa's – sounded very resigned when I got through to him and explained the situation – and I got the impression that nothing was going to happen very soon. So I settled in for what I thought was going to be a long wait. I figured I'd been lucky up to now but that my luck was about to run out again – that the real problems of being stuck in Turkey with no paperwork were about to manifest themselves. I had visions of growing old in the car park at Ankara customs while the price for sorting everything out would just increase as the days went by.

Resigned to this I put the kettle on and sat with Richie drinking gallons of tea and coffee. We ran through different scenarios, options and ways to while away the days – or even weeks – I might have to spend in Ankara. We discussed how much it might cost in bungs, and how many people might have to be paid, but the scale of the problem made the permutations too horrific to think about.

Eventually Richie's load was taken off and when his paperwork was returned to him he said something like 'Well, oi can oither stop 'ere with you t'noit an' 'elp you finish your beers, or you can drop your trailer an' come over to the Telex with me - 'cos oi'm boiying!"...when a miracle happened.

Lots of people appeared, suited and otherwise. Arms were waving, people were shouting, orders were being given, the seal was ripped off the back of my trailer – and I suddenly experienced a weird sensation of déjà vu!

I don't clearly remember the sequence of events that followed, but before too long the loading ramp on one of the warehouses was piled high with television aerials, my trailer was empty, I was allowed to leave, and before you could say 'Choc teşekkur abi' I was parked alongside Mr Thorne in the manky car park of Ankara's famed Telex Motel – grinning from ear to ear.

I never did find out who paid who. Or how much it all cost. All I do know is that I thoroughly enjoyed the belly dancer's Turkish delight, and of course several large helpings of Raki – a local aniseed-based drink five times stronger than aviation fuel.

What I don't recall too clearly is the eight-hour drive behind Richie's trailer as I followed him back to Istanbul with one of Asia Minor's worst-ever un-recorded hangovers.

Suffering at the hands of a Turkish driver's bottle of Raki

Ten

Of murderers and manifests

So – at long last I'd 'done' Ankara. Not under the best of circumstances, but at least I could now say I'd done it. All that remained was for me to get out of the country – which is easy enough if you say it quickly.

I had my bosh papers, which was a start. This is a piece of paper from customs that's loaded with the usual signatures and rubber stamps, and which confirms to customs at the border – or anywhere else – that the goods in question were actually off-loaded where they should have been and not in Ahmet Daley's lock-up.

I also had a completed carnet TIR – which is about as useful as a bag of pork scratchings at Kapik – two signed C.M.R.'s, a photocopied police paper with two stamps missing (Richie showed me where Kizilchammam TIR Kontrol was on the way back – police papers had to be stamped even when the truck is empty) and photocopies of my trip-tiks. And that was about it.

Alfa's had made a few enquiries on my behalf and told me what I had to do – which was quite a lot. They had pretty much washed their hands of me once their goods had been unloaded, so I knew not to expect too much help from them.

First I had to go to the police station at Avçilar to report the loss of my documents. The bits I had to be concerned about at this stage of the game were my trip-tiks and Turkish permit. The trip-tiks (carnet de passage) were used as a temporary import licence. I would need to produce them at the border to prove that the truck and trailer I was trying to leave the country with were the same as those I entered with. A photocopy could be 'mickied' and as far as customs are concerned I could have sold the truck in Turkey for a huge profit and be trying to sneak out with a ringer – a double.

The permit is an issued authorisation for a vehicle to enter and leave a country on commercial business. It is 'stamped in' on entry and has to be 'stamped out' on exit If a permit cannot be produced then, as far as the Turks are concerned, the truck is not authorised to be in the country. 'Parking, mister… You are not authorised to be in our country, so you do not leave!' (Perfect logic – like wheel-clamping a car that's blocking a road off).

Had I not lost my log-book, plating certificate and G.V.60 I could at least have confirmed that chassis and engine numbers matched up, and that the photographs on the G.V.60 matched the trailer I was pulling. But again, without the trip-tiks to prove I came in with the same truck as on those other documents – who's to say they weren't 'mickied' and sent out to me? I'd had two new trip-tiks issued at Şişli, in Istanbul, but they, like the photocopies, were no good without the originals bearing a customs entry stamp.

Even the fact that those details had been entered in my passport meant nothing. Number plates can be changed, engine and chassis numbers can be ground off and changed… in short, I was well and truly snookered – so I set out to do the rounds and try to get it sorted before I left Istanbul, fearing the worst.

At Avçilar nick I had to explain everything a dozen times and even with Kasim doing the translating it was frustrating work. Then I had to wait while several statements were typed up – one finger at a time – and wait again for the boss man to show up so that they could be signed, stamped and countersigned. Then I had to sign them all myself. Then I was told to go and get them translated into English, which I did at Alfa's office. It was done begrudgingly, and I decided it would probably be best not to call on them for any more help. I then had to take the translations back to Avçilar to be signed, stamped and photocopied again.

Next I had to take the whole lot to the local Jandarma station (a kind of para-military police), where the laborious process had to be gone through again. The only luck I had here was the fact that the Jandarma were right opposite the Chef's caterpillar yard in Avçilar, so after a hard day's work signing things and explaining things in triplicate, it was only a short walk home to bed.

Then I had to go and do the same thing at customs, then at the cop shop nearest to Salimpaşari customs – then at *every* police station that

I'd passed en-route to customs on the day my stuff went missing! Copies of *everything* had to be given to the police, the Jandarma and yes – customs – all signed and stamped by each... It just went on and on like that for two whole weeks. It was a fucking nightmare and at the end of the day it got me nowhere. I began to think that I'd never be allowed to leave the country. Bribes were refused and so were my pleas for understanding and leniency.

Alfa's had pretty much turned their back on me, the chef was getting pissed off from having so much attention paid to him by plod and the Jandarma, and after Roy had authorised the issue of the two replacement trip-tiks (with different numbers on them) he turned his back on me too. Issuing the trip-tiks was about the last thing he could do to try and help me. He'd already sent another permit – which was also as useful to me as an Arabic calendar – and he'd sent copies of everything he thought might be of any use and, most important of all, he'd sent a goodly amount of beer vouchers. But at the end of the day there was nothing more he could do. It got to the stage one day when we all felt we were just banging our heads against the wall and he said to me on the phone 'Fuck it, John – there's nothing else I can do. I can't get you out of Turkey, mate – it's as simple as that. I'm sorry, but you're on your own...'

And that was that. I had no-one left to turn to then, including the British Embassy, who at the time had a big hand-written sign inside their door which said 'TIR drivers – do <u>not</u> come to us with your problems!' and that was when I ran out of patience. People had been telling me for weeks now that I'd never get the truck – or myself – out of the country, and I was beginning to believe them. A few drivers even offered to smuggle me out under their bunks, which meant I'd have to dump the truck and risk being locked up if we were caught at the border – which wouldn't have been impossible because too many people knew of my problem and somebody was bound to talk if I disappeared – so I said thanks, but no thanks. I then grabbed hold of Kasim one day and said, 'Come on – you're coming up to the border with me!'

Kasim was horrified and said, '*Wha'?* Issa me no go a'Kapiky you – issa big a' proberlum Gümrük. Nah, Chon. Wassa for you wanna me go a'Kapik 'en eh?'

'I've had enough of all this bollocks. I've got to try and get through that border and I need an interpreter, so you'll have to do. Come on – I'll pay you.'

'Nah, nah. Issa no possibawl you go a'Bulgaria. Issa possibawl kalabush (prison) proberlum – you anna kamyon kalabush proberlum.'

'Fuck it, Kas, I've tried everything else and got nowhere – and I'll be buggered if I'm staying in Turkey forever. You've got to come with me.'

He didn't like the idea one little bit but in the end he relented and with the chef's permission he jumped in the truck and came up to Kapik with me.

Mistake.

Kapikule border is a huge concrete compound totally devoid of character and divided in two by a chain-link fence. One half is for trucks only – the other for everything else. There's one main concrete building in the car park, surrounded by several smaller ones containing duty-free shops, banks, and some smelly toilets. Inside the main building is a walk-around bit with all the open-top, glass-fronted offices in the centre where all drivers – entering and leaving Turkey – had to push and shove, one 'window' after another to 'do' each stage of their paperwork. Off to one side at the end of the building was a çay shop, a corridor leading to some 'off-limit' rooms – and the director's office. So I grabbed hold of Kasim when we got there and dragged him straight in to see the 'Murderer' (Müdhür – director).

When we entered and did all the nodding and salaaming his attitude seemed to say, 'Yes – I've been expecting you', almost as if he were surprised that I hadn't turned up at the border sooner.

Sitting behind his overlarge desk with expensive-looking fountain pens sticking out like darts in front of a spotless blotting pad, I then chucked a ton of typed up statements and photocopied paperwork in front of him and said, 'Er – I've got a bit of a problem.'

He just nodded, then looked at Kasim. Kasim said something in Turkish – obviously introducing himself – and the Murderer nodded again.

He made me nervous and I tried hard not to look him in the eye: In Turkey, as in most Muslim countries, any underling, such as myself (especially considering the circumstances under which I was there in the first place) is expected to show lots of respect to anyone in authority. This is usually done by overacting the humble, grovelling bit. The Turks do it by wringing their hands, lowering their heads and looking down at the shoes they've turned into slippers by squashing the heels down. Basically they'll go out of their way to look as awkward and as uncomfortable as possible, but they will rarely, if ever, look someone – especially not the Murderer of Kapik – straight in the eye. It's taken as an act of defiance and, therefore, as an insult. It's humiliating stuff and only serves to give these guys a greater sense of control and authority.

Normally I'd just stare at the paperwork on the desk or look out of the window – or even at the TV that they often had on – but this day I decided I'd better swallow my pride a bit – you know, when in Rome, and all that – so I looked humbly at my flip-flops and held my hands behind my back.

'You understand that this is a very serious problem in my country?' he asked in perfect English, after I'd quickly run through the story.

'Yes I do.' I then explained that I'd done everything I could and motioned to the stack of paperwork. He listened quietly, nodded every now and again and eventually said, 'Come back after.' Then he got up and left. I didn't know how long a Murderer's 'after' was, so we went to the çay shop and waited.

Kasim was nervous – more so than I expected him to be. He kept fiddling with things, looking from one window to another, and he didn't drink any çay. I think the presence of so many 'chefs' was a bit unnerving for him. I can't remember how long we waited, no more than an hour or two I should think, but it seemed longer. Eventually, after hanging around his door after the Murderer's return, we were summoned.

'Very well,' he said, leaning back in his chair looking very much like someone of great importance. 'There is a way to deal with this problem, and I will now tell you what you must do.'

I took a breath and waited, fully expecting him to say something silly like, 'Five hundred marks for this – one hundred for that', etc. But he took me totally by surprise when he said, 'First you must go to the man at such and such office, then you must…' and so he went on, going through a list of things I had to do and people I had to see in order to 'deal with this problem'. I could hardly believe it! Here was the director of Kapikule border, a man with the power to extract enormous bribes, or to impound trucks, trailers and their loads, and even have drivers imprisoned, telling me *free of charge* how to get out of his country with no paperwork!

He then turned to Kasim and went through it all again in Turkish, which had Kasim red-faced and trembling with awe. It was the first time I'd ever seen him speechless. When he'd finished I 'choc-teşekkured' him several times (thanked him very big) and shot off to do the rounds.

When a driver enters Kapik, as at most countries' borders, the first thing he's given is a 'kontrol card' or, to employ the more commonly used German word for it, a 'Laufzettel'. This control card has, apart from driver's name, nationality, registration nos. etc., a series of 'boxes' on it, all of which have to be stamped and signed at each 'window' by successive 'chefs' – i.e. the permit man, the trip-tik man, the 'Polis', and so on. This card, when completed, then has to be handed in at the exit barrier where the kontrol card chef himself checks it to make sure that each 'box' has been signed and stamped to prove to him that all of the given procedures have in fact been carried out. If one single stamp or signature was missing, that truck would be promptly turned back into the border *without argument.*

Welcome to Kapik.

My mission now was to fill up that bingo card – but it wasn't going to be easy. Getting a full house on the Laufzettel could be a daunting task at the best of times – the building was always heaving with drivers of all nationalities – each trying to get his papers shoved through a small slot in the window. There is no such thing as queuing here – it's every man for himself – and each window could take ten minutes or two hours to 'do'. And it was push and shove all the way. Having the added bonus of no proper paperwork and the chore of trying to explain why – even with the director's blessing – to bolshy, disinterested, money-grabbing officials, did not fill me with cheer. The fact that we also had to go and knock on doors along the forbidden corridor made the prospect even less pleasant.

It was 'Catch 22' right from the start. At every window we tried to explain the situation but nobody was willing to be the first to sign or stamp my Laufzettel. I was constantly told – 'You must do dis first...'

Dis first would then aim me in another direction and say the same thing, and so on until, after Allah knows how long, my Laufzettel had still progressed no further than name, rank and number.

That was when Kasim lost it and decided to take control of things – which got us nowhere even faster. Instead of speaking to these people and explaining what the Murderer wanted us to do (even the mention of the word Müdhür could instil fear and co-operation), Kasim, being Kasim, just barged in mouth before brain and started ranting. I kept telling him to calm down and shut up – but I was talking to a mud-brick wall. His nerves had got the better of him. As a result he got everyone's backs up and we were promptly told to sod off and come back on Monday. Kasim then lost it big time. He stormed back into the director's office uninvited, looked him straight in the eye and went into one… Goodnight and thanks for coming.

That evening I stuck Kasim on a bus and told him to fuck off back to Istanbul before he got us both locked up. I then made my apologies to the Murderer, went back to my truck and settled in for the weekend. Fuming.

Normally, Kapik is a seven-day-a-week, 24-hour border, so for the usual run of things nothing actually stops for the weekend. But in my case one of the problems, I discovered, was a genuine 'weekend' problem. The large manifest book, into which my trip-tik serial numbers had been written three weeks previously, was now full and had been locked away in someone's safe. The person in charge of the key was one of the normal office bods who worked in the forbidden corridor and only did the nine to five bit, Monday to Friday. So, until he turned up for work on Monday morning, there was nothing I could do except wait.

***

The trip-tik manifest chef, when I got to see him on Monday morning was, to my surprise, fully aware of my problem and only too willing to help! He was almost saying – 'Why didn't you come to see me first?'…I could have screamed.

After confirming that the photocopied trip-tiks and my name corresponded with the entries in his manifest (serial numbers, date of entry, etc.) he was willing, and able, to put the first of the required signatures on my bingo card... But there was a catch - first I had to 'do dis'...

And that's how it went on all day again, with every chef at every window telling me to go away and do 'dis first'. And, yet again, I got nowhere. So I queued up to see the Murderer again, hoping that he wasn't still pissed off with Kasim's outburst.

After shrugging my shoulders and explaining that I'd had a knock-back at every window, he got serious, summoned someone into his office and gave them a loud bollocking! Five minutes later I was being escorted from one window to the next where this guy, in turn, doled out bollockings to everyone else and started acquiring the stamps I needed on my Laufzettel!

Before long I almost had a full house and my head was spinning. After I'd acquired the first of many stamps, the process seemed to take on a life of its own and people were only too willing to offer their assistance. I could hardly believe it. I kept expecting one of them to say no and turn me away, but soon - less than a couple of hours I think - I was ready for my final port of call - The Murderer.

He sat behind his desk looking like a Cheshire cat and seemed amused when I re-entered his office. He motioned for me to put everything on his uncluttered desk and then he just sat there and let me stew. I was shaking like a leaf inside and felt like saying 'Hurry up you smug bastard'. But I had to keep my patience. This man's signature would mean the difference between driving out of there, or parking in a field and turning the truck into an apartment for the homeless.

Eventually he leaned forward, waved a hand at the crowd of people that had gathered at his door to watch, and picked up one of his pens. My heart was thumping as he artistically signed my Laufzettel like he was signing a finished painting, and said solemnly, 'You are free to go now. Please, do not be so careless next time. Goodbye.' And that was it! I picked up my get out of jail free card, Teşekkurred him a thousand times, with lots of bows and nods, and almost ran back to my truck – I was a free man again!

I don't know if I was just lucky, or if it was because I'd actually bothered to do all that running about and form filling back in Istanbul. Perhaps I'd genuinely completed all the legal procedures there and he was obliged to let me leave the country. Or perhaps he was just in a generous mood. I'll never know. At the time I didn't care – I was free to go.

I've often wondered since what would have happened if I'd just gone straight to the border and chanced my luck instead of enduring all that rigmarole at various police stations and stuff. But I'll never know that either. I can almost guarantee it would have been a very different story though.

Just before daylight, after passing the final kontrol box at the exit barrier, I'd entered the dimly lit, pot-holed, but imaginatively named 'Kapitan Andreevo', Bulgarian border, adjoining Kapik. Most of the staff there were either drunk or sleeping – all of them had camp-beds in their dingy little offices – and those that were actually awake just weren't bothering to work. It was the normal run of things for the Bulgarians, but I was buzzing around like a live wire. After more than three weeks in Turkey I just wanted to get rolling. I wanted to get my trailer *kontrolled*, and get the hell out of there… But nothing happened until eight or nine o'clock after the shift had changed hands – by which time I was fast asleep over the steering wheel.

By about midday I'd left the border, bumped and crashed my way through Plovdiv and was steaming up the motorway towards Sofia at Mach 2. There was a white DAF coming up in the opposite direction, pulling a yellow trailer. It looked familiar. As it drew closer its lights started flashing and the driver was hung out of the window waving frantically. I thought this guy might have a problem, so I backed off a bit and was just in time to hear Richie Thorne screaming 'Alroit Bub?' as we passed each other.

Eleven
Of backpackers and flat batteries

Roy eventually forgave me for that little episode, but it didn't happen overnight and it was a while longer before he let me live it down.

I think the thing that went in my favour at the time was the fact that I'd eventually managed to get his truck back in one piece, *and* found a decent return load to come home with as well. That in itself hadn't been too difficult - I'd simply scrounged some mickey permits then made a phone call to our shipping agent in Italy.

I couldn't have loaded from anywhere outside the EU at the time without incurring great expense. It meant I'd have to pay out to 'manifest' the load at each border until I got to the EU itself, where I could then T. Form it. But bringing back a load from Italy was cheap and simple because that could go all the way back to England on just the T. Form – which our agent used to very kindly supply free of charge. And, more importantly, I knew I could draw some much-needed beer vouchers from him at the same time – so it was the obvious place to go.

I then drove 'empty' up to Reggio Emilia, collected a full (and expensive) load of crystal ware, drew some cash, booked a ferry back to England on his account and went back home. I think Roy was a bit surprised when I rang from Dover one day to say that I was in the country bearing gifts – and could I come back home please?

The thing he seemed pissed off about more than anything else was the loss of his G.V.60. For some reason he seemed to place more importance on that one item than all the time, money and aggro the whole incident had cost in the first place. It made little sense to me at the time, especially when there were other, more important things to be angry with me over – but to keep him happy, and also to keep my job (Roy used to sack us all every couple of months, whether we needed it or not) I offered to pay whatever it would cost to have it replaced. Which I did. From the next trip's run money…

It was during that next trip that I bumped into Vanessa. I'd done the usual run to Turkey, tipped at the Otosan-Ford plant at Hyderpasha, and then gone up to Romania to pick up a full load of cheap ladies' knickers for Marks and Sparks.

At the time Lawrabian drivers were still forbidden to run home through the rest of the Commie Bloc – Hungary, Czech, DDR – because Roy continued to say that he didn't want any of us to be out of civilisation and communication for any longer than was necessary.

Because of that ruling, I'd then had to drop all the way back down through Romania to Yugoslavia which, yet again, was an extra unnecessary day's work. I then had to spend the usual two days or more at Moravita border, south of Timisoara, just trying to exit the country, which was *miles* from 'civilisation' and had no bloody communications at all! But there you go.

En-route through Yugo, I called into the 'Hotel National' at Belgrade, as most English drivers did at the time. The 'National' was – and still is – a not very special 'Hotel-Camping' set back behind some trees on the outskirts of town. It was always crawling with expensive (and ugly) 'Doris's' (slappers), lots of local thieves and a host of pig-ignorant coppers with violent dispositions. The food was good, but dear, and the phone and telex – when they worked – were extortionate. All of the waiters were called George by the drivers – except for Georgina, the hairy-legged waitress - and the small car park was a smelly, dirty shit-hole.

Most trucks that pulled in had to park on the slip roads where their windows and cabs were in danger of being done at night, and where the drunken coppers used to enjoy beating up drivers every now and again during the early hours just for being parked there in the first place… But it was a good meeting place come watering hole, and we liked it.

Again, even though it's a hotel, it's not a place where drivers took rooms - TIR drivers rarely, if ever, take rooms anywhere. There are the odd occasions for sure, like when the wife or girlfriend is in tow, but other than that there's no point in taking a room. The 'Camion Hotel' is as good a place as any – and a lot cheaper. All trucks that do any kind of long-haul work these days have beds in them – some even have 'double-bunks', one above the other (but behind the seats, not in a 'caravan' nailed to the back of the cab, as the Americans are fond of). The cabs themselves can be equipped with cookers, coffee machines, TV's – even a cocktail cabinet if a driver wishes (or at least a crate of beer on the roof-rack). So who needs hotel rooms? And anyway, the rooms at the National were nearly always full… with refugees.

Most of these refugees – and escapees – were from neighbouring communist countries like Albania and Romania, but there would often be an assortment of others like Arabs for instance (mostly women); blacks from African countries that were either in civil war or whose authorities just enjoyed persecuting people; there were professional people, peasants, AWOL soldiers, political prisoners, mothers with babes… All sorts, and it wasn't uncommon to see these people sat at the breakfast tables in the larger of the two restaurants swathed in bandages, or crying, trembling, staring… And the hotel never seemed to have a shortage of guests. Our questions about these people were rarely answered. Most of the time they were simply ignored – so we took the hint and left it at that.

My alternator had been playing up at the time so I needed to pull into the 'National' anyway because my batteries were as dead as a dodo and I wanted to get it fixed. I'd already had to keep the engine running non-stop for the previous three or four days because I'd had nothing to repair the alternator with and it was really pissing me off. I'd had no sure way of getting cheap or reliable spares in Romania either - even though F. Troop ran some 89s of their own, the country couldn't afford original parts or replacements, so when things went wrong they generally just bodged and made do. Hence, finding one of 'F. Troop's' barracks or any other workshop that could have handled such a simple task without fucking it up or trying to rip me off, was about as likely as Martians landing in Whitby to buy fish and chips.

So, seeing as I was on my way home I headed for Belgrade running the engine twenty-four hours a day on cheap Bulgarian diesel (bought at our regular fill-up – a large lay-by just outside Sofia – where we were met by a huge man in a scabby old Lada whose boot was loaded down with Jerry cans of diesel freshly stolen from the local bus garage). And anyway it was a good a reason as any to park up for a day and have a 'Bip Kontrol' (the local beer) with some of the lads.

The 'Terrible Twins', George and Hughie MacLennon, were in attendance when I got there. The two little Welshmen were literally blocking off half the car park. The gear-box from one of their 89s (a popular truck at the time) was in a million pieces all over the floor along with tools, bits of wood, rags and empty beer cans. The pair of them were covered in oil but quite happily sitting in the dirt playing with cogs and getting pissed.

It was always good to see George and Hughie so I parked next to them, killed the engine, breathed a sigh or relief, scrounged a beer, and set to work.

As I was laid under my front bumper listening to, 'No, no you stupid busstud, that doesn't go there…' Catweasle (Roy Marsden) pulled up in one of Roy's Scania's. Sat in his passenger seat was a pretty, freckled, fair-haired girl in a baggy T-shirt. As nearly always happens when there's a woman present, drivers – some of whom I didn't even know were there – began to appear from the woodwork, combing hair, and wiping hands on the bums of their jeans.

I couldn't move because Roy, recognising my truck and seeing a pair of legs sticking out from underneath, had purposely parked just inches from where I was laid.

After the usual round of hello's from all the drivers that were laying siege to his passenger's door, somebody mentioned beer, whereupon this girl was hauled out of the truck and escorted into the restaurant under tattoo-armed guard – and I was left sprawled under the 89.

I continued to *kontrol* my alternator problem once they'd gone until I heard the familiar clip-clopping sound of someone trying to walk in clogs. All I saw then as I looked round was a pair of furry animals with feet in them as they parked themselves next to me. Roy Haxell (Axles), another Lawrabian driver, squatted like he was about to have a spread-axle shit, looked at what I was doing, smiled and shook his head.

Roy, a tall quietly-spoken Northerner with a dry sense of humour, a '50s quiff, and a disgusting taste in music, sat there on his haunches like a cartoon cowboy and drawled, 'Are tell yer what, John – wah don't yer leave that fer now 'cos ahm on me way back too, an' we can roon t'gether. You can roon on mah batteries, an' are can roon on yours an' charge 'em oop. Then we can swop 'em over again when they go flat.' (Batteries can be taken on and off with a diesel engine running).

Then, 'Fook thee alternator, you'll not get it done cheaply 'ere anyway an' we can be 'ome in a few days - 'ow's that sound?'

Minutes later, having combed my hair and cleaned my hands on my jeans, I was parked at the 'English table' in the restaurant interviewing a Bip.

'Y' fixed y'problem then?' the girl said to me in a strong Australian accent from across the table.

'Er, sort of' I replied, not wanting to admit that I'd abandoned the project in favour of a beer and some female company. So I tried to play it cool. I remember trying to look clever by flipping the cap off another bottle of Bip for her by using my cigarette lighter… and broke the lighter: Proper TIR drivers rarely used bottle openers – they used to open a bottle by grabbing it round the throat and, using the forefinger as a lever, prise the lid off with the arse end of a fag lighter. The trouble was that the lighter got destroyed bit by bit with use, and when I tried to do it, a great chunk fell away from the bottom and the lid refused to budge. I felt a right prat but luckily she saw the funny side of it and we got talking.

It turned out she was on her way back to England from Khatmandu, in Nepal, and needed a lift. Catweasle had given her a lift up from Istanbul but couldn't take her any further because he was due to change trailers at the National and do a 'turn-around' – which meant he had to go straight back down to Turkey. He knew there was bound to be one or two English drivers parked in Belgrade, so he'd suggested that if she travelled with him to there, she was bound to find another lift.

The Bips flowed.

She told us of her travels around the Himalayas with 'Top Deck' – the Australian-run, English-based travel outfit that do overland trips for fare-paying passengers to loads of weird and wonderful places in old London double-decker buses. She'd 'done' Nepal, India and Bally-go-backwards, and then had flown into Turkey with one or two of the British contingent from the bus hoping for a lift to the UK, (Brits had to fly back over Iran at the time because the Iranians had a strop on and wouldn't give us visas), and I was impressed.

There was also talk of the disaster that had happened at Zeebrugge when the Herald of Free Enterprise had keeled over not long before and claimed the lives of 193 people. The incident was a shock to many of us. It brought home again the fragility of our existence as drivers and was enough in itself to be a subject changer.

It turned out that several drivers we all knew had genuinely been due to sail on the Enterprise that day, but had missed it for whatever reasons. I found out ages later that Richie Thorne had been one of them. Luckily his liking for beer had steered him in another direction – which had saved his life.

I'd been in Turkey at the time, two thousand-odd miles away, but it still sent a shiver up my spine when I heard about it. It could have been any one of us, any day of the week. Ninety-odd percent of TIR drivers shipped to and from Zeebrugge at the time and though I didn't personally know anyone on board when she'd rolled I could, on any other sailing, have known half a dozen – or even been on board myself. So we all had a drink in respect and got slowly pissed.

At sometime during the evening I offered Vanessa a lift back to England – and she accepted! Later that night, while the rest of us were still enjoying our Bip Kontrol she, and her 'I-belong-to-the-SAS' backpack moved into my truck which, at the time, I thought was very sporting of her.

The trip home from there was a scream. Twice a day we had to stop and change batteries with Roy because, as the ones I was using got flatter and flatter, the lights would dim, the wipers would take ten minutes to cover an arc, and the cassettes ran slower and slower. We were listening to some of Roy's country and western tapes and all we could hear on just about every tape *and* on what we thought was a haunted radio was... *'Well, aahm a trurk draavin' cowboy...'* being sung in slow motion underwater.

We constantly took the piss out of his furry clogs, which he took like a truck drivin' man, but when we found some bar stools in 'Pauline's' at Golling, near Saltzburg in Austria, that were covered in the same material, we were convinced that his clogs were going to fall in love and elope and it cracked us up for days.

We ran home through Luxembourg that trip to top up with cheap diesel and because Vanessa hadn't been there before. But instead of fairy-tale castles perched on valley slopes and princesses swanning around on horseback, all she got to see was the countryside of the Ardennes at 90kph… Drivers rarely have enough funds left on their way home to go sightseeing – on their way down it's a different story, but our destination was Dover.

When we went to drive off the boat in England the truck wouldn't start. I'd purposely left the engine running when I pulled onto the ferry in Zeebrugge, but they weren't very impressed with that – even though I'd squared it up with the authorities beforehand. The Enterprise disaster was still fresh in everyone's minds and safety measures were of prime concern, so they called me up on the tannoy as I was about to tuck into steak and chips, and I had to go back down to the loading deck and switch the engine off. I also got a severe bollocking from 'sir' for being a fire hazard and for choking all the crew members with diesel fumes.

Then the tuggie who came on board at Dover to give me a jump start couldn't understand why we were laughing, after Axles staggered over in his oil-stained clogs and nodding slowly with a serious expression said, 'See – are told yer t'get it fixed at t'National…'

Mr Tucker was waiting on the dockside to greet me again as we rolled off the ferry. After another falsely polite interview – where had I been, etc., and the usual check of my international road permits, we were allowed to carry on. I felt his eyes burning into my back as I drove up to the 'Waterguard' (Customs and Excise).

Vanessa had been really good company. It was great to have someone in the truck who not only enjoyed making sandwiches but who could roll a cigarette *and* carry a heavy-duty twelve-volt battery.

As we sat in the 'Wheelhouse' (it may have been called 'Barnacles' then, I can't remember) - the so-called drivers' restaurant at the eastern docks – waiting for customs to clear our carnets for the loads we'd brought back, Roy said to Vanessa, 'If y'enjoyed y'self wi' John, lass, wah don't yer go an' do a whole proper trip wi' 'im? Are know itter be foon, an' ahm sure our John 'ere won't mind.'

Vanessa had already told me that she had things to do in the UK, so I fully expected her to turn the offer down but, after just a moment's thought she simply smiled, shrugged her shoulders and said, 'Aah… yeah – okay then. Why not!'

And, sod's law, that was when Roy Bradford dropped one of his most unexpected bombshells as he announced that from that date on, Lawrabian drivers would have to avoid Austria at all costs – and start running through the Commie Bloc!

Horse and cart with stray dogs in tow

Roman on TIR plates outside Romania Combi S.A.

Twelve

Of kontrols and Kalashnikovs

After all the times Roy had said, 'Fuck the Commie Bloc – I don't want you lot going through there... You'll all end up on the missing list for weeks shagging the tarts and spending my money on the piss...' and so on, he was now saying, 'Fuck Austria, it's too expensive, you lot are costing me a fortune... I've got the permits now, so you've all got to go through Czech – Hungary... It's cheaper; there's no transit taxes and all that shit... It's only a day longer... Now, I want no fucking about – just get through the borders, don't upset anyone, and go like fuck 'til you're out of there, understand? AND KEEP IN TOUCH! ALRIGHT?'

No, it wasn't alright. I had Vanessa with me. I wanted to have fun and go the usual way; the way most of us went when the sun was shining, i.e. straight through Austria and Yugoslavia to Greece, then onto the beach at Kavala without passing 'Go'. Any other time I'd have jumped at the chance to 'do' the rest of the Commie Bloc, but now, with Vanessa in tow, I wanted to take things easy and show her a good time – not to go traipsing off into unknown territory. Especially not fortified 'enemy' territory on the wrong side of the Iron Curtain.

When I told her the good news I expected her to be pissed off, thinking she had the same ideas as me about beaches and beers with umbrellas in but, after quick consideration, all she said was, 'Aah, yeah, that'll be good...'

I thought fuck me, I can't win!

For the Commie Bloc we both needed visas. One or two we could buy at borders, but for Czechoslovakia and Bulgaria we had to get them in advance. The 'Bulgy' visas we could get at a consulate en-route but the Czechs could get funny about it, so we trotted off to their Embassy at Kensington, armed with the usual unflattering passport photos and a few bob for the pub next door.

The Commie Bloc - The Communist countries of the Eastern Bloc. I'd been to Bulgaria and Romania a few times, but that was all. I knew what shit-holes they both were, but I knew sod all about communist East Germany, Czechoslovakia or Hungary. I just assumed they'd all be pretty much the same and wasn't really looking forward to finding out, especially not with an Australian woman in the passenger's seat which I thought might complicate things.

Yugoslavia, though a socialist country, was never really considered a part of the Commie Bloc. If anything it was always classed as the alternative route. Poland and Russia were never really on the TIR drivers list either. Not enough people ever went that way (except for the Vikings who regularly transited Poland from Scandinavia), and for Russia it was nigh on impossible to get permits anyway. So, for transit purposes, as far as UK TIR drivers were concerned, the Commie Bloc consisted of the remaining five: East Germany (DDR), Czechoslovakia, Hungary, Romania and Bulgaria.

The problem for me lay in which way to go and which borders to use. One route was as good as the next as far as I was concerned – seeing as I didn't know any of them. I never even had a map to give me a clue. Believe it or not, most TIR drivers didn't carry maps! It may sound daft, considering the distances and amount of countries involved – but most drivers know where they are going. After all, a transit route is a transit route. It's like going to the shops. Once you've been there you know the way – but if, like me, a driver hasn't been somewhere before it's simple enough to get directions from someone who has – and even simpler to tag along behind someone who's going that way... So who needs a map?

Normally I'd have just shot off to Dover and seen who was about, or hung around for an hour or three until someone showed up... but the day before I was due to ship, Her Majesty's Customs and Excise had decided to go on strike and nothing was moving in or out of the country! Dover was at a standstill. As was Ramsgate, Harwich, Portsmouth... Customs were refusing to process paperwork for import or export and drivers were stranded at ports all over the country.

Plan B.

Roy said he'd heard on the grapevine that a skeleton staff of Customs and Excise officers would be manning the rubber stamps at Felixstowe in a stalwart effort to keep things moving – So I was duly dispatched to 'Give it a try, John – tell 'em it's an urgent diplomatic load or something. They'll never know the difference – probably spend all their time on the golf course... won't know a diplomatic load from an 'ole in one...' And off I went.

When I got to the docks at Felixstowe I was surprised to find the place relatively empty. I'd expected to see hundreds of trucks parked all over the place, but I guess most had decided to sit it out at home and wait for the strike to end, and that few, if any, had heard the same grapevine news as Roy. So I went to the freight booking office to find out the score.

I was told 'No chance mate. We can't issue you a ticket until customs have done your paperwork – and they're not doing *anybody's* papers at the moment!'

Vanessa looked at me as if to say 'Roy was lying – looks like we're in for a long wait!'. So I asked where customs was.

Sod's law, it was miles away.

When I eventually staggered in the place seemed deserted so I caught my breath and bought a coffee from the machine. By the time I'd stopped sweating nobody had showed up, so I started knocking on doors. Whenever somebody answered my knocking and I explained what I wanted I was laughed at – until a big fat guy (skeleton staff?), a bit like an older version of Billy Bunter, came to a door. He had lots of gold bits on his uniform, and looked pretty important – so I said hello, apologised for disturbing him, and asked if it was possible for someone to stamp my papers because the boat was waiting for me.

'Certainly,' he said, 'But we have a bit of a problem at the moment. All our staff have buggered off and I'm afraid I've been left holding the baby, as it were.'

I commiserated with him and repeated the lie that I was holding the ferry up because I couldn't find anyone to 'start' my carnet.

'I'd gladly oblige, Mr er... but it's not my usual place of work you see, and frankly, I haven't the foggiest how to go about it.'

I'd got him. 'Oh, it's simple enough,' I said. 'I can show you if you like...' My heart was pounding. I'd expected a remark like that to get right up his nose, but all he did was raise an eyebrow and say, 'Jolly good show – follow me.' And off he went!

Vanessa couldn't believe it. Here we were being escorted into the offices of Customs and Excise by one of the big chiefs who was willing to let *me* show *him* how to complete an important customs document in the belief that a cross-channel ferry was straining at the leash for my arrival!

And I could hardly believe it either as we both ran back across the compound minutes later laughing our socks off.

We were still laughing as we struggled up the stairs, sweating, and plonked everything on the shelf outside the booking office window.

'I don't believe it!' The guy said when I told him I'd 'done' customs and could I have a ticket please – one driver, one passenger?

'But they're on strike – they're not doing any papers. These guys have been here for two days…' He pointed at the bored crowd.

'What strike?' I said, as we both burst out laughing again, whereupon dozens of bum-sore drivers dropped what they were doing and stampeded towards customs… Poor Bunter.

Roy had lied, but it proved worthwhile because we, and just one other truck, were actually packed off on the next boat to Belgium. The only problem with this was that the 'one other' driver was bound for somewhere local in Western Europe, and I was the only TIR driver to arrive on Belgian soil that day heading east… There was nobody else about to interrogate.

At the time, before customs did away with internal EU border controls, drivers running under a carnet TIR were obliged to nominate which border they intended to leave a country from. That name was then written on the carnet by customs when each page is completed and torn out (one page 'in' – white – one page 'out' – green). At Zeebrugge I had to nominate the border at which I intended to leave Belgium, so without thinking I said Eynatten – the Belgian side of the motorway border crossing into Germany at Aachen Süd.

Nominating Eynatten pretty much ruled out going to East Germany because of geography. For the sake of directness I'd have needed to use a border further north for that, such as Venlo in Holland (at the time the Benelux countries, Belgium, The Netherlands and Luxembourg, had no internal border controls for transit traffic, much like a forerunner of the recent customs union agreement in the rest of Europe, so had I nominated Venlo I could have transited Belgium into

Holland and thence the German border, without having to stop, go to jail, or pass go. But, seeing as there was nobody for me to tag along with I named the border I normally used.

I could have changed my mind en-route and gone another way. The border that is nominated was, strictly speaking, only an 'intended' border of exit and shouldn't have meant a driver was obliged to go that way just because it's written on the carnet (I mean, what if war breaks out somewhere, or the roads are blocked?). But, in practice, using a border other than that stated, or being over the stated transit time could cause problems – more so in Eastern Europe than anywhere, it must be said, but it can still cause problems. Customs men can – and often do - get very shirty about it, especially if they've had a bad day. And they have the power – often abused – to turns trucks away, refuse to complete their documents, or impose ridiculous 'on the spot' fines (contrary to TIR regulations).

But I wasn't obliged to use East Germany anyway – I only needed to avoid Austria, which I could do by using Czech and Hungary. The reason drivers went DDR was because they could get across W. Germany within the amount of driving time allotted to TIR drivers (eight 'on', eight 'off' at the time), and because the E. Germans, bless their canvas socks, had no *kontrols* on red diesel, which meant drivers could start running on red much sooner. It was also a matter of personal preference. Some guys went that way because they reckoned that the borders were easier.

I wasn't really concerned with any of that. Eight hours was far too much to drive in one day, I thought, and if I needed to run on 'cherry' I'd simply start pumping it through wherever and whenever. And as for the borders…

Our first port of call was the Total garage just up the road for a free coffee and to see if anyone else was about. There was no-one, of course. Nor was there on the boat that came in after ours. Nor did anyone show up on their way home either… I soon began to regret my enthusiastic departure from Felixstowe – but it still never occurred to me to buy a map.

Next we went to the 'Wally Stop' at Eynatten, a small truck-stop two k's from the border where there was an explosion and a terrible fire some years back that killed so many people – driver Keith Hill among them.

Surprise, surprise – the Wally Stop was devoid of English TIR drivers, so we had a meal and called it a day.

At Aachen border the next day, after completing customs on the Belgian side, I once again had to nominate my next border of exit – this time from Germany. I'd been told that most English drivers running the Commie Bloc were using a border called Fürth im Wald to transit from Germany to Czech. So I promptly pissed off the German customs officer by pronouncing it completely wrong… Having made my day I merrily entered the Bundesrepublik and headed east on the autobahn – running on red.

It wasn't until I got to Tennenlohe truck stop, near Nüremberg, that night that I actually bumped into another 'white man' – Chris Hooper, who was on his way home. The best I could do was pour some beers into him and interrogate 'Billy Big Pockets', as he was known at the time (because of his superb ability to spend vast sums of money and have sod all to show for it), for directions and 'do's' and 'don'ts about Czechoslovakia.

Needless to say the hangover and accompanying memory lapse saw us well and truly lost in Bavaria the following day on steep, twisting country roads.

I eventually found Fürth im Wald by luck more than judgement I think, and was pleasantly surprised to find that there wasn't much of a queue. There were one or two 'Bubbles' (Bubble and Squeak – Greek), a few 'F. Troop', some 'Charley-Sads' (CSAD – the Czech State transport fleet), a couple of Wombles and a smattering of Erics (Germans, no idea where the name came from). In an hour or so I was safely out of German customs (they didn't check my 'running tanks') and heading across 'No-Man's-Land' towards Czechoslovakia for the first time.

'No-Man's-Land' was nothing more than a bumpy two-hundred yard uphill run to the monstrously thick, rusted 'barber's pole' barrier that signalled the entrance to one of Western Europe's frontiers with the Iron Curtain. There wasn't much to see, but even the small things were immediately noticeable, like flaking green paint on the guard's hut; the watchtowers in the near distance; the shabby condition of the buildings; a strange flag on a pole, and soldiers with Kalashnikov assault rifles.

I didn't really know what to expect, but the sight of a German copper with binoculars who'd been constantly watching things across No-Man's-Land from the moment we'd arrived, led me to suspect the worst.

The system wasn't entirely new to me – I'd entered and transited communist countries before, but there was a difference. They, Bulgaria and Romania, bordered only other communist countries or the Black Sea, Turkey, and Greece. I was now crossing the barrier from 'us' to 'them' at a place close to home; a place where Nato had spent millions of dollars on sophisticated surveillance equipment, on military hardware, tank traps, barbed wire and German binoculars. This was front-line Europe – the place where it was all supposed to happen if the cold war ever warmed up and the countries of the Warsaw Pact got stroppy. This, I thought, was where the really strict *kontrols* would have to be endured.

I'd already heard all the horror stories about dogs, minefields, cab searches, body searches, interrogations and so on; of the mean-tempered bastards waving guns and Geiger-counters at everything and screaming at everyone. Of the coppers and customs men who delighted in scaring people and making everyone's life a misery.

As I left the car park on the German side I had visions of old spy films with Michael Caine legging it into the West with a bag full of Russian secrets, as sirens wailed and searchlights scoured the fields; of army officers screaming orders as soldiers loosed off hundreds of rounds, with tracer bullets zinging and ricocheting everywhere, of vicious dogs howling and straining at the leash…

It turned out to be a load of bollocks, of course.

Yes, the place was dark and gloomy but only in comparison to the clean, well-lit well-ordered German side. In reality the entrance to Czechoslovakia was no worse – and in the end no more daunting – than the entrance to a shitty old Victorian factory that could have been anywhere in England.

Two young lads in baggy uniforms with Kalashnikovs slung over their shoulders smiled at Vanessa and couldn't get the barrier up quick enough as we drove up the hill. If that wasn't enough to throw me off guard the Czechs, who drive on the right like everyone else in Europe, directed me to park on the left of a little brown brick building that could only be described as an overgrown toilet block.

An unshaven bod in a brown uniform came up to the cab, attempted to salute, and asked for our passports, which he disappeared with. I was then told to go to a small window in the dingy 'main' building next door to 'do' my papers while the dogs had a sniff around Vanessa's handbag.

The place was small, unlit, and not over-friendly, but I didn't get much feeling of oppression or of any of the hatred that I'd expected – just one of boredom, indifference and a certain regimented system in operation. Nothing was hurried and no-one shouted. In fact very few people actually spoke. Not even to one another. They seemed fed up, just going through the motions.

These people didn't look like much of a threat. They were bored shitless. If anything I think they would rather have been in Germany enjoying a beer, not defending the ideological claptrap of communism and being afraid to say or do otherwise. The biggest threat, I realised, came from within their own borders, which is why *kontrols* behind the Iron Curtain itself – as in Bulgy and Rumo – were a lot stricter than they were here, on Communism's 'supposed' front line of defence.

That was when I realised Eastern Europe had more to fear from its own people than it did from anything else. The borders, the strict regime, the fear, the barbed wire, the oppression – it was all designed to keep their own in, not to keep us out.

I'd also expected the Czechs to give Vanessa a hard time of it, but soon both our passports were handed back with a grimace and a lazy salute, and that was about it. We were allowed to go – no screaming, no pushing and shoving, no cab-control, no being dragged off to a back room for a body search and a grope… so to cheer her up I promised her one later and off we went.

And then I got lost again. The roads were narrow, unpainted, unlit and bloody slippery. The signposting was shit and when we came to the first sizeable town I professionally took a wrong turning, and spent the next two or three hours trying to find Plzen (as in Pilsen beer).

It was hard work. All the tiny, twisting roads seemed to go uphill, and I couldn't make head nor tail of the signposting. If we stopped to ask directions all we got was a shrug of the shoulders, a funny look as if we were mad – or simply ignored. So we just plodded on, arguing between us whose sense of direction was better.

Vanessa won, and when we finally reached the outskirts of Prague I had to admit defeat. I wearily reversed onto some roadworks, said something like, 'Fuck Czechoslovakia' – and crashed out over the steering wheel, knackered.

My passenger was not impressed.

I woke up a few hours later with OVLOV imprinted on my forehead from the steering wheel, and a bad crick in my neck. Vanessa was fast asleep in the bunk, so I fired up and headed off, following the signs for Brno and Bratislava. I thought, I'll show you…

There's a big hill going down into Prague. It's about two or three kilometres long and quite steep. As it was now daylight I was paying more attention to the sights than to the road. I noticed the contrast between some lovely old buildings with towers and balconies and all kinds of architectural oddities which, in their day, must have been grand old houses lived in by nobles and the like, and the shabby, cloned apartment blocks with lines of washing strung up all over the place, and knackered old Skodas parked out front.

It all looked as if it was falling to bits. Paint was flaking off walls, grass grew up between cracks in the concrete pavements, there were broken windows, slack and dangerous-looking power lines thrown up all over the place… It reminded me very much of Islington. Then I realised the engine was screaming. I looked round and saw that not only was the rev counter in the red, but so was the traffic light in front of me… and I'd let the truck run away! I panicked. I stood on the brakes and anchored up so hard that Vanessa was violently thrown out of bed and almost tossed through the windscreen – bum first.

From Prague we joined the concrete section motorway that runs East-ish all the way to Bratislava, gathering Pot noodles and trying to clear other debris from under the pedals – and we bumped along in silence. She was convinced I'd turfed her out of the bunk on purpose.

We stopped at a place known as the 'Airfield' – a two or three-kilometre stretch of motorway with no central crash barrier. It was just a strip of concrete six lanes wide (four lanes, two hard shoulders) plus the bit where the central reservation would have been. They're common in E. Europe – they are, quite simply, emergency landing strips – or take-off strips, should the need arise. I didn't stop to admire it – I stopped because there was a huge parking area next to it and I wanted a brew.

The parking areas (staggered – one on each side of the 'strip') would have been used as marshalling yards in war situations, for refuelling craft and so on – but they'd have had to get rid of all the lorries first. There were dozens of drivers parked up all over the place, changing wheels, cooking, sleeping.

It turned out to be a regular tea-stop for a lot of English drivers too, and when one of them saw us parked as he came from the opposite direction, he didn't hesitate to anchor up on the hard shoulder and run across for a cuppa.

I don't know who he was but I interrogated him anyway. He cheered us both up by telling us we weren't allowed through Bratislava and that the detour took us over a 'bloody great mountain…' It was signposted off the motorway (TIR in small letters with an arrow) but that it was a steep climb and 'Watch out for the Vicious Bastards at the bottom.' (VB was the initials on the doors of all the orange and white police cars).

So - cheered by this news, we set off again.

The motorway had been hard work from Prague. It was all up and down – a two-kilometre climb up, the same down, two up, two down – and so on. Beautiful scenery and all that, but there wasn't a flat bit on it until we got past Brno. That was when I put my foot down and got stopped by the Vicious Bastards in an orange and white car.

They were arseholes. They screamed, they shouted, they demanded our passports and then sat us on the hard shoulder for twenty minutes trying to scare us into paying silly money. So I did what all sensible Englishmen do in such situations – and put the kettle on.

If there's one sure way to wind up a copper when he's doing his utmost to be an arsehole, it's to put the kettle on and pretend you don't care. Communist policemen are not – were not – prepared for such blatant insolence and rarely knew how to react. They were so used to people cowering and shaking in their boots, that the sight of someone shrugging their shoulders and saying, in effect, 'Fuck you, you can shout as much as you want' really threw them off balance.

Some of them could turn nasty, hence the nickname, and more than one of them have pulled guns in the past, or coshes, to enforce their arguments —but that sort of behaviour didn't cut much ice with most British drivers, and they soon learnt that using physical violence, like slaps or a poked finger in the chest earned its own rewards, as on the day Joby, a jolly, fifteen-stone 'Forester' knocked one of them out on the roadside.

I'd 'brewed up' many times in Bulgaria and Romania and it nearly always had the same effect. First came the stare of disbelief, then the dropped jaw and outstretched arms, which said. 'I know he's doing something wrong – but *what*? Often the lips would go up and down as they tried to think of something to say but it nearly always stumped them – after all, making a cuppa isn't illegal, and if we hadn't been stopped by *him* in the first place, we wouldn't be doing it… Then they'll walk away shaking their heads. Minutes later, not knowing what to do, and not wanting to look stupid in front of their colleagues – and nearly *always* before the kettle had boiled – they'd walk back, airmail the passport through the open window at Mach two and bark instructions to move on.

Vanessa had been a little unnerved by it all at the time and kept looking at me as if I was mad, but once we drove off she couldn't stop laughing.

It may seem a silly thing to do at the time, but it's meant to. It's the sort of thing the English do. Frequently. And it works, they just can't get their head around us.

Pulling the curtains around the window works even better…

The 'mountain' we'd been warned about turned out to be nothing more than a short, twisting climb through the foothills of the Carpathians and although it added an hour or so onto the journey, was nothing at all like a mountain and all it did was get me lost again.

There wasn't a single signpost for the border I was aiming for – Rusovce, the Czech side of the border commonly known as Rajka. All the other borders were 'signed-up' – but no – not mine. And again, all the: 'Excuse me mate – where's Roosovsee?' from Vanessa just went ignored…

So we blundered on, turning left instead of right, stopping to interrogate the locals for directions, getting lower and lower on diesel, getting annoyed.

Eventually, after passing a couple of bored-looking squaddies in a dilapidated sentry box by the side of the road, I saw the arse-end of a trailer. In front of him was another trailer – and another… We'd found the queue for the border!

Hand-drawn map by John Nevill

Thirteen

Of warning poles and pot-holes

It was a relief. Not because we'd finished Czech and made it to the border, but because I could put the handbrake on and not have to drive anymore. What would normally have been one day's work had taken us nearly two and I was exhausted. A lot of people think that because TIR drivers cover such huge distances that they can regularly spend days behind the wheel knocking out the miles; that they can do 1,000kms a day with matchsticks propping up their eyelids; that going from A to B in 'one hit' is the norm... Bollocks. Four or five hundred k's a day in a knackered truck is good going by anyone's standards over there. The M6 motorway doesn't extend all the way to Eastern Europe – Carlisle to Coventry in one hit may be okay in the UK but to cover the same distance on what would largely be classed as 'B' roads is bloody hard work, and I don't mind admitting it.

A round trip to Istanbul is roughly 6,000 kms. It can take from two to four weeks. In the UK and Europe some drivers regularly knock out that kind of mileage in a week or so... Not me. Anyway, I got to the queue at 'Rajka' and fell asleep. I was knackered. I'd done less than 500 k's in two days, and it felt like 5,000.

The border itself was a relative breeze. Again, after queuing for 8 or 9 hours, police and customs weren't exactly friendly but they didn't give us much hassle. The Czechs and Hungarians shared the same border, and had their offices next to one another, so it was a simple matter of chucking all the papers into one window then, when they were stamped and rudely thrown back, of changing permits over and rudely chucking everything through the next window.

The only annoying thing was that the Hungarians always demanded a copy of the CMR and sometimes of the invoices. Strictly speaking they didn't need them – all the relevant information for customs is on the page of the carnet TIR that they tear out and keep. But, on the

CMR's and invoices are the names and addresses of the buyers, the shippers and the consignees of the goods. And sometimes the freight charges. The Hungarians then used this information to go poaching our work at cheaper rates. And they're still doing it. 'Foul play' I hear you cry. Yes it is. But that's transport, and until we handed over photocopies of everything they flatly, and rudely, refused to process the paperwork. 'Parking, mister.'

Our cab *kontrol* consisted of a young squaddie poking his nose in the passenger's side, asking for a packet of fags… and being told to 'Fuck off'. Again no screaming and shouting, no Kalashnikovs being waved about as we'd half expected, just 'Marlboro, English?' There was even a little snack bar inside the border which sold fags, soft drinks, stale cheese or salami rolls and delicious Hungarian coffee, which is different to any other coffee I've tasted. So, at the time, it was all quite civilised in a way. And cheap - it hadn't cost us more than a quid so far! And I think that was for visa photos, which they used to take in situ.

While we were at the border, Vanessa picked up a free tourist map of Hungary. It was only a small thing – just a bit larger than A4 when unfolded, and full of indecipherable words. I said we wouldn't need it. She just turned and looked at me as if to say, 'Yeah? Like you didn't need one in Germany and Czech?'…So I shut up.

Hungarian roads are pretty good – which was a nice surprise. Most of them are wide enough for two trucks to pass without smashing wing- mirrors, they've got some white paint on them, and best of all – they're flat! The only pot-holes and tramlines we found were in the towns and to make things even better, we didn't get lost!

The signposting was good, but unpronounceable – there were names like Szekesfehervar (known as 'sexforever'), Kiskunfelegyhaza, Hodmzovasarhely… Listening to Vanessa trying to pronounce these names with her Australian accent was hilarious. It's such a weird language. It bears little resemblance to any other language I'd encountered. Even common names and words that can be understood in different tongues, like café, hotel, police (polis, polizei, etc.) were completely alien to me. (Rendörseg – police!!?)

Budapest was a different story – the roads were shit and the traffic was murder. A lot of the trucks were dinky little draw-bars that bumped and weaved along at Postman Pat's pace, and most of the cars were knackered old Moskoviches, Wartburgs, and Ladas, all of which screamed about in clouds of smoke at full pelt creating traffic chaos. It was like Toy Town in slow, slow, quick, quick, slow motion.

There's a motorway that by-passes Budapest now but it wasn't built then and a lot of TIR traffic that didn't use the cross-country transit route went straight through the middle of the city. It could be hard work dodging the lunatic taxi drivers and erratically driven 'bendy-buses', but we had to go to the Bulgarian Embassy for visas – so there was no avoiding it.

Budapest is a pretty old city (two cities actually: Buda and Pest), though a bit run down in places. It reminded me of a mix between Paris, Edinburgh and Islington. So we got our visas then went for a nose around – and were pleasantly surprised. This was supposed to be a run-down communist country, a nation under the thumb – but there was little sign of oppression here.

Unlike its neighbour, Czechoslovakia, which had a real dinginess about it and had pictures of Lenin stencilled all over its crumbly walls, Hungary had brightly lit shops full of stuff, people were out and about in droves looking for all the world like normal 'westerners', there were colourful advertising boards all over the place which were nowhere to be seen in Czech, unless they sported the hammer and sickle and, as far as I could tell, there was no propaganda blatantly staring us in the face.

It was only four to five hours' driving time to get across Hungary, but it took us the best part of three days all told, (nothing to do with Russian tanks slowing everything down) and we'd really enjoyed it.

Attempting the three-point turn

It was a pleasure to drive on good roads for a change – even if we couldn't make head nor tail of the signposting, and it was even nicer to be able to just pull up at one of the many superb, roadside restaurants whenever we wanted a cheap, decent plate of goulash. The Rendörszegs didn't bother us once – and of course 'hallo' means 'goodbye'!

I'd decided not to transit Romania after 'doing' Hungary (a) because I didn't need to (Roy told us to avoid Austria and its one hundred pound transit tax – he didn't tell us to avoid Yugoslavia's), and (b) because the arseholes had a compulsory money exchange system in force for anyone who wasn't a driver – ten dollars a day I think it was – which meant we'd have had to give away perfectly good money to the *Rumos in exchange for a fistful of useless 'Lei', for Vanessa, (or make her drive the truck into the border as a 'driver'), and (c) because I couldn't stand the place anyway and any chance I got to avoid it, I jumped at.

I knew we'd have to go into Rumo on our way back anyhow because that was where I usually got sent for a reload, so it saved a couple of bob and anyway, I still had plans of heading for the beaches in Greece. It meant it added even more time onto the trip… but what's a couple of days between friends?

Vanessa had already been through Bulgaria with Catweasle, but was a bit surprised when, after we'd finished in Turkey and were on our way home, I had to transit north through the country to get to Romania instead of west to Yugo – the way she'd gone before.

Bulgaria's a very run-down place. The roads were, and still are, incredibly bad. The signposting, which is nearly all in Cyrillic, (or acrylic, as some say), is nigh impossible to decipher from just a quick glance while on the move, and the coppers could be out and out pigs. Stop in the wrong place for more than a couple of minutes and they would appear, shouting, demanding to know why the truck had stopped, what you were looking at, who you were talking to, did you have a camera… and so on. They were arseholes.

There was sod all in the shops, most of which always seemed to be closed anyway, and the restaurants only ever served food after it had gone cold and lumpy. Diesel could only be bought with coupons – when they had them, the Doris's were demanding Deutschmarks, but the beer was good and it was reasonably safe to park up at night… in certain places.

I was always glad to get out of Bulgaria. I often felt like I had a weight on my shoulders while I was there which was only lifted when I exited the border, and I think Vanessa was glad to get out of there too. 89's are a hard ride, they kick a driver in the back on every small bump, and poor old Ness had been thrown all around the cab like a rag doll for over five hours.

I warned her to expect even worse in Romania. To start with I'd told her we could expect to spend eighteen hours or more in the border queue just trying to get into the country as the Rumos took each truck to bits looking for 'Bomba', 'pistole', 'hashish' – and 'second' passports, which could have been used – or sold – to get a Romanian citizen out of their own country – a country from which very few people were ever allowed to leave. I warned her that the roads, especially the ring roads and TIR routes around some towns, were even worse than the roads in Bulgaria, that there was fuck all in the shops apart from sardines, and that the coppers were complete shits. I warned her about the poverty, the peasants and the hoards of scruffy, barefoot kids. I also warned her about the thieving that went on, from trailer boxes, from tilts that got slashed open at night – and from cabs left locked, but unattended.

I also warned her of the dangers presented by horse, oxen and donkey-drawn carts, of canvas-covered wagons, (original 'tilts'), and of the mobile haystacks, all of which trundled along unlit on the dark, unmarked roads.

I told her of the time I'd taken a friend to Romania with me the year before, Clive Kirby, a wacky, out of work musician from London. We were on our way back across country when we came across a road accident. A car driven by a Hungarian had run into the back of an unlit donkey cart. Sticking out of the back of its huge load of hay was a long wooden pole with a piece of rag tied to it as a warning marker, which is as useful as a chocolate ashtray when it's dark and a car comes up from behind at 80kph.

On impact, the pole and its useless warning flag went straight through the car's windscreen, into the man's chest, out of his back, and straight through the rear window, missing his two kids in the back seat by inches.

Amazingly, he was still alive when I stopped and ran over to his car. There was blood everywhere, and his wife and kids were hysterical. There was little I could do. Moments later a crowd appeared on the scene and lit everything up with their car headlights. It was a mess. The guy was gurgling – dying. A van pulled up, and the locals decided to get the driver into the van and rush him off to hospital. But they didn't take account of the twenty-foot pole he'd been impaled on. As they clumsily dragged him out of the car, the rough treatment killed him. Messily.

Nobody apart from the poor family and myself (Clive refused to leave the truck) seemed to give a shit. The wife and two kids were understandably distraught, screaming, covered in the man's insides and bits of glass, but all the locals seemed to care about was the donkey, which was lying in a ditch, honking.

So, suitably warned, we exited Bulgaria, and drove across the huge rusted bridge to the border of Giurgiu expecting the worst. And what happened?

Sod all.

We sailed through Giurgiu in just a few hours, the roads were empty of mobile haystacks (harvest time was months away), we only got pestered by a couple of kids at the factory in Floresti, and all that got stolen from us was a GB sticker off the back of the trailer – even after I'd slashed it with a razor blade so that anyone patient enough to peel off six dozen diamond shapes of plastic was welcome to it!

I'm sure Vanessa thought I'd been exaggerating the truth a bit, but it was just sod's law. We went in, got loaded and buggered off – just like that!

The highlight of our trip was at Nadlac border on our way out when customs insisted on opening the trailer for a *kontrol* – as they did to all trucks. The only problem with this was that I'd picked up a full load of car tyres.

Tyres have to be stacked properly in a trailer – especially in a tilt trailer, or they shift around and settle wherever they can after having crashed through the first couple of pot-holes. By the time I'd driven 400 odd k's from the factory to the border on roads that wouldn't have been out of place in a quarry, my trailer looked like it had mumps -

there were bulges sticking out all over the place and the superstructure was shaped like a banana.

For a packet of Kent cigarettes a squaddie at the barrier would open up the trailer and re-lace it again after customs – or at least the squaddie himself – had checked the load for hidden people. It was the squaddie's job anyway, but they were more than willing to be extra helpful for a packet of fags. It saved getting covered in shit myself, and Kent cigarettes were bloody awful, so I was always glad to get rid of the last of them.

Everything was paid for with Kent, from speeding fines, to getting the carnet stamped up. Coffee worked just as well, but at only a fiver a carton the fags were much better value. They could ensure rapid, although not always competent loading, pay for a phone call – or even buy the services of a local Doris. Long live Ceauşescu's bad habit.

When the squaddie covertly asked for a packet of Kent I gladly obliged and warned him to be careful when he opened the back of the trailer. He shrugged it off as if to say, 'For Kent, this is not a problem.'

He was wrong.

As soon as he started unlacing the back end the tyres began to shift, straining and bulging against the back of the trailer. Another soldier was called over to help. I looked at the spotlessly clean customs officer who was standing expectantly at the back of my trailer, with my carnet in his hands, grinned, then tactically moved to one side.

Suddenly there was a scream and the rear end of the trailer seemed to explode. The backflap flew up in the air and the squaddies on the ladder were sent flying as dozens upon dozens of tyres erupted from the trailer like buckshot and went bouncing all over the place.

Vanessa went one way, I went another and the customs officer legged it towards Hungary. It was chaos. Tyres went rolling all over the compound, bashed into cars, trucks, people and buses, and bounced into the brook that ran alongside the border… And I suddenly got a fit of the giggles.

Most of the tyres were eventually rounded up but one or two landed in the boots of police cars, and those that ended up in the brook simply stayed below water, where they probably remain to this day.

The poor squaddies then had the job of reloading all the tyres that had gone walkabout, and the customs officer who'd legged it in the wrong direction was now covered in shit.

Several hours later we rolled into the Hungarian side of the border with a straight, even-sided trailer. We were still laughing that night after the Hungarian customs man took one look at the carnet and said, 'Lastik? No problem – go!'

Amongst a collection of classics

Messing around on a scooter, killing time at a border

Fourteen

Of roadtrains and roping off

So now I'd 'done' four-fifths of the Commie Bloc. Four countries down, one to go – East Germany, which was reputed by other drivers to be 'a piece of piss' – a more down to earth, and honest, appraisal of what lay in store than the descriptions I'd been given of elsewhere.

Czech and Hungary had been nowhere near as daunting as I'd been led to believe, but I realised later on, on subsequent trips, that our ease of passage had been partly due to luck (we'd caught them on a good day) and also partly down to the fact that Vanessa had been with me. Instead of complicating things as I'd first feared, her presence in the truck had actually had the opposite effect. Giving drivers a hard time on their own was one thing, doing it in front of 'civilian' passengers, and female ones at that, was a different matter.

But I didn't have to put up with it much longer. On our trip Vanessa and I had already discussed plans for me to give up driving and travel with her to Australia!

I won't say that what we had was any kind of whirlwind romance, but things happened quickly and the thought of going to live on the other side of the world quite appealed to me, so when Vanessa suggested it one day I said yes without *really* considering it.

Well it seemed a good idea at the time…

She stayed in England after that trip and got herself a job at the Australian Embassy in London – issuing visas! I then carried on driving for a few months more just to get some loot together for the move… and that was when we began to drift apart. I didn't realise it at the time, but our lives belonged in different worlds – literally. Hers was with her friends and family down under – mine was on the road.

Blind to our differences I announced to Roy, Fred and Ernie one day that I was going to bugger off to Australia and drive roadtrains, rope kangaroos, wear a floppy hat and learn to play a didgeridoo.

Roy was really good about it. He called me a silly bastard, shook my hand, told me to keep my eyes open for business opportunities and wished me luck. Fred was just as enthusiastic. He made me promise to keep in touch, send postcards and leave the sheep alone. Ernie was more down to earth – he just lit a fag, screwed up one eye and said, 'Fuck it… I'll have to find another driver now!'

During my last few trips for Roy, Vanessa and I gradually grew farther and farther apart. Even though I'd go and stay with her at the house she shared with her Top Deck friends at 'The Lodge' in Dollis Hill between trips, things weren't going well. I should have got the message and cancelled the whole thing, but by now I was so fired up with the idea of setting up a new life in the Antipodes, that I ignored all the warning signs, telling myself that things would somehow work out at the end of the day…

They didn't. At least not in the way I'd expected.

On 23rd of October 1987, nearly two years after starting for Roy as a 'novice' TIR driver, Vanessa and I landed at Bangkok airport for a two-week stop-over in Thailand before going on to Aus. It was a great trip – she pretended to sleep most of the way, or just buried her freckled nose in a paperback book.

After three days in Bangkok, swilling large amounts of Singha beer to keep from sweating to death (and nearly dying from the hangovers), we boarded a bus and headed south to the island of Koh Samui, where we ended up in different grass huts on the beach.

Thailand was – is – an incredible place, and I should have been enjoying every moment of it, but our dying relationship put a dampener on things for the first week. After that I gave up all hope of sorting things out with Vanessa and settled in to enjoy the delights of the island before having another three days in Bangkok.

Consequently, when we got to Australia, Vanessa stayed in Brisbane and I ended up in Melbourne, 1,000 miles away, skint.

I had a friend in Melbourne, Dave Roebuck, whom I'd met on his travels the previous year when he landed in the Malt and Hops for a drink and ended up working there. We became good friends and he'd always said, 'Come on down to Aus – anytime…' so I did. I rang from Brisbane, explained my side of things, and he said, 'Great – see you when you get here!' So off I went for a thousand-mile trip on a non-smoking bus…

Dave was living with his mother out by Ringwood in the eastern suburbs and she generously agreed to take me in. She turned out to be a lovely lady and I've never really thanked her properly for the kindness she showed to a complete stranger. Even if she did keep beating me at Scrabble.

The split with Vanessa was beginning to turn into a bit of a feud, but Dave didn't care – he was just really pleased to see me in his part of the world – even though I was 12,000 miles away from home, jobless and skint. So I promptly went out to look for some work.

I couldn't find any driverless roadtrains in Melbourne (there aren't any – they're not allowed in) so I gave up on that for the time being and wound up with a job on the trucks for Ansett Ridgeways as driver-come-shifter-come-dogsbody… I hated it.

It was bloody hard work so needless to say that didn't last long, but at the time it paid some rent to June, Dave's mum, and put a few Fosters vouchers in my pocket.

Dave was an electrician working at one of the big hospitals in town – Alfred's I think it was. When I was on the job hunt I'd often meet him during his lunch break for a coffee and a 'letch' at the girls passing through Flinders St. Station. I told him one day that I'd found another job to start on the Monday, so his afternoon of changing bulbs and fuses went straight out of the window and we went to the big pub on the corner instead and got pissed.

The job was driving a Japanese-made flat-bed Tonka delivering steel and pipe fittings all over the Melbourne area. I obviously didn't know Melbourne very well – but I was used to that sort of thing. What did turn out to be a ball-ache was learning the ropes – literally!

Nearly everything on a flat-bed trailer has to be roped down. That in itself wouldn't have posed a problem – I'd done my fair share of roping and sheeting in the past, but that was in England - here in the UK drivers tie their ropes off to 'U' shaped hooks beneath the bed of the trailer, but in Australia, instead of hooks, all trucks have rails which drivers have to tie their ropes to.

So what's the problem? Well 'tying off' to a hook was simple: Drivers use what is known as a 'Dolly Knot', made by a series of twists and loops that enable the rope to be pulled against itself, thereby tightening the rope and securing the load. The remaining length of rope is then tied to the next hook along and thrown back across the load ready to be 'tied off' on the other side. Simple.

Here lies the problem. Ropes can be anything up to 100ft long. And more. Forming a loop and tying off to a hook was one thing, but it's not possible to tie a loop to a rail – at least not the way I was doing it.

The method of tying off to rails is actually quite similar – but with one or two variations in the initial method, ie. how the 'knot' is first formed. Get it wrong and there's no way of tying it off. And could I figure it out? Could I heck. I tried this, I tried that, I tried hard to remember how I'd seen other drivers do it, I asked people – but I just couldn't get it. In the end I thought fuck it, and gave up. I then 'invented' my own method of tying rope to rails, Heath Robinson style, which meant I had to thread every single inch of those bloody ropes through the rail before I could toss it back over the load and start again.

I've been shown how to do it properly since – but can I get the hang of it? It's just one of those things I seem to develop a mental block over – like electrics. I can change a fuse, but I can't understand what it's all about – especially when the fuse goes bang and welds itself to my thumb.

Before long I had my sights set on driving artics again. Most of the trucks running around Australia are American jobs - Kenworths, Macks, Peterbilts, etc. And some of the yellow-plated trucks on Interstate work are a sight for sore eyes, so I thought, I'll have some of that, thank you very much! But there was a problem - I needed an Australian licence… so that was my next project.

It was actually quite simple. I just booked in for a few lessons, Dave paid for it, and I took a test. As easy as that! The driving test in Australia is a breeze. All I had to do was aim an empty flat-bed trailer around the block a couple of times, back it into a side turning, then head back to the test centre. I was allowed to cross my hands, zoom across junctions, pick my nose and scratch my arse. It was great. I then had my mug-shot taken, paid my penny, and waited for the postman to deliver my 'Heavy Articulated' driver's licence.

In the meantime I swiped Dave's car – a well-preserved Austin 'Frog-Eyed' Sprite and zoomed off (with the roof down, of course) to the western suburbs of Footscray and elsewhere, knocking on transport managers' doors for a job.

I was like a schoolboy in a sweetshop as I drove into some of those transport yards. There were 'prime-movers' (tractor units) that were longer than the rigid truck I'd recently given up driving – or 'given away'. There were huge-bonneted Peterbilts, Macks, Kenworths, all with very tidy paint jobs, lots of chrome, sparkling exhaust stacks and monstrous bull-bars. Some had the distinctive 'caravan' sleeping compartments nailed to the back of the shed, and *all* of them were screaming out to have their 400 and 500 horsepower engines thrashed up the Hume Highway towards Sydney (a.k.a. Humorous Highway, or Sesame Street).

After the Mack I thought I could live without American trucks, but with the sight of these monsters sparkling in the sunlight of a Melbourne summer, I just wanted to climb in one and go and play. Immediately.

But could I get a start?

In Australia, as I discovered the hard way, getting a foot in the door of road transport is not easy – unless a person has contacts. But I only knew Dave and his mum – and Vanessa. Day after day I went from one firm to another figuring, as I'd learnt in England, that it often got things done quicker than simply phoning or writing. But I was wrong. I was constantly fobbed off with stupid comments like, 'Yeah, but in Europe you've got café's every half k…' or 'Aah, but can you handle a thirteen speed Fuller?' or '…But have you ever driven across a desert?' (on perfectly good tarmac – not sand). And so on - it made me spew!

I even tried to wind one guy up into giving me a job by betting I could beat him to Sydney – but it still got me nowhere. Before long I'd visited a large percentage of transport yards in the western suburbs and round Campbellfield and other places in the northern suburbs… and got absolutely nowhere. I just couldn't get a start on the 'Interstate' for love nor money. Eventually I ended up driving a knackered old bonneted Ford 'semi' delivering piping for a firm in Port Melbourne – which included roping and sheeting…

By the middle of January I'd had enough. Money was tight, Dave and I had moved into a small house in Northcote and the rent had to be paid, I was still no closer to landing a job on the interstate and as for driving roadtrains and roping kangaroos…

I knew I had to go back home. Dave was great company, and had been more than understanding with me, but I felt awkward and out of place. I wasn't happy with my work and seemed to be constantly broke, and I was putting on Dave more than he deserved. I was also missing the job. So I made a decision one day and told Dave that I was going to try to get back to the UK.

'How're y'gonna do that with no money?' he slurred.

'Don't know – I haven't got that far yet.'

We were sitting out in the back yard at the time, fighting off the flies, drinking a rather nice cask wine, admiring our shrivelled tomato plants and getting slowly pissed. It was scorching hot.

'Take y'awhile to save the fare.'

'Yeah. It will if I keep drinking this stuff.'

'Whaddabout Roy?'

'What about him?'

'Well, y'said he's a friend – would y'reckon he'll lend y'the money then y'could maybe work it off when y'got back?'

'…Er…' It got me thinking. Would he? I'd quit working for Roy months earlier – he had no reason to put himself out for me – yet…

'S'worth a try,' Dave said, looking cross-eyed. 'He c'n only say no.'

Halfway through the four-litre cask the idea got better and better. I'd phoned Roy often enough in the past for a draw – usually from the Austrian border of Spielfeld, and for never more than a couple of hundred to pay the tax and buy some beers – but this wasn't quite the same.

'Aah – give him a tinkle. He'd be glad to hear from y'anyway.'

'Yeah. Trouble is it's about three o'clock in the morning over there – I don't think he'd be too impressed.'

'Oh, yeah.' Then Dave got a fit of the giggles. 'He'd sure tell y'what to do with y'request.'

And that was it for the afternoon. We sat there giggling, finished the wine, pissed on the tomatoes, then opened another cask until the pair of us were too stupid to move.

Sometime the next day Roy got the strangest call for help I think he's ever had.

'You're where?' he screamed.

'Er – Melbourne.'

'Where's that?'

'Australia.'

'Fuck off – you're winding me up. You're in the yard next door ain't ya? You're gonna walk in 'ere in a minute and shout 'gotcha'.'

'Wish I was.'

'Whaddya mean?' He went a bit quiet then.

'Er, well it's like this Roy…'

'What? What?' he interrupted. 'What's wrong?' He sounded genuinely concerned.

'Well, I need to ask a favour.'

'…Go on.'

'You know what it is, don't you?'

There was silence for a minute, and I could almost see him smiling, then he said, 'Ask me anyway.'

When I put my request forward Roy just burst out laughing and yelled, 'I fucking knew it! You can't keep away, can you? I knew it – I fucking knew it!'

He was still roaring with laughter as he handed the phone over to Fred to get my details. No questions asked. No grilling, just, 'You useless little bastard – talk to Fred – I'll see you when you get here.'

And that was that. Roy didn't think twice – he knew I was in a spot and that I needed his help – so he gave it without question.

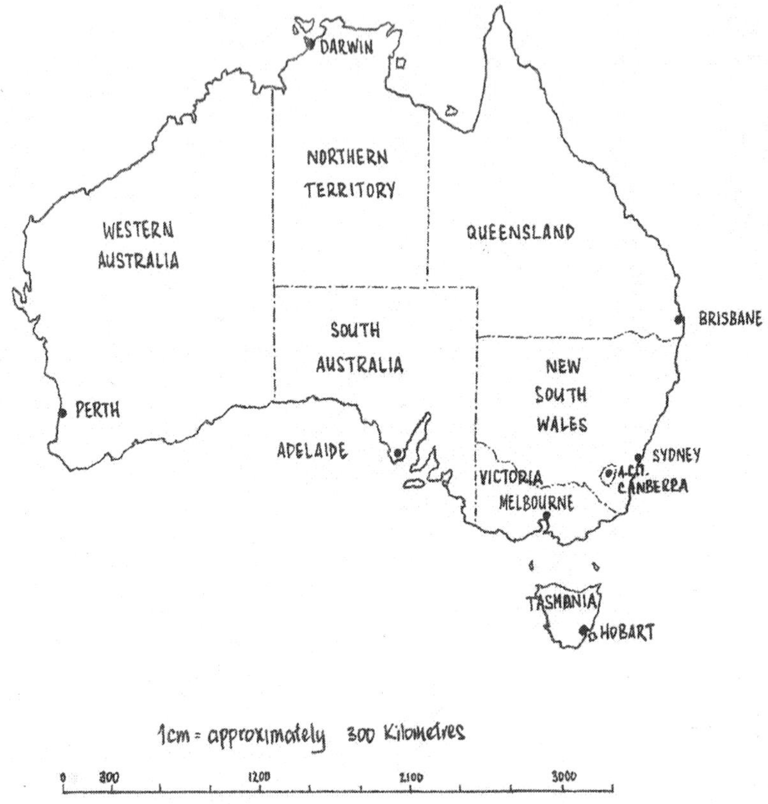

Hand-drawn map by John Nevill

Fifteen

Of stale bread and cobwebs

I was potless when I landed at Gatwick at the beginning of February '88. I was that broke I'd had to borrow twenty dollars from Dave to pay the departure tax at Tullamarine airport.

But it didn't matter – I was home! The biggest problem I faced then was the cold. I'd just left an Australian summer where daily temperatures were touching 40° Centigrade, and here I was plonked right in the middle of an English winter where temperatures were struggling to reach 40° Fahrenheit! I was bloody freezing.

I couldn't face going outside right away so I rang Roy at the yard and asked if he had any trucks in the area that I could scrounge a lift from, 'today or tomorrow, mate' – I wasn't bothered. It was warm in the airport.

Predictably, the reply I got was, 'You cheeky little bastard! Get on that road and stick your thumb up in the air – I want your arse over here – *NOW!*'

I thought, 'Oh well, at least he'd let me reverse the charges.' I then searched out the nearest lorry driver, scrounged a tachograph disc off him in place of sticking a thumb out, and used it to hitch a series of rides back to sunny Barking.

When I arrived at the yard, having walked all of a mile since leaving the arrivals lounge, I strolled into the portacabin feeling really pleased with myself, casually said hello to everyone and helped myself to a mug of proper coffee from the pot that Roy always had on the go.

Everyone was staring at me in silence. Roy just looked me up and down slowly, then said sarcastically, 'You made it then?'

I got the feeling I'd done something wrong, but couldn't figure out what – perhaps the coffee-pot was now off-limits to drivers, I didn't know, but something wasn't quite right. Then when Roy couldn't contain himself any longer, he suddenly screamed, 'Right Nevill, put that fucking coffee down and get your arse on the back of that trailer out there! You're going to work off every penny if it kills you – RIGHT?' He screamed so loud I nearly spilled the coffee – just as everyone burst out laughing. After that it was handshakes and pats on the back… but he still made me get on the back of the trailer!

For the next two or three weeks Roy put me through hell, tipping trailers, loading them, shunting them round the UK. Fetching, carrying, humping… It was good to be back at work, but it was a bloody nightmare. Roy was paying me a wage, and leaving it up to me how much I paid him back each week. No pressure, no hassle. He didn't even ask what had gone wrong until he figured I was willing to go into it all – two weeks after my return.

Paying half my wages out each week was playing havoc with my social life – especially with the price of beer in England and the scarcity of duty-free fags so, when Roy came out into the yard one day and said, 'Right, Nevill, drop what you're doing now – you're shipping out.' I thought '*Yes! At last – fuck all this UK crap!' and ran to get my kit.*

Roy had already told me he never had a spare truck, and Ernie himself had somehow managed to find a Turk months before to take over his 89, which is why I'd been stuck working in England, so I asked, 'Er – what in?'

Roy said, 'Phil Houghton's gone and got himself locked up in Belgium, the silly bastard, so I want you to take his motor down and finish the trip for him. It's all loaded and ready to go.'

Phil was one of the 'originals' who I'd already met, a typical 'Ealing 'B' film' middle-aged rogue. A youngster in ageing bodywork. He reminded me of Jimmy Edwards, the actor, with his (greying) wing commanders moustache, rosy cheeks, infectious, 'guffaw' type laugh, a wonderfully eccentric sense of humour and a (well) adopted 'I say chaps' kind of accent that was designed to take the piss out of *everything…* which he did.

Phil was a 'one-off' at the job. Still is at the time of writing. Loved nothing more than finding 'new' ways around old problems, and excelled at executing them – like when he destroyed a German petrol station and conned the owners into accepting a micky Turkish insurance…

'Oh, okay,' I said. 'No problem. Where is it?'

'Dunno. Somewhere in Belgium – you'll have to go and find it!'

I thought great, what next?

'Anybody going down to Dover, then?' I asked, knowing what the reply would be.

'What's wrong with your fucking thumb? Haven't broken it have you?' So I took the subtle hint and started to get my gear packed. As I was preparing to leave, bag over my shoulder, tacho disc in hand, Roy said, 'Oh, by the way, you've got a passenger.'

'Female?'

'No – Phil's boy. He's in the truck waiting for you. He was going to do a trip with his dad until they locked him up… Now, the boy's a bit worried what with his old man being carted away an' all, so don't leave him sitting there for too long, okay? And,' he added, 'go easy on him – he's only a young lad, and I know you haven't had any for a while… ta ta!' And with that he disappeared! He didn't even bother to tell me where the truck was loaded for, let alone what had happened to the money or paperwork…

I didn't know why 'Old Phil' had been locked up – I didn't really care too much at the time either, I was just glad to be getting away from the 'UK shunting'. And anyway, I hadn't bothered to ask and Roy didn't volunteer to tell me. I wasn't too surprised at the news either. Drivers often get to spend a night in the cells every now and again for whatever reasons, it's an occupational hazard, (believe it or not) and I figured his son would tell me all about it if and when I found him – and if he knew.

After an amazing piece of detective work I found the truck, a tidy-looking Ford Transcontinental, which had been conspicuously left in the Total garage at Zeebrugge, two minutes from the docks. Phil's son, of the same name, was sat in the driver's seat looking bored, but not at all worried as I'd expected. So I introduced myself, dragged him off to keep me company over a beer and began to interview him.

'Where's the run money?'

Phil, a gangly, dark-haired lad from 'Skem' (Skelmersdale) pulled out the remains of his dad's run money with large ET lookalike hands and handed it over. As I picked it up I asked, 'What's your dad been banged up for?'

'Oh, der fookin' Dootch are after 'im for a trook 'e bought,' he said, as I was having a roll call. 'Er, I spent some o' da mooney by der way.'

'What's criminal about buying a truck?' I asked.

''E didn't pay f'rit.'

'Looks like he paid for it out of this.' I said, noticing there was a fair bit missing.

'Yeah – 'e 'ad to pay a fine.'

'Is he okay?'

'Yeah, 'e's okay. Day've given 'im a phone, a fooking telly an' everytin'. 'E may be banged up for a few weeks, but 'e's bedder off dan we are.'

'You can say that again, we're going to struggle on this.'

'Wize da?'

'Have you been down the road before?'

'Yeah.'

'So you know the score then?'

'Er, sord of.'

'What do you mean?'

'Well, it was a while ago.'

I thought, here we go. 'Was it?'

'Yeah. Me daa took me to Iran.'

Iran? The Middle East? You bastard!

'That was nice of him.'

'Yeah, but I don't remember much – I was priddy yoong ad der time. I never even 'ad a passport so me daa 'ad to smooggle me in an' out…'

Fucking hell, I sighed…

The trip itself wasn't one of those you'd have written home to mum about. Young Phil - as he came to be known – obviously did remember some of his trip to Iran as a youngster – most of which manifested itself in his expectations of me to work the same way as his 'daa' - to do the same things, drive the same way, stop at the same places, etc. But it doesn't work that way. We all have our own ways of doing things; our own peculiar habits, our own ideas of how many hours constitute a day's work, and so on. So when Phil thought I ought to be doing it like this, that or the other, and I didn't, it began to create a certain amount of friction.

The fact that we were short of money didn't help. We kept some bread and cheese in the truck to try and cut down on food bills, but Phil wasn't impressed with having to perform 'mould kontrols' with a blunt knife before we could eat penicillin-free cheese sarnies.

A certain amount of friction is always to be expected when two people have to spend all day together in a truck. It's another reason why most drivers don't like 'doubling up', so when we'd finished in Turkey and headed up to Radauti to pick up yet another load of cheap, nasty barbecues (that looked a bit like the Martians on the 'smash them all to pieces' advert), for an English public that rarely use barbecues, I decided to lighten things up by dragging Phil off through the snow for Saturday night out at the town's 'hot spot' – the Hotel Nordic.'

We'd been told by the lads at the factory that this was the place to go, hinting that the music was good and the local talent even better. We soon discovered that the reason it was the town's hot spot was because sod all else was open. And the local talent was conspicuous by its absence. But what a night we had. We arrived early – about 6 or 7'o clock, fully expecting a long evening. There was one large room, the 'restaurant' where we could get a drink, and where half a dozen locals sat around in bored silence with nothing in front of them.

We parked ourselves at one of the round, wobbly tables covered with filthy, mismatched tablecloths nearest the door (ready for a swift exit if anything went off) and ordered two beers, half expecting to be refused.

The place was falling apart. It looked like something out of an Addams Family film and it stank of the toilets. Phil kept looking at me as we sat down as if to say, 'What time does Dracula appear?' The walls and ceiling were cracked and flaking, the manky lino curled up at its joins like stale sandwiches, the lights, with bare wiring, kept flickering on and off, and the yellow-stained lace curtains with rips and burn marks in them which fluttered in the draught really added to the spooky atmosphere – it was brilliant! There were even Hammer House of Horror cobwebs in the corners!

The locals just glared at us in silence, and nobody talked to anyone else – not even the ugly waitress with a snot-stained apron and grubby ankle socks, and when she came over and plonked two label-less bottles into the rusted, unstable ice-bucket that stood next to our table and they went 'Clunk, clunk' on the bare metal, Phil just cracked up.

And things got even better. At 8 o'clock the 'live' music unenthusiastically fired up to an audience that had now swollen to about ten. The band itself turned out to be three Herman Munsters dressed in crumpled, ill-fitting tuxedos (two black – one red) with an unplugged electric guitar, a cello with a broken string and a set of yellowed drums that were bashed with something that looked like balding paintbrushes.

Still everybody was silent and nobody got up to dance. Most of the noise that night came from me and Phil as we got rapidly pissed and hooted with laughter, expecting all the time to be bitten on the necks or thrown out.

At nine o'clock on the dot everything packed up – just like somebody had thrown a switch – so we bribed Nora Batty with a packet of Kent to fetch us a rake of beers, which we sat and greedily guzzled as we waited for a vampire bat to come and evict us.

The dancing only came about that night after we'd left the 'hotel' when Phil was given an impromptu lesson in singing Russian military songs as we goose-stepped back through the thick snow to the truck… in hysterics.

Welcome to Romania – Komrade!

The night out had had the desired effect – Phil and I had let off steam and the tension between us had eased a lot. Life in the truck became a lot more bearable – even if the cheese sandwiches didn't improve. The most memorable event of the whole trip however, and the reason I describe it all, is that it was the cause of one of the worst periods ever in my driving career. When we got back to England after that trip, I got grounded.

It happened because just before 'old' Phil was let out of nick in Belgium, stories of our trip kind of got a bit twisted - of how we'd not got on, of where the money had gone, of how I'd forced Phil to live on stale bread and cheese… Roy got the wrong end of the stick about it and, consequently, I got the wrong end of a fist. As punishment I was told it was high time I got myself a proper driving licence, and then promptly demoted to UK work only – something I despise – which meant driving the dreaded 'sixteen tonner' – an uncomfortable, hopelessly underpowered 1628 Mercedes box van – 'Hitler's revenge' – which, like an earthbound spirit (and because of its lack of any other useful ability) was condemned to roam the highways of Britain eighteen hours a day, seven days a week – for ever and ever…

Welcome to Hell!

Sixteen

Of pride and procedures

Roy was gloating. Not only had he placed me on 'Jankers' (shit duties) for the duration, but had rubbed salt into the wound by insisting that I take an official Department of Transport driving test first.

Had I known what was in store for me in the months to come, I think I'd have been tempted to move to Reykjavik and buy an ice-cream van.

The British Heavy Goods Vehicle (H.G.V. as was) 'class one' driving test for articulated trucks was, and still is, reputed to be one of the strictest in the world. To say I was a trifle miffed at being forced to take such a test at this stage of the game would be a bit of an understatement. To say I was scared witless would not.

With all the 'bad' habits I'd picked up through continental driving or, more to the point 'forced' to adopt, due to the nature of the beast, I was more than convinced my chances of passing a road test now were slightly less than zero.

I pleaded with Roy, saying that the three licences I held (American – 'Tractor Trailer'; Australian – 'Heavy Articulated'; and British 'Class Three' – for rigids and roadtrains) were more than enough to cover me for the countries we visited. But all I got from Roy was 'Bollocks! They changed the rules, so you're taking that test whether you like it or not! Okay?'

I then pleaded poverty, saying I simply couldn't afford to do it (apart from being one of the strictest tests in the world, it was one of the most expensive. And still is). But Roy had that angle covered too. He'd already paid for it. All I had to do was get through the test and he'd dock it off my wages later.

Simple, huh?

My one saving grace was the fact that I was booked in for a week of lessons first. This was all to be done through a friend of Roy's – a local one-man-band with an ageing 'D-Series' Ford, powered by an incredibly noisy V.8 Perkins engine, and with suspension that a Vickers tank would have been proud of.

Day one got off to a flying start. I was put behind the wheel and simply told to 'Just drive normally' - which I did. I then managed to cover a whole two miles before nearly coming to blows with my instructor.

I'd been heading for the roundabout beneath the 'Threepenny Bit' flyover at Canning Town when the dickhead suddenly leant over from the passenger's seat and applied the 'dead-man'!

My heart nearly skipped a beat as the trailer bounced up and down with the wheels locked on, and I thought I was going to nut the windscreen!

'What the fuck do you think you're doing?' I screamed. 'Are you mad?'

'You were about to drive onto the roundabout,' he said casually.

Huh?

'Drive onto the roundabout? Of course I was! That's what it's there for! What do you think I'm gonna do – push the fucking thing round it?'

'That's not how you approach roundabouts,' he continued calmly. 'You could have caused an accident.'

'*I* could have caused an accident? Anyway the fucking roundabout was empty!' I couldn't believe what I was hearing.

'That's not the point. There is a correct way to negotiate a roundabout, and that wasn't it. If you'd done that on your test it would have been an immediate 'fail'.'

The smug bastard was obviously trying to prove a point, and I was taking bets it was one of his favourite little tricks, but I couldn't figure out what I'd done wrong. I'd been told where to go, the road was clear, so I simply 'dropped a cog' (a gear) and went for it…

Wrong.

I was informed by anorak that the correct approach is to 'drive' to the roundabout, using the gears, and my mirrors, a million times in the process. The objective then to enter the roundabout without coming to a stop at the give-way line!

No. I couldn't figure that one out to start with either! I'd had no intention of stopping the bloody thing! If he hadn't hit the dead-man I'd have been halfway to Southend on Sea by now!

And so it went on – procedures for this, procedures for that, check your mirrors, don't cross your hands over the steering wheel, you're in the wrong lane, you're speeding, you're driving too slow – lack of progress, lack of progress… until he'd made me feel like a complete novice and I just wanted to clump him to see how much he would bleed!

At the end of that first day I was about ready to quit. I was knackered, angry and totally confused. I couldn't understand how or why I'd done so many wrong things, even after I'd made a conscious effort to keep my 'bad' habits in check. Everything he said seemed contradictory or pointless and I couldn't get my head round any of it – until he made a simple comment, and the penny dropped.

'Mr Nevill,' he said in his calm, measured way. 'We still have a lot of work to do and only four days left in which to do it. Please remember, I'm not here to teach you how to drive, I'm here to teach you how to pass the driving test. There's a difference.'

Not here to teach me how to drive…

Of course! It made sense now. The Heavy Goods Test is basically a *conversion* test for people who can drive already. It's not so much about logical, sensible, everyday driving, but a test designed to prove to an examiner that you can actually do what is required at set standards. Nobody really expects a person to drive like a fail-safe robot for eight or nine hours a day – it just has to be proved that you can do it!

All I had to do was accept that fact and suddenly everything fell into place. If the test involved swerving around a coven of mothers-in-law, blindfolded and in reverse, so be it! Get on with it, prove to an examiner you can do it, then roar through as many puddles as you like at a later date.

After that I was able to knuckle down and eagerly did everything I was told to do, whether it made sense or not, and by the end of the week I was deemed ready to be tested.

The test itself, as with the lessons, was to be taken with an empty trailer – a 30' flatbed. Yet another aspect of the 'Heavy' Goods test that makes little sense to me… but I was getting used to it by now.

Anorak turned out to be a decent bloke, and was there to give me encouragement and last-minute advice. 'Just do what you've been taught, nothing more. Give the examiner a 'comfortable' ride and you can't go wrong.' etc. He wanted me to get through this as much as I did. Pass rates are a matter of professional pride among instructors.

The test really is as demanding as people claim. And as nerve-wracking. Everything is monitored and ticked off; every look in the mirrors, every gear change, every use of the indicators, the wipers, the washers, every anticipated move to be made by other drivers, every assessment of road conditions and actions taken, every line of approach, every… *everything!*

Even when I wheeled back into the test station at Thurrock thinking my ordeal was over I was bombarded with questions re-testing me on the Highway Code.

It had been an ordeal alright, and I don't mind admitting it. I'd put every ounce of effort and concentration into doing it right, and in the process used up a month's supply of adrenaline in a little over an hour. Only one thing remained now – the result – and my examiner wasted no time or formality in passing on the good news: Failed.

I can only imagine the look of disappointment on my face, but I could see it quite clearly on the face of my instructor. It racked me with guilt. I felt as if I'd let him down, as well as myself, and I was gutted enough for both of us right then.

I wanted to apologise but he cut me short. He was good about it – I'd only failed on one point, he told me. Nothing to be ashamed of. He then went to the office and booked me in for a re-test the following day.

Fuck it. I'd failed, and I was on a 'downer'.

Roy was really understanding and took the news quite well – he simply called me a useless little tosser and threw the coffee pot at me.

Oh well, I thought, it could have been worse. At least the coffee pot was empty.

The following day I was taken back over the test route by my instructor to iron out any wrinkles, and fine-tune any relevant manoeuvres before that afternoon's re-test. I felt a lot less confident than the previous day, and twice as nervous – I was terrified of fucking up a second time.

It's easy to say after the event, but I needn't have worried so much because the re-test was over and done within just fifteen minutes! The examiner only wanted me to cover the one point of the original test failure, and that was it. He passed me – just like that!

The relief was sudden and physical. After being wound up tight enough to launch a rocket for the past eight or nine days, I went weak and wobbly at the knees, and felt light enough to float. The only other time I'd felt such a strong emotion was when my daughter was born before the ambulance arrived and I had to catch her in the slips before she went over the boundary rope. Hearing her little lungs eventually fire up was such a relief I nearly dropped her.

Seventeen

Of early mornings and health warnings

My joy at being the proud new owner of a class one H.G.V. licence was to be very short lived. Roy made certain of that.

After grunting his approval at my test pass he promptly announced that there was to be no reprieve from my 'Jankers'. I was still grounded, which meant that I was now to be installed in 'Hitler's Revenge' – the dreaded Mercedes box van – a sixteen ton 'rigid' that had seen better days, and was covered (under the old licensing system) by the class three licence – which I already held…

I was now to be plunged into new depths of misery and torment, because driving in mainland Britain – especially in an underpowered Merc – has to be one of the most frustrating and soul-destroying jobs in road transport.

Apart from having to crawl out of the pit at criminally unsociable hours, drive like a lunatic against the clock *and* suffer the world's worst food, the biggest enemy of the great British lorry driver is, and always has been, public opinion.

The British public for whatever misguided, misinformed or purely snobbish reasons, have always hated the sight and sound of heavy commercial vehicles on this country's roads, and looked disapprovingly down their noses at the people who drive them.

This is only too obvious in the shit manner in which road haulage in general, and drivers in particular, are treated in this 'great' country of ours. Wherever a truck goes in Britain these days it's greeted with anger and complaints; with weight limits, time and parking restrictions; with extortionate parking costs; with persecution from the police and Ministry of Transport; with high fuel prices, and even with loud public protests from greenies with placards and broom handles that were delivered by a truck in the first place!

Even the arseholes accepting a delivery would moan and groan, whether the load was a day early or five minutes late – and it's always the driver that has to listen to the earhole bashing!

So when Roy 'grounded' me, by condemning me to shunt around the UK in 'Hitler's Revenge' for the duration, my system was in for a bit of a shock.

I'd done plenty of work in the UK in the past, but it had been a long time before and I'd quite simply forgotten most of the horrors. I managed to escape from it all in 1982 when I went on to 'T. Forming' around Germany and Italy in a furniture wagon (a T. Form was the Customs document used in W. Europe), and was able to push the torment of UK work to the back of my mind. Two more years 'doing' Turkey and the break in Australia had also contributed to the mental block-out.

Consequently, when I had to get up at 1 a.m. on my first day and go haring off to the Lake District with a truckful of 'Made in Taiwan' trinkets for the tourists yomping around Lake Windermere, I felt like I'd had electrodes clamped to my nipples!

The work was physical and gruesome. It involved unloading all the overseas containers and groupage trailers (trailers with mixed loads) that arrived in Roy's yard, transferring parts of those loads – usually by hand – onto the Mercedes, then zooming off to exciting places like Grimsby or Pontefract to deliver the bloody stuff!

It was awful. I was always knackered by the time the Merc was loaded and just wanted to curl up in the bunk and sleep, but that was never possible – the goods had to go up the road.

It was always multiple deliveries and ninety percent of it, after being handballed on, had to be handballed off again – fifty boxes here, a hundred there… By the time I'd finished, at whatever time of the day or night, I'd just try to find somewhere to park and then keel over into the bunk, often kicking off my boots and crashing out fully clothed. Eight hours sleep was a luxury – a rare one – but a bigger luxury was actually finding somewhere sensible to park.

In Britain 'proper' parking areas for trucks are few and far between. Nine times out of ten drivers are forced to park up on industrial estates, or on a shitty piece of waste ground, or in small lay-bys inches from the main road where it's not only dangerous to jump out for a piss, but nigh impossible to drink a cup of coffee – let alone sleep properly – because of the noise and the violent rocking motion caused by passing traffic.

Drivers don't choose to park in these places because they like them. More often than not it's because they've run out of driving time and simply *can't* go any further by law, or because there's nowhere else to park where some arsehole isn't going to come banging on the cab door demanding money. Most 'off-road' parking has to be paid for in the UK. Motorway service areas – the only parking areas on any of Britain's motorways – where a lot of drivers are forced to park due to the nature of their work, charge a fee. About £8.00 at the time of writing. All so-called truckstops charge for parking. Even shitty little 'transport cafes' (greasy spoons) with muddy, pot-holed car parks charge for the privilege of pulling the curtains.

A lot of bosses wouldn't – and still won't – pay for this highway robbery, so if those drivers decide, or are forced, to cough up, it comes out of their own pockets. If you're out for five or six nights a week it comes to a lot of money.

Some bosses will oblige. They'll say, 'Yes, pay it and we'll reimburse you'... At the end of the month. Maybe. Or a driver may simply not have the money in his pocket and is left with no choice but to park elsewhere... inches from the flow of traffic.

I begrudge paying for parking *anywhere* in the UK for a number of reasons. Firstly because there isn't a single parking area I know of that can actually guarantee secure parking – the kind of safe 'sleep easy' overnight parking that would justify having to pay a fee in the first place. Most 'secure' parking areas aren't that at all. Trucks, trailers and loads frequently get stolen under the 'watchful' eyes of security guards and video surveillance; trailers get slashed open, cabs get broken into, diesel goes missing, wheels do the same disappearing act – I even know of an Eminox exhaust stack that went on the missing list one night!

Secondly I, and many others, think it morally wrong to expect a driver to shell out hard-earned money for the so-called privilege of parking at a place where he – or she – is probably going to spend money on food and other things anyway – especially when the sign on the wall says 'All drivers park here at their own risk'.

It's a load of bollocks.

Sure, a lot of places have a high ground rent to pay on their one and a half acres of 'prime' pot-holed waste ground… So what? If they bothered to improve the food a bit – or a lot – they could 'up' the price of that, double their custom, knock parking charges on the head and *still* cover the cost of some tarmac!

As a rule the Europeans don't charge trucks for 'overnighting' at their truckstops and roadhouses – why should we? And European truckstops are *never* empty.

There is no other justification for charging overnight parking in the UK other than greed.

There's even one 'greasy spoon' in the Midlands that puts a padlocked chain across the car park entrance/exit at only six or seven p.m. – *after* they've closed the café, collected their parking fees and left everyone to it. And the chain is only removed when they come to work next morning – an hour before they open for breakfast! And that is supposed to be classed as 'service industry'?

I once pulled into a small 'transport café' (as the sign boasted) near a J.C.B. plant in the Midlands. I'd finished early one day. I also had a passenger with me, and we were not only hungry, but wanted somewhere to stop for the night. The tiny, muddy car park was empty and, surprise, surprise, the café was closed – as if transport only works nine to five. There was nowhere else to go that we knew of, so the truck stayed put and we walked to a pub.

First thing the next morning we both went in for breakfast. We were still the only ones there and apart from the owner's car, ours was the only other vehicle in the car park. As we walked in the first thing the guy said – instead of hello, or good morning or something – was:

'Is that your lorry out there?'

I told Einstein it was.

'Well I normally charge for overnight parking,' he growled, as if I'd committed a crime.

He got my back up straightaway, so I said, 'Oh do you? Well we normally have breakfast. Ta ta.' And walked out.

We got fed elsewhere. He lost two customers. Simple. If more drivers did things like that somebody might eventually get the message.

Britain's catering industry – especially where transport is concerned – has to be a contradiction in terms, and should carry a government health warning. I got so angry and frustrated with it all while I was grounded with the Merc that I used to dread stopping anywhere for a feed. It even got so bad after a couple of months that I took to cooking in the cab again. Not just to avoid the costs, but more to avoid the disgusting 'chips with everything' culture.

It developed into one of my pet hates. I'd walk into a greasy spoon that stank of vinegar and chip fat, then join the queue with the rest of the inmates to be 'served' ('no table service here mate – this is England! Wassa matter, got broken legs 'ave yer?'). Then before I could open my mouth, and without being asked, a Nora Batty type would plonk a mug of tea down in front of me. So I'd look at it and say:

'What's that?'

'Tea! What's it look like?'

'I didn't ask for tea.'

'Well why didn't you say?' she'd growl angrily.

'Say what?'

'That you didn't want tea!'

'Well why didn't you ask?

'Ask what?'

'What I wanted?'

'Well what do you want then?' as if I was putting her out by being there.

'Coffee please.'

A mug of instant coffee would then be slammed down in front of me, so I'd look at it and say:

'What's that?'

'It's coffee! You asked for coffee!'

'Yes I did.'

'Well there you are then.'

'But I didn't ask for milk. Coffee's black, not white.'

'But you have milk in tea!' was the regular non-sensical answer.

'I don't drink tea! – that's why I asked for coffee.'

'But…'

And so it went on.

Ordering a meal was just as complicated. I'd get comments like:

'You want beans *and* tomatoes?' Or, 'What's wrong with black pudding?'

Then it was often a case of taking a raffle ticket – which spoke volumes – and waiting at an uncleared table for the town crier, again in the form of a lumpy tart in a snot-stained apron, to scream out 'Egg, chips and beeeans!' or, 'Number twenty-eight where are you? Ain't you 'ungry?' whereupon the 'customer' is duty-bound to get up and fight his – or her – way back to the counter again.

After a while I got bored with winding them up, so I stole a set of spanners (knives and forks) one day and invested in a camping stove.

Apart from the risk of having cremated beans on toast, or an 'Ashes Test Cricket' standard roast potato bowled at me by a fast-pacer with a cob on, other hazards of 'UK shunting' are manifold.

After a mostly sleepless night in a lay-by not much over nine feet wide (all trucks are just over eight feet wide) I'd have to join the Wacky Races on a motorway somewhere, with bleary eyes, and drive like Ayrton Senna to avoid causing an accident.

I'd been used to European driving, i.e. plodding along at 70 to 90 kph (45 – 55 mph), and I thought that was fast enough. But here, on the motorways of Britain, there were fully freighted trucks belting up the middle lane at 110kph (70mph) and more! It was terrifying! I kept thinking Christ, if one of these guys has a front-wheel blow-out at these speeds it'll be Armageddon! Amen! I figured it would be unwise to try pulling out into the middle lane to overtake anything while these lunatics were trying to break the sound barrier so, against all my better instincts, I soon found myself driving at the same speeds just to keep things moving.

Another headache was being stopped by the police – a regular occurrence – which was worrying because I'd made a temporary tax disc from a label off a beer bottle; or being hauled in for a spot check by the ministry of nuts and bolts, paperwork and bad breath; or getting caught in another traffic jam with no fags…

And I always seemed to be chasing the clock. It played havoc with my nerves. And that's how it went, day after day, night after night. I'd drive flat out to get somewhere, manhandle the goods off the truck, try my hardest to let customers' complaints transit straight through to my opposite ear, zoom off to the next drop, etc. Then, when everything was closed for the day and I was either parked on someone's warehouse doorstep, or in a poky little lay-by with the wing mirror pulled in, I'd warm up a tin of Atlantic Salmon à la Caspian Caviar sauce and spaghetti hoops, set the alarm, and zonk out in the bunk.

It was Hell.

It went on like that for five months or more and all I could think about was Reykjavik. I was ready to quit. I'd paid my dues and more than done my bit – but I'd seriously had enough. I'd decided to pack it in and leave Roy as soon as I could seek salvation elsewhere, so I was more than a little surprised when he came stomping across the yard one day in a bit of a panic, and bellowed 'Nevill! Drop whatever you're doing right now and grab your kit – we're flying to Turkey!'

Eighteen

Of spies and black eyes

I'd never flown in the posh end of an aeroplane before. All my air miles had been done squashed up in the smoking section of refugee class sat next to non-smokers.

Club Class was something else. Cruising towards the 'Gateway to Asia' at 35,000 feet and at more than 500 mph in one of British Airways' finest, with outstretched legs and a large scotch to hand, was a whole new experience – and I couldn't fault it. Fuck Hitler's Revenge… this was the way to travel.

Roy had explained the situation as we hurtled round the M25 to Heathrow in his wife's sports car at warp factor six. Apparently he'd had an unexpected phone call from Turkey, 'I'll not mention any names', warning him that one of his newly acquired drivers was spitting the dummy about something and, more seriously, was threatening to dump Roy's truck in Istanbul.

As I've said, dumping a truck abroad is a big no-no, especially in Turkey – and definitely not if you worked for Roy. It's tantamount to treason, desertion, heresy and a kick in the nuts all rolled into one, and can incur fearsome punishment. So it was no great surprise to find myself boarding a flight to Istanbul with Roy, just three hours after hanging up the phone.

Full credit to the man. A lot of bosses would have gone into one in the office and spent a fortune on phone calls, or simply ignored the warning as drivers talk and gone home biting their nails. But Roy wasn't like that, he didn't leave things to chance. He preferred action, certainties, actually trusted most of his drivers enough to listen to them – and the call also gave him a damn fine opportunity to make up for a long-promised business visit.

Jayva was there to meet us at Atatürk airport with a friendly greeting and a private car. 'Jay' was head-shed at Alfa Shipping. Only young and with hateful good looks, spoke flawless English with a gentle voice, had impeccable manners – the type peculiar to educated Muslims, perfect dress sense and the wherewithal to accommodate it, and an obvious attraction to women that made you want to punch him.

It was early evening when Jay escorted us out of the airport, still light and quite warm. I felt at home straight away – it was nice to be back.

I'd been under the impression that we'd go zooming straight off in search of Ahmet, the alleged dummy-spitter, another Turk – one with German connections – that Roy had found from somewhere while I was floundering down-under. Well, it was a reasonable assumption at the time considering the urgency with which our mission had so far been conducted… After all, why go to the effort of transiting from Barking to Istanbul in six hours, only to go and park up at such expensive digs as the Hotel Maçka (pronounced Mach-ka), a three or four-star carpeted jobbie in the posh end of town, if we weren't on an urgent call?

But mine was not to question why as one of the 'abi's' (friend – brother) took an oil-stained bag up to my double room, as Jay, Roy and I parked our bums at the round, open bar, and dispatched several more drinks on expenses.

The spies had been out and about. Ahmet's whereabouts were well known, surprise surprise, and, we were assured, there was less chance of him doing a bunk than the guy from 'Auf Wiedersehen Pet' winning the Eurovision Song Contest. So Roy had decided to tackle the matter first thing in the morning. Tonight was for business, small talk – and whiskey.

After a typical breakfast of soup, cheese, fruit, trip-tik bread (flat stuff folded over), juices, boiled eggs and olives, most of which Roy declined (wot – no fry-up?) and loads of piping hot Turkish coffee which did sod-all for the hangovers, we jumped into Jay's car and were whisked off to a Scania workshop at Florya, between the airport and the Londra.

Ahmet was in attendance along with his truck, an ageing 141 Scania – ROO 108W – which was in for repairs. The look on his face when he saw us told me he'd been forewarned of Roy's flying visit and that he was expecting a little bit more than just a quiet word in his ear.

I was told to keep out of the way so that Roy could conduct his business in private – which was fine by me. But I didn't really want to see Ahmet get a clump. He was half Roy's size and suddenly looked quite pathetic as they squared up for the showdown. My heart went out to him and I wanted to say something, but couldn't. Besides which, I just hate loud noises and the sight of blood when I'm hung over.

I was also beginning to think that all this had been a bit unnecessary, suspecting that the stories of the truck's fate and of Ahmet's intentions to smuggle himself out of Turkey and trek back to Germany alone might have been just a teensy bit exaggerated. But it was all too late in the day to adopt a guilty conscience now. Roy and I were there, two thousand-odd miles from home and at not inconsiderable expense. Something had to be done, actions had to be justified, pride had to be saved – and Ahmet's job had to go.

The conflab went on for more than an hour, with lots of pacing up and down, vertical take-off rehearsals and raised voices, by which time I'd smoked the last of my fags, counted every breeze block in the building, and was in dire need of a livener.

I'm relieved to say that Ahmet didn't get a clump. Roy obviously knew the score and tried to do the 'right' thing while trying to save face. Whatever it was, he never confided in me – and I never asked. All he did say at the end of it was 'Nevill, you are now in charge of this truck. Take the keys – Ahmet's out.'

Suddenly the ecstasy of being taken off UK work, and of our James Bond mission from the A13 to Atatürk, paled into embarrassed insignificance. Ahmet was now out of work. I'd been put in charge of his truck. It didn't feel right. The man had just lost his livelihood, rightly or not, and I felt partly responsible.

He'd done me no harm, and by now I was quite convinced that he had no intentions of dumping the truck. We've all been pissed off with things before and said so over a beer – but it's usually forgotten in the morning. Most of us don't lose our jobs over it.

That night we all landed at the Londra, and it felt like a long-awaited homecoming for me. A few of our lads were already there – Alan Wood (Red Leader One), Black Nev, a real-live Baloo the Bear,

Dave Gracie (who I can't say too much about because if I did he'd have to kill you in the morning), and one or two others who, for some inexplicable reason weren't the slightest bit surprised to see us...

Ahmet was there too.

The night was on Roy, bless his Fred Perry socks. Roy didn't get to spend much free time with his drivers, and it had been years since he'd last paid a visit to Istanbul, so we very kindly let him enjoy himself and all got deliciously pissed at his expense.

At some time during the evening Roy pulled me to one side. He covertly stuck £200 into my hand and whispered, 'Have a drink on me. Just take that truck out of here when it's ready and get it back home. And don't let the Turk anywhere near it... I'm leaving it all up to you, John.'

That was music to my ears, 'I'm leaving it all up to you...' It meant that Roy trusted me. Meant that I'd been accepted! You can't imagine what those words meant to me at the time. After all the cock-ups, the stress, the worry, Roy was now saying, in effect, 'welcome aboard, I'm trusting your judgement – don't fuck up.'

I had absolutely no intentions of fucking up. I'd already decided what to do. I'd get the truck home – not the way Roy wanted – but I'd get it home. I looked across at Ahmet, smiled and winked at him. He simply nodded. We understood each other.

Thanks to Roy the next morning's hangovers were worth writing home about. I'd plotted myself up at the Londra's hotel (opposite the restaurant and next to the swimming pool) because the Scania was still in hospital and I had nowhere else to kip. That morning I took a well-earned lie in. The 'Scanny' wasn't due out for another day or three, so I just hung onto the room keys and decided to take things easy for the duration.

Lounging around the swimming pool and the outside tables at the restaurant, sunning myself and gargling Efes couldn't exactly be classed as punishment, but I was under instructions to have a drink on Roy – and orders are orders! I'd also been told to go to customs with Ahmet and get the truck details transferred from his passport to mine – which is easy, when you say it fast enough. But some orders, such as this, just begged out to be disobeyed.

It's not a simple process, or at least it wasn't. In fact it could be a bloody nightmare, and an expensive one at that. We already had our plans for getting the truck out of Turkey, and for getting Ahmet home to Germany. It meant going against Roy's orders but, as he said, he was leaving it up to me – trusting *my* judgement. And I wasn't going to make things hard for myself, was I?

Roy only stayed on in Istanbul for a few days. On his last night there he decided he wanted to take us all out to an expensive restaurant. Naturally we pleaded with him not to be so foolhardy as we all bundled ourselves into the fleet of waiting 'Taksi's'.

The meal itself only served to convince Roy that he still didn't like Turkish food, though the rest of us thoroughly enjoyed it and, just to round off a good time, the day after Roy left I met Jan.

Four or five of us were sitting out in the sun, topping up the tan and putting the world to rights over a crate of Efes. Suddenly this girl breezed across looking like something off a Boddington's advert. She had long reddish-brown hair, greeny eyes, a smile that could melt a Trabant at 100 metres, and a figure that wasn't too well hidden under slacks and a baggy T-shirt.

To me she looked like a stunning cross between Kate Bush and Koo Stark, and I suddenly realised my mouth was open as she asked, 'Hi there, are any of you guys English?'

There was a resounding 'Yes!' from all of us at once.

'Er, I don't suppose any of you know a truckie by the name of Alan Wood, do you?' She asked, looking at each of us in turn. When she looked at me my stomach knotted.

Then, in my best 'hi – take notice of me' type English, I blurted out something like, 'Actually he's just gone to squeeze his pecker – he should be back any minute!'

I could have kicked myself. It just came out, uninvited. I knew instinctively that it would have made things worse if I'd started headbutting the table-top – so I shut up, accepting my fate.

Apart from being embarrassed, I felt jealous! What, I asked myself, would a beautiful girl like this want with a wrinkled old fossil like Woodsy? How did he even know her? Should I way-lay him before he got back from the bogs? And who was she anyway? Australian, that much was for sure, and drop-dead gorgeous to boot - *But Woodsy?*

Alan rounded the corner moments later, pulling up his zip. As soon as Miss Australia saw him it was yelps, whoops, hugs and kisses… And Woodsy got the lot.

I suddenly hated him.

'Red Leader One' as he'd been nicknamed after he unfortunately tried to take control of a situation at a factory in Inonu, Turkey, when twenty-odd trucks – twenty-six I think it was – all got stranded, waiting to tip. They'd been there for more than a week, with more turning up all the time, and everyone was running short of patience – and beer vouchers. So Alan did some phoning around to organise hotel rooms and a 'draw' for everyone – except that the only person who didn't get to draw any money was…?

And now, here he was being slobbered over by a bundle of arms and long hair. There were shouts of, 'Oi, Woodsy, your flies are undone,' and, 'Alan, stop dribbling!' But it didn't work so a chair was dusted off, a beer shoved into her hands, and both her and 'Rot Führer Eins' were ordered to sit for the interrogation.

It turned out, luckily for him, that she'd met Alan *and* his wife, Lesley, months earlier when she'd first visited Istanbul. Now she'd returned on her way back to the UK and had just popped into the Londra on the off-chance. She was plotted up alone at a two-bob hostel in Sultan Ahmet, having done the rounds of Turkey, and was due to go down to Athens in a day or so to collect left-luggage.

But I wasn't having any of that. I didn't want her to go, for whatever reason. I tried to persuade her that it would be a lot more fun to stop on and have a drink with us, rather than traipse all the way back to town alone; that Sultan Ahmet was boring on a Thursday, that bus fares had just gone up, and that there was an horrendous traffic jam outside because of flash floods…

But it didn't work.

She didn't comment on my lavatorial way with words though, bless her, and did at least promise to come back the following day for a drink.

That was on the afternoon of September 12th.

By the 13th I was acting like a March Hare.

When the bandages were removed and ROO 108W was expensively discharged, I signed a piece of paper for Roy to cover it – via Alfa's – drove her all of two k's from Florya to the Londra, hooked her up to the loaded trailer in the car park – and went in for a beer. I figured I'd done enough work for one day.

Jan, nicknamed Koo by the others, kept her promise and did return from town to the mystic delights of 'Londra Camping', for a bit of culture and some sensible conversation.

We had a good night – we always did when the fairer sex was in attendance – and especially when our bare arms touched at the table and I didn't get belted in the ribs for it. That night I offered her a lift to Greece. Not all the way to Athens, mind – that was too far off route – but to Thessalonika (Saloniki) where, I assured her, I could guarantee her another lift to Athens in one of the English trucks that regularly went there via Yugoslavia – and she said yes!

Ahmet and I had already laid our plans: He would simply drive the truck out of Turkey with me as passenger. No hassle, no fucking around at customs getting passports altered – and no backshish. From there on in we'd simply take it in shifts until Ahmet and all his kit was safely back home in Germany. Easy peasy.

Well I saw no problem with it. Roy only wanted Ahmet kept away from the truck in case he had ideas of taking revenge for being fired – such as sabotage. But, going against Roy's orders, I put my trust in Ahmet as a fellow driver and took the obvious way out. I even agreed to let him stay in the truck as I endured the rigours of the hotel.

Anyway, why would he let me down? If he made any attempt at sabotage he'd have no sure way of getting back home – especially with all his kit in tow – and it certainly wouldn't have ended there. Not only would there have been recriminations (it *is* a small world out there) but at the time, remember, the truck, the trailer and load were still *his* responsibility. All the details were stamped into *his* passport. Not mine! For all intents and purposes I was just a tourist. So he couldn't simply burn the truck, destroy the paperwork, or fuck the engine and then bugger off home. It really wasn't that easy. And anyway he was enjoying himself – he liked his beer as much as anyone else.

It was only at the eleventh hour that he let me down:

'No possibil Chon,' he said sheepishly.

I was a bit shocked. 'What? Why the hell not Ahmet? It's my lorry now mate, remember? – I can do what I want!'

'No, no, not dat. Iz no possibil for me to go to Yunanistan (Greece).'

'Why not for fuck's sake? I'll be driving from there – all you have to do is curl up and go to sleep. It's only six or seven hours to Saloniki!'

'No Chon – no vizum.'

'What?'

'No vizum. Vizum peroberlum Yunanistan.'

'Bollocks, visa problem. You're a driver – of course you can get a visa.'

'Cannot Chon. Sorry.' He shook his head solemnly. Mine was spinning. Ahmet looked upset – and I just wanted to scream. We'd kind of cemented a bond between us in the few days since Roy's departure, and he must have felt as if he was letting me down. He said,

'Chon. Must have letter from chef to say me go Yunanistan – for embassad, yes? Must then wait – maybe yes vizum, maybe no. And me have no chef to make letter!'

It meant that he needed to prove he was an employed TIR driver with a valid reason to enter Greece before he could apply for a visa. Even if we'd 'mickied' an 'official' letter for him, because the trailer was loaded for the UK he could – and probably would – be refused a transit visa, simply because he was Turkish, and the load had no need whatsoever to go through Greece – apart from Miss Melbourne and my honourable intentions!

Greece and Turkey, as everyone knows, have never exactly seen eye to eye over things, except at scimitar-point when the Seljuks swept into Asia Minor in the eleventh century – and especially not since the hoo-ha in Cyprus. And, consequently, small things like day to day cross-border niceties, international co-operation, dreadful results in world-class football and nights out at the local taverna, could be turned into major headaches.

So what to do?

I'd already gone against Roy's wishes and promised Ahmet a ride home. We'd trusted each other and basically he'd done alright by me. So I couldn't let him down now, could I? Honour, and all that. But I'd also promised Jan a lift to Yunanistan, and a door to door jobbie to Athens.

I knew deep down that work had to come first. I really couldn't afford to fuck up after Roy had put his trust in me. And Ahmet had similarly committed his trust – but for different reasons. There was honour at stake. And black eyes.

The truck had to go home and I knew I couldn't do two things at once, simply because I'd fallen in love – even though she'd packed her sandwiches, left the hostel, and was now parked in my hotel room waiting for her ride out of Turkey.

Suddenly I wanted to curl up in a ball, don a wig, pretend to be someone else and just slip out of the back door. But simply saying, 'Me? I know nuffin',' wouldn't solve my dilemma – I had to face Jan.

She was silent and turned away to face the wall after I'd nervously tried to explain, and probably gained ten out of ten for making it sound like a 'goodbye' in the process. And I could see her eyes getting wet. I'd broke the news as honestly and as diplomatically as I possibly could, but she made me feel like I'd just been caught stealing my nan's purse. Especially when she shrugged off my attempted cuddle.

I'd only known the girl for a few days but in that time I'd grown extremely fond of her. She was different. One of the 'boys' – and now I was letting her down. It made me feel awful.

Tony Meddins was in attendance that week, en route to Kuwait again with another load of choccie bars, so I grabbed hold of him and 'Baloo' (Black Nev) for a pow-wow to try and sort something out.

They were both brilliant, fully understood my situation, and couldn't offer enough assistance,

Nobody that they interrogated was due to leave Turkey right then to transit Greece – all of the lads were either waiting to tip, waiting for paperwork and a draw, or had backloads to go for from E. Europe – so we couldn't find Jan another lift. Even though Pat Seal was in the car park fast asleep in his 'stretched' 88, and may have been going that way. Pat, a rather large man with enough wild, gingerish hair to stuff a mattress, a pair of boots that would put the tyres on a JCB to shame, and the temperament of a Saturn rocket with anyone who tries to rouse him from hibernation, was parked at the Londra in possibly the oldest, and most cared-for truck in the middle east (about 28 years old at the time of writing – and still going strong).

The reason being that Pat could have taken anywhere from ten to fifteen days to get there, whether from Dover or Doha, and he liked his sleep. It's why he had the cab stretched – and anyone who disturbed him was in danger of having their necks stretched… so we left him alone.

Pat – actually a gentle giant of a man in Sasquatch footwear – would probably have taken longer to reach Saloniki in the 88 than the local donkey express anyway, so we settled for the obvious solution. A bus. One of which left Istanbul every day for Athens.

I had to go. I'd overstayed my time anyway and the carnet TIR – or at least the amount of transit time we're allotted after loading and clearing customs – was about to expire. Tony, bless his woolly hat, was also due to leave that day, but decided to 'cancel' on mine and Jan's behalf, to take her to the bus station the next day.

So I departed, leaving Jan in the capable hands of Black Nev and Tony Meddins, who both looked like out of work Texan railroad workers, with a cigar stuck to Nev's lip – and a roll-up stuck to Tony's, knowing I could trust them.

So I left Londra Camping in the passenger seat of 'Roo', with Ahmet at the wheel. Koo waved goodbye… then turned her back on me and I had a bit of a lump in my throat.

Pat Seal, illustrated by John Nevill

Nineteen

Of square wheels and square deals

To my surprise Jan actually got in touch when she arrived back in England. I thought she would have kicked me into touch after leaving her in Istanbul, so I was more than chuffed when I strolled into the office and Fred gave me the good news.

She'd actually been on the phone before I'd even left Ahmet in Germany, but the message itself got a bit garbled having been committed to Fred's memory instead of being written down, so it was a few more agonising days before we actually spoke again.

When we did get together over spaghetti and a bottle of wine at her place, she told me how Tony, good to his word, had taken her to the bus station and seen her safely onto a *Kamikaze* bound for Athens. She also told me I'd been forgiven for abandoning her at the Londra, that she understood the situation, and knew I couldn't have done anything else.

Very sporting, Australian women.

She hadn't spent long in the Greek capital after collecting her kit – she's already done Athens, and just wanted to get back 'home' to the UK. So she jumped on the next plane to England and promptly took up residence with another Aussie lady, Jo, at a flat in Acton, W. London… And all this before I'd even left the Bundesrepublik!

By rights I should have beaten her back to Blighty – or at least arrived at roughly the same time. After all, I did have a day's headstart *and* the 'advantage' of being doubled-up, i.e. two drivers instead of one…

Ahmet had been really good about everything. Once he'd accepted his fate he just got on with the job at hand, and gave me no aggro whatsoever. He took us out of Turkey, I drove through Bulgy, then Ahmet let off a little bit of steam by belting up through Yugo at 70-odd mph. Bless him.

But doubling up rarely works the way most people expect it to. It may have advantages in Britain or W. Europe, but does nobody any favours elsewhere. It doesn't speed a truck's passage through Turkish or E. European borders, for instance. Nor, once through these borders, does it mean that two can keep the wheels turning any more than one – especially when there are driving bans in force. A person can only stay awake for so long – whether he's driving or not, and trying to sleep in a moving truck while it's crashing in and out of pot-holes and bashing over bumps, is not easy.

Before long, both drivers get tired and wound up, and need to sleep. Then there's only so many miles to go across one particular country before there's another queue to join, another border to contend with, passport controls, cab searches… Or you might simply bump into other drivers somewhere and end up at another party.

Jan and I got on really well after that and continued to meet regularly. We also kept in touch with Red Leader One and Lesley, as drivers and wives often do 'off the road', and we soon had a steady relationship going. The only drawback to that, I realised, was work itself. For a while I was torn between Jan and the job, and for the first time in ages I found I actually wanted to spend more time in England than I did on the road.

She was very understanding and tried not to let 'us' interfere with my work. Although it didn't actually affect the job too much. If anything it made me try to knock the trips out that much quicker – though 'try' is the operative word – and even though I still had dreams of doing the Middle East, I didn't bother to chase it up too enthusiastically… at least not for a while.

Jan decided one day that she wanted to come on a trip with me – which actually turned into quite a few trips. This temporarily solved the problem of wanting to be at home with her, and gave her the opportunity to see what it was about the work that grown men seemed to find so irresistible – and she loved it! She enjoyed the sense of freedom, the anarchy, the company and the laughs. And she saw places and experienced things in a completely different light.

We shipped out once just before Ramadan, the Muslim observance of fasting for 30 days during the hours of daylight – when basically sod all work gets done. Roy had said 'Take your time, you won't get tipped 'til whenever, so you might as well make a holiday of it.' Which we did. Jan could hardly believe it when I got off the boat, dropped the trailer, and bobtailed up to Brugge for a weekend's holiday.

During this time I seemed to bump into Richie Thorne nearly every trip. After the fiasco with my lost paperwork Richie and I became good friends, and every time we were in either Greece or Turkey our paths seemed to cross. We used to go downtown a lot and do the night-clubs where we spent an absolute fortune, and before long our night-clubbing in 'Stanley Bull' became something of a ritual.

Actually most of our nights out started in mid afternoon down at the Pudding Shop, necking a few beers, from where some of the lads would always insist on going up to 'Pig-Alley' – Istanbul's red-light area - for a gawk at all the flabby tarts with stretch marks and un-ironed legs. Then it was off to the expensive end of town for loud music and flashing lights.

To get into most night-clubs in Istanbul, men were required to be in the company of ladies, which, for obvious reasons, wasn't always possible. One particular evening when Jan wasn't with me, and we couldn't find any other drivers' wives or girlfriends to escort us in, we grabbed hold of a new boy – who looked a bit girlie anyway – tarted him up with some borrowed make-up, dressed him up a bit, hung him on our arms and went to see if we could get into the Hydromel – a late-night disco by Taksim Square – and it worked! The guy even seemed to enjoy it all, especially when the Turks started showing an interest.

Things were going really well for me by this time. I even got to complete my personal run of the Commie Bloc countries when I tagged along behind Mickey Johnstone one day, who was on his way through East Germany.

DDR was nowhere near as intimidating as some spy-writers would have us believe, even with the miles of barbed wire, armed watchtowers, searchlights and dogs. The roads weren't exactly the best in the world, especially the lumpy, concrete-section autobahns, where drivers had to P-dink P-donk along for miles on end. The bouncing, juddering motion made it feel like being in a clown's car with square wheels. It played havoc with a truck's nuts and bolts, and even worse with half-digested breakfasts.

The uniformed bods at the borders were no problem most of the time, except when British drivers used to toss biscuits and sliced ham to the friendly sniffer dogs. Sure, they screamed and shouted a bit, especially when we simply grinned and shrugged our shoulders. But Roy used to shout a lot too – and he could be much more intimidating than red-faced communist 'Polizei' and customs men. A lot of them – police, immigration, customs – even proved to have a sense of humour, which was more than could be said for their counterparts in the west.

Getting through East Germany's Grenzübergangs (main borders) in a truck required very few James Bond tactics. Most of the time a driver didn't even need to get out of the cab, and it could be a relative breeze compared to borders elsewhere. I was never bullied or intimidated enough to put me off going that way and after a while I started using DDR as a matter of course.

Soon Jan and I were getting on so well that we rented a small flat in Muswell Hill and moved in together. My old Nan in Wales would have disapproved, saying we were living in sin, bless her heart, but we were happy, and at the time I thought things couldn't get much better, until Roy unexpectedly pulled me to the side one day and made me an offer I just couldn't refuse.

'I want a quick word' he said, walking me away from the portacabin. From his expression I thought, Oh-oh. Here we go. I'm in trouble again, so I asked what was wrong.

'Nothing. Nothing's wrong,' he said in a lighter tone. 'I've got a proposition for you, that's all.'

'Oh yeah?' I was getting suspicious.

'Yeah. It's like this. I've got three units up for grabs. One of them's yours if you want it. I've already made the same offer to Axles and Catweasle – now it's your turn.'

I was confused. I didn't have enough cash to buy a second-hand car, let alone a truck, so I said as much.

'I know you haven't – now shut up and listen.' He looked serious again. 'You lot have stood by me in the past. Fuck knows why but you have, and it's appreciated. You've helped to get me established – now it's my turn to help you. Here's the deal. If you want I'm willing to help you three set yourselves up as owner-drivers. I've got the trucks, I've got the trailers, and plenty of work. The other two have already taken me up on this offer, they've got their trucks now and I'm offering you the third – the one eleven' (Scania)

'What I'll do is get you underway. I'll sort out the insurance and everything and lump it all into one package. All you have to do is take the Scania off me and treat it as your own. I supply the loads and you pull my trailers! Simple as that. It's up to you John, but you won't find another offer like this. If you agree we'll sort out a price and we can work the payments out trip by trip… Interested?'

I was stunned and all I could think to say was 'Fucking hell Roy!'

'Right. Have a think about it - there's no rush. Get back to me when you're ready.' Then he turned and walked away.

I felt like I'd been belted across the head with a four-by-two. What to think? It all sounded too good to be true – Me! An owner-driver? Just like that?

I went walkabout for a bit, to shake out some cobwebs, control the adrenaline – then I ended up at the tea caravan outside the container base where I bought a takeaway coffee – without milk – and then spent the afternoon walking around Barking in a bit of a daze.

I got back home a bit late that night with several pints under my belt. I hadn't phoned Jan to tell her what had happened – I'd decided to keep it a secret and went and got myself pissed instead. It wasn't until I put the key in the door that I thought, oops! What if she doesn't like the idea? Because, knowing what women are like, with their ability to compute everything in less than a hundredth of a second and point something out that you've just spent hours racking your brain over – and missed – I suddenly got a bit of a panic attack.

As I wobbled in Jan squealed and rushed up to me beaming from ear to ear, as she always did when I came back off a trip.

My ticker pumped at nineteen to the dozen as we hugged and I slurred something like, 'Hello darlin'. Guesh wha'?'

'What?'

'…I juss bawt'a tru-*hic*!'

Twenty

Of windscreens and wigs

As I prepared to become the world's latest millionaire by visiting expensive Chinese restaurants in Acton, and spending most of my imminent fortune in advance on Jan's plastic, Roy had been a little more realistic and spent the week negotiating a new contract.

The contract – a verbal one in all likelihood, because the only things that came in black and white in this job were the bills – was for us 'Lawrabian' to start running Ford's car-body parts to an assembly plant in sunny Portugal.

Running to that part of the world was a teensy bit off our normal beaten track – several thousand kilometres off to be more precise – but it must have been a good deal because to get me off to a flying start as Britain's newest owner-driver of the world's slowest ten-year-old, left-hand drive, one eleven Scania – BNO 30T – I was given the usual, 'Just get there…' etc. and aimed in the general direction of Lisbon.

Jan was really pleased for me, and quite excited when I asked if she wanted to come along for the ride. I told her that most of the gang from Lawrabian would also be on the same mission, some of whom seemed to regard it as a form of punishment.

A few of the lads had already left and were well ahead of us, and others would be following up behind. I suggested to Jan that it would be fun going somewhere different for a change, that the Port was original (one of her favourite tipples), that it should only take about ten days all told – and that a bit of moral support never goes amiss.

She rang the agency she worked for to book the time off, left a 'Dear John' for the milkman, turned the gas off and had a bag packed before I could say boo.

A move she soon came to regret.

Nipping down to Lisbon should have been a nice quick way to get the ball rolling as an OD – but Lisbon isn't just round the corner, and it's not the sort of place you can just 'nip down' to… not without Prat and Whitney jet engines and the blessing of the gods.

I'd been to Lisbon once before so I thought we might at least be in with half a chance – but that had been for a holiday in an ageing, umpteenth-hand Citroen Dyane which kept falling ill, and from which passengers were obliged to get out and walk when it came to a hill… and which eventually caught fire.

I also had BNO 30T which, slow, old and showing signs of senility as she was, had, until very recently, belonged to a certain Mr David Gracey – 'Auntie Gracey' (who I can't tell you too much about, etc.) and which had been reasonably well cared for, so I set off with all the enthusiasm and gaiety of a new-born lamb… to the slaughter!

The trip got off to a racing start. I loaded, filled up with red in a leaking belly-tank, which weighed half as much as the load itself, shipped to Calais, gave the 'Douanier' (customs officer) the usual fifty francs (coffee money, or café) not to look too closely at anything then managed to get all the way to Paris – a whole four hours' driving – before things went pear-shaped.

Roy had 'asked' me not to drag my heels too much on the way down because Red Leader One, bless his Shirley Temple perm, was stuck in Lisbon waiting for us – skint. He'd somehow managed to overspend and had been forced to phone in for a draw. Roy couldn't arrange a draw for him in Portugal, seeing as he had no contacts there and couldn't pronounce the word 'Ethcudoth'. So I'd been given an extra few hundred in cash for him, and faithfully promised not to hang about too much.

And I meant it at the time. After all, I *was* on a mission of my own.

Anyway, we got to the marvellous ring road system in Paris with Jan at the map, and got *seriously* lost! And it wasn't down to me this time. I'd invested in an atlas of Europe and my beloved had been doing the navigating, bless her down-under-orientated sense of direction ('Well, the sun's in the wrong place…')

First we did a complete lap of Paris, took a wrong turn and ended up on some narrow cobblestoned roads heading into town. Then, when we found the motorway again and went past Charles de Gaulle airport for the second time, I began to smell a rat. Especially as we convinced ourselves that the plane we watched coming into land was the same one we saw take off earlier.

We just went round and round in circles getting hopelessly confused by the signposting, cursing everyone from Joan of Arc to Napoleon – before I drove into a busy underpass and broke down.

My tooth-marked steering wheel took a severe thumping, and they must have heard the screaming as far south as Bordeaux. If the devil himself had appeared at that moment I'd have poked him in the eye, swung him round by his bloody tail and chucked him into the fast lane – I was fucking fuming!

...And Jan thought it was funny!?

She'd been lost with me plenty of times before, and it wasn't the first time she'd seen me crawl under a truck in the dark with a hammer and a fist-full of spanners, hoping to bodge something while she made coffee. But two of Nescafé's finest and several scraped knuckles later her sense of humour soured a bit when I got back in the truck, covered in oil and grease, and told her that we really were stuck because I thought the clutch had packed up.

On board I was carrying a grand total of just three tonnes of cargo – body parts are nice and light. Even with my tonne and a half of red diesel it's actually sod all in terms of weight when you consider that most artics carry twenty-four tonnes! In fact three or four tonnes isn't even enough to keep the wheels on the road in winter.

Calculating the weight of everything – truck, trailer, diesel, load, spare wheels, tools, Pot Noodles, etc., and the fact that neither of us had been for a dump that day, the whole outfit, top to toe, couldn't have weighed in at any more than eighteen tonnes. Sod all. I could have doubled that and still been able to load the roof-rack with beer! A truck with an empty fridge would probably have weighed more.

Surprise surprise, I had no tow-bar with me, but I did carry miles of rope and by now I could tie it to hooks, to rails, to a gnat's dick and a puff of smoke, so I strung out rakes of the stuff, wound it around the tow-pin on the front bumper, doubled it over umpteen times – and waited for a semi-articulated knight in shining amour to come galloping up.

...And waited.

I know I didn't really look like a medieval damsel in distress praying for Galahad to come to the rescue, but let's be honest – a British-registered twelve-metre trailer, with 'Long Vehicle' plates reflecting in everyone's headlights, sat on the hard shoulder of a French underpass waving four-way orange handkerchiefs in the middle of Paris' rush hour, isn't exactly inconspicuous – is it? I mean, it's like saying, 'Ooh! What armed robbery was that then?' as hooded men in black run around firing off shotguns!

Yes – I'd already tried to flag down some assistance, of course I had. I'm not going to just stand there like a lemon expecting someone to stop out of the goodness of their hearts, am I? Not in France I'm not. Anyway, I soon decided that I was still quite attached to my right arm – and went to Plan B instead.

A few English trucks had already zoomed straight past me without even slowing down, conveniently blinkered as most of them seemed to be, but that was – and still is – about par for the course in this part of the world. I wasn't too worried about it, the next English truck would have to run me down if he wanted to get past.

It didn't happen in the next five minutes but when I saw an English-registered 142 Scania bearing down on me, I didn't hesitate to stand right out in front of him and play windmills… Almost shitting my pants in the process.

The driver had little choice. He had to slam his brakes on. He'd never have run me down if he could possibly avoid it. It goes against all of a driver's instincts, like swerving into the next lane without looking… or so I told myself.

Anyway, I didn't let it get that far. I backed off at the last minute. He'd seen me, he'd hit the brakes, now all he had to do was stop. It wasn't wet, he wouldn't 'lose it', didn't need to swerve – just stop, inform me that he was a fully qualified Scania mechanic, salute, then tell me everything would be hunky-dory in a jiffy!

But Matey wasn't impressed as he pulled in – I could tell. But so what? I was in trouble.

The driver didn't bother to get out of his cab. Fair enough. So I legged it up to his door and said, 'Sorry mate, I don't make a habit of doing that, but I've got a problem and need some help.'

'Yeah?' he snarled, giving me a dirty look.

Okay, I thought, he's pissed off with me, so I politely said, 'Look mate, I really do need some help. I've been stuck here for ages. Me and my girlfriend are gagging on the fumes, and I just need to be towed out of this tunnel. Please? I've already tied up loads of rope, I'm light, you won't even know I'm there. All you need to do is back her up a bit, I'll tie her on, then we can go. You don't even have to get out of the seat – what do you say?'

He just looked down with a sneer, as if he was above people like me. His window was halfway up, and his engine still running. I realised I'd been shouting at the top of my voice just to make myself heard. Had he opened the door I'd have bet money that he was wearing furry clogs over white socks.

He shook his head. 'Nah, can't, I'm loaded.' He growled, displaying true grit.

He was loaded, but not 'heavy', I could see that – any driver could. Though it's not the point. Today's articulated trucks can pull 70, 80 or 90 tonnes – bog standard. That's their capability, it's what they're designed for. Legal weight limits and manufacturer's limits are two completely different things, and between the two of us we wouldn't have grossed more than 40 or 50 tonnes. So I said as much.

His reply, surprisingly, was, 'I've got nothing to tow you with.'

'Mate, I've already told you, I've lined up enough rope to pull a fucking Jumbo Jet! It's really not a problem. I just want to get us out of here and breathe some fresh air again.' I really couldn't believe I was having to plead with this guy. 'Look,' I continued, 'I'm not asking you to tow me a million miles – just fifty yards. Please? All you have to do is pull me out there,' I pointed, 'then dump me on the hard shoulder.'

He thought about it for all of five seconds, said, 'Nah. – ain't got time.' And with that, he slammed into gear, dropped the handbrake, gunned it and roared off, belting me with exhaust fumes.

'YOU CUNT!' I screamed at the top of my voice. *'YOU DIRTY NO GOOD…'* But I was wasting my breath. I suddenly found myself trembling. I then stormed back to the truck, incredulous and seething with anger again.

I couldn't believe all this was happening to me. My first mission as an OD! Why? What did I do in a previous life to deserve all this? I'd set off with all the best intentions – I'd dipped the oil, wiped the windscreen… Now, four hours from the boat, it was all going tits up.

Jan was smiling as I got back in. She said, 'Well done. Is he dropping his trailer and coming back, or something?' thinking we'd worked out a plan.

'No!' I said sharply. 'He's fucking not!'

'Well, where's he gone then?' her smile faded.

'He's gone.'

Her smile disappeared. 'What do you mean, he's gone?'

'He's fucked off. He won't help us.'

Jan went quiet for a moment as she took it in, and tears began to well in her eyes. I felt for her and all I could do was give her a hug, which ruined her T-shirt.

Obviously confused she simply asked, 'Why?' But I couldn't give an answer. All I could do was shrug, and I suddenly wanted to bury the ignorant bastard that had made Jan's eyes water.

Jan wasn't used to this sort of behaviour – especially from 'fellow' drivers. And particularly from other Brits. She'd been with me in the truck all over Eastern Europe, the Balkans, Turkey. She'd met the lads, seen with her own eyes the people who were only too willing to don overalls, open a toolbox, lose a day, no questions asked. She'd seen these people get stuck into it when one of us had a problem, and had come to accept this kind of behaviour as the norm.

But this was Western Europe. T. Former's territory. A completely different kettle of fish – and Jan was trying hard not to cry.

I spent over four hours – half a day's work to any normal office bod – in that stinking, choking underpass. Nobody else bothered stopping for me, including several more British trucks, one of whom had the gall to toot as he went by, and at the end of the day I actually managed to drive myself out!

The problem turned out to be with the hydraulics, not the clutch itself, though it didn't make me feel any better for knowing that. I'd have been much happier to discover the problem under different circumstances. As it was, I'd spent half a day getting wound up, covered in shit, breathing carbon something-ide, scraped lots of skin off my hands, put Jan through it – and gained another unwanted prejudice.

After struggling to a local garage by starting her in gear and crashing through the box without using the clutch, I laid out more than I thought was reasonable to have my hydraulic system pressure-bled – which didn't solve the problem – gained a grey hair or two and another wrinkle in the process – and put myself a day behind. Blinding.

Neither of us was in the best of moods when we eventually got rolling again. Not that it mattered too much because, apart from one good night out with some of the lads, things actually got worse instead of better.

We – or at least I – was under instructions to meet up with some of the gang on the way down to interview each other's wallets and swap paperwork (don't ask) which we eventually did – I say eventually because all the others were running behind schedule too – at a rather nice, friendly, roadside café somewhere near the Palace of Versailles.

Black Bill was there, *aka* 'Billy Block of Flats' because of his enormous American jobbie with added shiny bits and a second storey nailed to the roof; plus Jimmy Ellis, a south-London ex-rugby player with an enormous sense of humour and a beer-belly to match; a German that worked for an English firm, myself and a couple of other 'professionals', all of whom displayed lots of plumage in front of Jan and two ageing, but gorgeous, French waitresses.

We did ourselves really proud, as British drivers do abroad, by downing large quantities of local vin and being loud, speaking in 'Del-Boy' French trying to impress the women. Like 'Mange tout darling, 'may we' 'ave le din dins, silver play?' So Jan stepped in, spoke a slightly more acceptable form of the language and ordered everyone a cheese omelette.

In Spain, we bumped into 'Hoss' – a 'good ole boy' who always had a cheroot stuck to his teeth, and a mismatched syrup (wig) stuck to his head… except when the wind took it one day as he poked his head out of the window, whereupon his syrup took to the air and promptly attached itself to a passing Yugoslav's windscreen.

We were in hysterics as he told how, when he ran back to retrieve it, the Yugo driver was trying to poke it off his windscreen with a stick, believing it to be a live animal!

He warned us to 'watch the bastards' as he told how, on his way back from Lisbon, he'd been pulled in and 'set-up' by a Spanish cop for something or other. El Plod, apparently, had not only parked him up and 'spot-fined' him for something he hadn't done – but also had him wheel-clamped for parking where he'd stopped!

So, suitably warned, and laughing our socks off for the first time in days, we headed deep into Clint Eastwood country, found a bloody great hill to go over – and broke down in the overtaking lane.

By now I knew what the problem was, but it didn't cheer me up to keep crawling underneath the truck with a 10mm ring spanner while Jan pumped the clutch pedal… especially not with traffic passing on both sides.

As soon as I got it going, it went again.

Then it went again on a rather steep hill in Portugal – which we shouldn't have been on in the first place (printing error on my map).

Then again – when I'd run out of hydraulic fluid and had to use water.

By this time Roy was going apeshit about the time it was taking me - but he wasn't sat on the roadside covered in shit, and let's face it, I'd been told the 'Scanny' was up to the job.

When we eventually got to Lisbon, about a week overdue, Woodsy's perm looked like a fruit tree in blossom, and he also seemed a bit underweight.

The load was 'tipped' rather rapidly (I think they'd been waiting for it) then we threatened Woodsy that we weren't going to give him a single penny until he promised to take us out for a beer, which he did – at the cheapest spit and sawdust bar he could find in the whole of Lisbon.

And things didn't improve.

Our planned excursion of the capital, the weekend in the Algarve, the swimming, sunbathing – *and* the visits to all the local wineries turned, not unexpectedly, into a rabid 'Get the fuck up the road, Nevill! You're loading in Strasbourg on Friday, or there'll be hell to pay. *OKAY?* And I don't want any excuses!'

All I could say was, 'Er – where's that?'

Then I found it on the map.

Strasbourg? France?... Bollocks! An impossible task. Forget it. Not on your nelly. Pull the other one...

'Roy – I'm in fucking Portugal!' I said when I rang back. 'I've got no chance. Do you know where Strasbourg is? It's fucking miles away!'

I got the predictable reply.

Strasbourg is the best part of two thousand kilometres from Lisbon. There were two borders to contend with, and most of the route seemed to be uphill. And to get there at the 'agreed' time, i.e. before the weekend started, I'd have needed to drive at Mach two, on empty roads, for umpteen hours – non-stop!

We gave it a try. We set off from Lisbon following Red Leader One, who 'knew' the way, so we got lost en-route to the Spanish border. On the Portuguese side we bought some duty-free Port to make up for our lost visit to Mr Trenchcoat's winery. Then Jan, poor thing, nearly got arrested on the Spanish side because her visa had expired – which wouldn't have been a problem had Woodsy not brought it to their attention!

After narrowly missing the arrest of my sweetheart, we followed Alan up to Madrid – and got lost again.

Following a dodgy meal at a rough and ready 'transport' restaurant in an area of Madrid that isn't even on the map, we headed east and went over some bloody great hills – and that's when it started to snow.

Jan, bless her, was hung out of the passenger's window, cackling and squealing with delight, trying to catch the flakes! She'd never seen snow falling before, which I found really amazing as I clenched my arse-muscles, tried to control my knees, and politely screamed at her to close the window.

We then lost ages at the Spanish-French border at La Jonquera because we drove up the wrong lanes and didn't know which 'windows' to go to.

Then, after we exited the border, we zoomed off through Southern France's worst-ever traffic jams, pulled into a service area near Lyon – and broke down again.

By this time I just wanted to curl up into a Smarties tube and cry... then I had a very weird experience.

As Jan was pumping the clutch pedal in her sleep, I was laid on my back with a mixture of hydraulic fluid and H_2O running up my arm, when this bloke, looking rather like a Pakistani in a suit, walked over to me, bent down and, with what looked like a microphone to hand said, 'I say,' in perfect Oxford-English, 'would you mind awfully if I took the liberty of recawding the saynd of your lowwy engine?'

I then realised I'd been wasting my time because at that very moment the awful truth dawned on me, I'd just died lying underneath my truck and gone not to Heaven or Hell, but to the Mad Hatter's tea party in Wonderland! It was obvious – what other explanation could there be? *My fucking engine wasn't even running!!*

All he needed to say next was, 'I'm late, I'm late…' and I'd have leapt out and strangled him with his mike-cord.

'DO WHAT?' I screamed in disbelief.

'Yes, I work for the BBC,' he continued casually, as if protected from reality. 'My colleague and I are pwesently touring certain parts of Europe in an effort to collect saynd recawdings of certain things – for our tape banks, you know – and I was wondering if it wouldn't be too inconvenient…'

'You see, when the Beeb has to use saynd effects for their pwogwammes they like to have them to hand, instead of having to rwush awf and wecawd whatever it is they need at the time – which can be awfully inconvenient. Don't you agwee?'

Agree? I couldn't believe what I was listening to!

'Mate, if I could listen to the 'saynd' of my engine running right now – *do you seriously think I'd be lying under here getting covered in shit?'* I yelled.

'…Oh! So you can't start your engine for us then?' he asked, sounding disappointed.

I think I screamed then.

I shuffled out from under the truck, head-butting something en-route, and was about to confront 'Not the Nine O'Clock News' in 'Not the Queen's English', when the sight of him suddenly deflated me. Five feet two, skinny, suited, and standing in the rain smiling, with a microphone aimed at me… 'Say hello to the boys…' And I simply gave in, panting, close to tears.

He left soon after, walking across the car park, not hopping two feet at a time towards the bushes, with the required 'saynds' on his tape, and a few words to the boys… and I felt like I'd just been conned out of my dinner money!

Jan had missed most of this being semi-comatose over the wheel, and only caught the arse-end of it all – but it seemed to cheer her up a bit. I think it was the first time she'd seen me calm for a week, staring at the heavens, listless, dripping wet.

When we reached Strasbourg, thoroughly broke, tired, and covered in shit, I shrugged off Roy's bollocking about catching the weekend, told him I had no more money for phone calls, hung up and settled in for what was left of it.

There wasn't much we could do about being broke, short of food and nearly out of smokes, so we wandered around town for a bit, looked in all the cake shop windows and went 'home' frothing at the mouth. Which is when Jan really put the lid on the whole trip as she put both feet on the dash, stretched and yawned – and kicked my windscreen out…

I'd done my best, but my best obviously wasn't good enough. I'd got there and I eventually got back as well. A round trip that British Airways can do in about five hours – and it had taken me nearly a month!

Jan wasn't impressed. Roy wasn't impressed. I had a hydraulic system with attitude, which I told Scania's was a design fault (and got the obvious fob-off) so they weren't impressed. Fords weren't impressed either, simply because I'd delivered their load a little bit late, and the chemical company I'd backloaded for weren't impressed either.

And of course, it was all *my* fault!

But didn't I really do well for myself? I had a windscreen that looked like a 3D map of the Mekong Delta; a boss that didn't want to talk to me; a girlfriend that was threatening never to get in the truck with me again; an urgent desire to become a travelling salesman – and a pay-cheque that didn't even cover the bill for Jan's plastic!

Twenty-One

Of Deutschmarks and diesel

Jan did come out in the truck with me again, bless her, I knew she would. In fact she spent the best part of 1989 in my passenger's seat being chauffeured around Europe, Greece and Turkey.

She not only enjoyed the weather, the beaches, and the laid-back (lazy) attitude in Greece, especially at 'Maria's' – a regular watering hole 12 k's from the Turkish border – but actually liked running through the Commie Bloc too!

Of course, this had nothing to do with the cheap supply of original 'Budvar' (as in Budweiser), a 'Plzen' (Pils) beer native to Czechoslovakia that was available at just ten Dm. (Deutschmarks) for a splintered wooden crateful (and a couple of bob back on the empties). And she didn't mind one little bit if I drove or did roadside repairs while she grabbed another round the throat and carried on drinking the stuff!

She also liked to pig out on the tonne of dumplings and gravy that the Czechs serve up with just about everything they eat – lovely stuff that sets like concrete within minutes and makes you feel pregnant. And to my disgust, she actually *ate* the chewy-spewy dog turd and toenail sausages that were common fare at all the tatty, green-camouflaged snack bars. There's only one other person I know of in this world who could stomach such delicacies, and that's 'Buttons', because he's an out and out dustbin and will eat *anything* – dead or alive – if he's hungry. Which is always.

My sweetheart took full advantage of life on the road, trying everything that was new to her and, though I won't say she was spoiled, was one of the few people I know – male or female – who could get Buttons to share his 'Bakey-Boiley cake'.

She got on great guns with the rest of the tribe too, all of whom were perfect gentlemen and treated her like one of the boys. Like Dave Davenport (Penfold) who used to hijack her for the communal trailer-box breakfast before I was awake; 'Joe 90', a tubby, rosy-cheeked northerner, who stood sentry outside the manky showers at the Telex Motel fighting off the Ted who pretended to mop the floor, because of his predictable habit of sticking his nose over the top of the door for a peek; and Barry Barnes from Hampshire, a cross between Jack Dee and Dave Allen with fingers, who had her in hysterics for weeks over the tragic story of Speedy – his dead tortoise.

It all seemed like an endless summer holiday at the time – swimming, sunbathing, laughing – but there was a catch. The party wasn't to last. In that year, 1989, the world and our working lives were to see some huge, unpleasant changes. Changes that, for a lot of us, proved to be for the worst.

There were rumblings in Yugoslavia which, it has to be admitted, made a lot of us uncomfortable. We began to hear daily of the unrest, the calls for separation, the street demonstrations – and of the number of police being murdered. (Civilians weren't mentioned).

Suddenly they didn't want to be Yugoslav any more. There was talk of Slovenia, Bosnia, Croatia, etc. It meant fuck all to me at the time. Yugo was Yugo – I didn't know any different.

Lech Walesa was stirring things up in Poland; Czechoslovakia began losing its citizens to the 'west'; Hungary, via a bottle of Bull's Blood, started giving their Soviet 'saviours' a hard time; East Germany said as much as their Kremlin-controlled press and the 'Stasi' would allow them to say; top men in Bulgaria began stashing large sums of money – mostly in the west – in readiness for the expected witch-hunts; and Romania stirred too. It sat yet another inch forwards on its un-sprung seat and watched – and waited.

The by-words on everyone's lips at the time were *glasnost* and *perestroika* – and our pet name for vodka – *Gorbachov.*

Things began to happen, the sort of things that just *did not happen* behind the Iron Curtain. Change was definitely in the wind, big change, and for 'us' it was just a matter of time.

It's difficult to remember the exact timing of events over ten years on, but for me I think it really all began when loads of E. European nationals, Poles, Czechs etc., began doing 'runners' from their homelands on an unprecedented scale. Something that didn't happen without dire consequences.

These people began to covertly – and expensively - exit the Commie Bloc in a hundred different ways. A lot of them with the aid of racketeers who offered, at a price of course, to smuggle them into the west, often with promises of jobs (on the 'game' or in sweat-shops mostly).

They came via West Germany, Austria and, to a lesser extent, Italy. I say 'lesser' because, according to the grapevine, the 'eye-ties' who took bribes to let them out of the ports and land borders aren't going to own up to figures, are they?

Things were afoot and suddenly border *kontrols* were tightened. Armed police were seen roaming the countryside and patrolling likely river crossings. Cab and trailer searches at borders from east to west became a lot less fun, as did paperwork and passport *kontrols*. Temperaments became even less pleasant – and *everyone* seemed to be armed to the teeth.

Shock may be too strong a word, but the frontiers of Western Europe were trying to stem a flow of illegal immigrants from communist countries on a scale they'd not had to deal with before – and I think it put the wind up everyone. This wasn't just a case of rounding up the odd one or two that flew over the cuckoo's nest in a microlight.

By enforcing stricter *kontrols* the Austrians were simply hoping to dissuade these people from trying to enter the west via *their* borders. And the Germans were hoping the same. None of them seemed to care too much where these people did go, just as long as it wasn't on *their* patch.

Day after day we heard stories of how ordinary people were risking their lives, those of their families and, more often than not, their life savings to cross rivers, trenches, barbed wire and machine-gun posts to reach the west. *Perestroika* and *Glasnost* had worked their magic and hundreds, possibly thousands, of communist citizens, on a scale not seen since the concrete was poured for the Berlin Wall in 1961, were all trying desperately to flee a sinking ship.

And rumours of revolution were rife.

For Jan all this really began when I took her on what I think was her very last trip with me. Again, I have to say that I don't remember dates, but putting an exact date on something as important (and as protracted) as the break-up of European communism at the arse-end of the twentieth century seems a bit academic here.

We'd been to Ankara to tip a load of plastic pipes after which I – we - were sent all the way to the town of Zadar on the Adriatic coast of Yugoslavia for a return load – of plastic pipes! Jan called it 'Planet Zadar' in a mechanical voice, because it was fucking light-years from Ankara – and, of course, we had to be there by Friday!

Not surprisingly the run to Planet Zadar turned into a bit of a mission, what with getting hopelessly lost – in Sarajevo amongst other places. Seeing what we were *convinced* were skinned sheep-dogs on spits, running out of diesel and, naturally, 'catching' the weekend and being too late to load!

But the biggest shock to Jan wasn't the lovely pizzas we bought in town over the weekend, (she didn't know the Yugos ate pizza!) but was when we eventually left Yugoslavia – after climbing some horrendous hills and cracking a cylinder head in the process – entered 'Eggy-Sheggyland' (Hungary) and had parked our bums at a very cosy, friendly, road-side restaurant for the night, right on the doorstep of the enchanting Lake Balaton.

The television was on (colour, no hissing, good picture – a rarity in E. Europe at the time). As we were feasting on a table-full of splendid tucker, deciding whether to go for a swim or interview a beer, everyone suddenly fell quiet. The volume was turned up and we all stared at the screen in silence. All we saw and heard was mayhem.

Everyone crowded in to watch. And they were silent. The tension and fear could have been cut with a knife. This wasn't murder and chaos on the other side of the world – this was local stuff.

I asked somebody what it was all about, and he pointed, almost crying. 'Yugoslavia,' he told me. In most 'border areas' – anywhere in the world – there are always the so-called 'ethnics' - people on both sides of a barbed-wire 'border' where live aunts, uncles, sons, daughters. So the concern of the locals was understandable.

The shit had hit the fan, big style. What looked to me to be a full-scale war was being 'conducted' not far from where we sat – and we'd just missed it, having exited Yugoslavia that afternoon not suspecting a thing.

It was at this stage of the game that the authorities in Yugo decided to back the police by mobilising the 'Black Shirts' – a kind of para-military police. Their job being to mount road-blocks, get pissed, intimidate everyone, steal what they could from just about anyone, answer to *nobody*, and shoot whoever they fancied under the guise of national security.

It wasn't funny. I rolled up to the *kontrol* post just outside Belgrade one day to be told about one dead German driver. The Black Shirts were off across a field chasing his friend. Armed, with 'safeties' off.

I 'paid' and left, feeling sick.

By this stage of the game – mid to late '89 – I'd actually finished working for Roy, which meant, obviously, that I was no longer an owner-driver.

Even though I'd run the 'Scanny' for the best part of a year, and had (miraculously) made a decent living out of her – even more so when I had a 'Vatican Mack' spoiler kit nailed to her roof in Turkey and cut down on fuel bills by about a farthing per trip – I still found, surprise surprise, that I just couldn't make it pay.

As the saying goes – if you want to make a small fortune in road transport, start with a large one! So I decided one day that life would be a lot less stressful if I chucked in the spanner and went to drive a truck that belonged to someone else – the 'Scanny' had to go.

I also still had ambitions of paying a wheeled visit to the Middle East, which I couldn't do with Roy. He was, by now, flatly refusing to send anyone further east than Turkey, and no further east than the Bosporus if he could avoid it. So I knew it was time for a change.

One day, after the best part of five years with Roy as 'Tanker International', as 'Lawrabian', and as a 'five-minute' owner-driver, I tearfully handed back the keys to BNO 30T (to cover loads of outstanding repair bills and the remainder of the original 'deal'), did an odd trip or three to see things out, and parted company. I had to - the sands of Arabia were calling stronger than ever.

It was around this time that, sadly, Jan's father Jim, died suddenly in Australia. He was a doctor, a good one by all accounts, and I'd never even got to meet him.

Due to the nature of the beast the first I knew about it was when Woodsy – who'd rushed Jan to the airport on just a minute's notice – rang me at the Londra to tell me what had happened, and to say that my beloved was in shock, 12,000 miles away attending the funeral.

By the time Jan came 'home' I was already working for Dave and Richie Thorne down in the Forest of Dean, in Gloucestershire. Richie had always said, 'If you wants a job, moi bub, come an' see me. Oi'll soon sort you out with sumthin.'

And, as good as his word, he did.

Dave, Richie's elder brother, was equally as good and even better to Jan when he and his wife offered to put her up for the duration at their place, the family pile in Lydney, because 'we' had nowhere to live. Or at least Jan didn't – I was practically living in the truck, being away most of the time.

To keep some pennies spinning Jan, bless her liver, took a bar job at the local pub, worked hard to pay her way – and grew quite fond of 'proper' English beer in the process.

I had been put in charge of an old, but charming, 'six-legger' F12 Volvo, a younger sister of the '89, and simply told to 'Get on with it, boy – she's all yours!'

Dave and Richie, and their younger brother Sammy, had been 'doing' the Middle East for a few years, on and off, so I figured it would just be a matter of time before I was posted off to a desert somewhere (Iran, Iraq, Saudi Arabia – anywhere, please – I didn't mind).

By now the situation in Europe was getting worse. It got to the stage one day when I had to tell Jan she wouldn't be coming in the truck with me any more. Things were getting silly all round to the point where I realised I couldn't guarantee her safety any longer. There was no protection, not even at borders, and I wasn't willing to take the risk. Though I did promise to bring her back a goodly supply of Budvar each trip.

My fears weren't unfounded because it was at this stage of the game that Jimmy Ellis took a severe beating in Yugo.

He did absolutely *nothing* to deserve it, seeing as he was stopped in the border queue at Tompa. He'd been in the queue for hours, waiting, shunting forwards, dozing over the steering wheel – when a police car suddenly smashed into his trailer. Three drunken coppers got out of their wrecked car, dragged Jimmy from his truck, and proceeded to beat the shit out of him – blaming *him* for the accident.

Yugoslavia, even though at war with itself, (and anyone else that happened to be there) and with raging inflation (a motorway toll that ran to several million Dinar, for example) was, surprisingly, still open for transit.

The bit between Hungary and Bulgaria was, and still is, Serbia, and although the fighting was about the rest of the fragmenting country – Croatia, Bosnia, etc., and Macedonia – which the Greeks are still in dispute over – the fact that our transit route didn't touch on anyone else's toes did, in effect, help to keep that route open.

Sanctions were imposed by the UN in a lame attempt at wrist-slapping, but they didn't have much effect at the time. Everyone – Serbs, Muslims, Christians, Croats and Uncle Tomasov Kobley, were all shooting at each other in total madness, ignoring pleas from mothers with babes, the UN and the rest of the world – and sanctions were being busted left, right and centre.

A lot of stuff, fuel etc., was entering Yugo not-so-covertly via shipping along the Danube, a part of the world the UN had difficulty policing. After all, the Rumos, Russians and others, all freely sailing up and down the Danube from W. Europe to the Black Sea, all on the lookout to make a few bob, didn't give a toss for the UN and its sanctions, did they?

And neither did anyone else that was running it in overland. Some by way of Greek fuel tankers that were filling up 20,000 litres at a time in Bulgaria, bunging everyone at the borders, then simply driving into Yugo to sell it all for hard cash. And even more came in via TIR traffic, all filled to the brims with cheap Bulgarian 'white', or even cheaper Hungarian 'red'.

Everyone was at it. Winter was fast approaching and fuel was at a premium. The Yugos were offering top dollar – and paying it – and anyone who wanted to make a pretty penny simply filled up with diesel (or petrol, which fetched an even higher price) in leaking top-tanks, saddle-tanks, side-tanks, belly-tanks – and even Jerry cans - drove it through the border, (no bungs from us, the Yugos were loving it) then waited for someone to flag them down.

The 'buyers' were often in charge of rusty old farm tractors and trailers decked out with empty 200-litre drums. All that was required was the patience to pump it over, make sure there was enough left in the running tank to get out of the country, take possession of a rather large wad of Deutschmarks, shake hands – and bugger off.

The actual buyers, most of whom we never saw because they sat in Mercs and BMWs with tinted windows at the ends of the lay-bys were, at one stage, paying two Dm a litre. Hungarian 'red' was only 25 pfennigs a litre and some drivers, on a two-way transit, were making three or four times their wages.

I was even 'forced' on one trip to sell my diesel to a grinning policeman, who made me wait for two hours at a peage until he'd gone off duty and returned with his friend's truck!

We consoled our consciences by saying that the fuel was going only to the needy, to the farmers and peasants who needed to keep the home fires burning – but none of us really knew. Yugo was Yugo, and a Deutschmark is a Deutschmark. So nobody really cared. Sure, some of it probably reached 'undesirables' but who knows? A small amount of it by way of friends, contacts or even neighbours, must have found its way to back-burners or pot-bellied stoves.

Before long the UN put its feet down with a firm hand and enforced the closure of Yugo's borders, which was a bit of a turn-up for us because it meant we had to find alternative routes to Turkey.

Basically there were just two options open to us: Becoming a 'Boat-Person' by taking the ferry from Italy to Greece – which is nice and civilised and all that, but bloody expensive – or by transiting Romania.

Most of us, still desperate to keep the work on and make it pay, decided to start running through Romania, the cheaper, less pleasant option of the two. But being the cheaper there had to be a catch.

And there was.

Romania wasn't geared for it, and neither did it care much. They were suddenly faced with an enormous increase in transit traffic – and they simply didn't want to cope with it. They'd been used to the lazy 'one-truck-an-hour' routine, and were now facing an unprecedented stream of TIR trucks trying to enter and exit their borders on a scale, and with an urgency they'd not had to deal with before – and they didn't like it one little bit.

It was chaos.

Then, when we all thought things couldn't get much worse, they did. In fact, the fucking floor opened up.

One of Richie Thorne's trucks, illustrated by John Nevill

Twenty-Two

Of heroes and villains

At the arse-end of the 1980s communism in Eastern Europe came on stage to take its final bow. The Berlin Wall was not only breached, but literally torn down in chunks. Lumps of concrete with hastily sprayed graffiti were being sold to gullible Americans as genuine parts of the 'wall' – and streams of smoking Trabants chugged westwards to make a killing of their own.

Yugoslavia was becoming a jigsaw of states with hastily erected sheds plonked on roadsides under the guise of international borders. Czechoslovakia was threatening to split into two, Greece moved tanks and troops to its Northern border with Macedonia, Hungary told Russia to fuck off out of its country, Poland went tits up, Russia – or the USSR as it was – threw a wobbler of its own and, just to put the icing on the cake, Romania - bless its tarpaulin ankle socks – went and staged a very sudden, and very violent, revolution.

Dictator Nicolae Ceauçescu after trying to do an ill-fated runner with his wife and somebody's family silver, was collared and executed (so we're told) at Tirgovişte Army Barracks on Christmas Day 1989 – the timing of which I personally find a bit suspect. I think it more likely that he was beaten to death at an earlier date, then simply thrown out for the cameras on the 25th.

But that's only an opinion.

Either way it made no difference because from that date on – Merry Christmas all – the 200 gates were open. After forty-odd years of oppression, free travel on the gas-buses, full, enforced employment and no contraception, the people of Romania had just won their freedom!

Whoopee. Great news for them, but a fucking nightmare for the rest of us. The animals were loose, law and order were nowhere to be seen, the screams could be heard in the dark —and Romania quickly earned the nickname of Jurassic Park.

Terry – I'll not give his full name – got caught up in it all in Timisoara, the city in SW Romania where the violent revolution actually started. For him it simply began – and then turned into a nightmare. It began without obvious warning; without build-up, and Terry was stuck right in the middle of it all.

He was there for whatever reason, tipping or loading, it's not important now, when crowds of people began stoning his truck for no apparent reason. Terry's a man with well over twenty years of experience on the road, but he didn't need to be Einstein to figure out that the best place to be was elsewhere – so he floored it and tried to escape.

But there was a problem, the roads suddenly became choked by thousands of people fighting, screaming – killing each other. So he took his only option and ended up scraping under some low, arched bridges. Not that it mattered because he was immediately brought to a halt by an army of fully armed riot police.

A blessing in disguise you might say. Well, yes and no: The immediate danger of being beaten or stoned to death had been averted, but a longer agony was about to begin because the riot police forced him to stop where he was – for four days and nights as the revolution took place right in front of his eyes!

He told me the story as we sat in my cab one evening interviewing a few tins of Guinness. I saw the horror in his eyes as he recalled the events of those days and nights. Of the incessant noise, the gut-wrenching screaming, the beatings and the other sounds – the gunshots. Corpses lined the streets, alongside the beaten, the mutilated, and the dying, illuminated by scores of fires raging uncontrolled.

He told me the story very quietly, almost as if I wasn't there, trying in his own words to describe how it felt to be totally alone in an unprotected truck, miles from home, watching and listening to hordes of human beings kill and mutilate each other.

More than ten years on he still wakes from the horror of it, gasping, sweating, seeing and hearing it all over and over.

There was no actual finish to his story. It didn't really need one. He just fell quiet and stared at the dark through the windscreen – and I was trying to hold back a tear. So we sat in silence for a while. We were parked in a scabby little Romanian TIR park at the time.

Terry wasn't the only driver in Romania when it all went off. A few of the lads were there, and all have stories to tell.

'Big T' was there. A jolly eighteen stone Mancunian. I don't know his story, but I do know he was lucky enough to get out of the country in one piece – only to lose his life in an accident on the M1 in England soon after.

The border queues to get in and out of Romania soon got worse. And more dangerous. The queues began to stretch – two kilometres… two and a half. Trucks were 'parked' nose to tail. Two days and nights, with nights being the worst.

Drivers were constantly being hassled by gangs demanding money with menace, going without sleep, getting into fights, always on nerves-edge and being totally ignored by the police, by our Embassies and, more often than not, by the guy in front.

Three k's… Three and a half… Four…

The rule that said 'no contact with outsiders' suddenly didn't apply anymore, and not only did the arseholes quickly make up for lost time, they didn't have to look very far, did they? After all, there were literally kilometres of 'rich' western TIR drivers queued up in the dark waiting to part company with their hard-earned cash, their clothes, food, cigarettes… their loads.

A lot of us took to running in convoy, working on the premise of safety in numbers – but it didn't help that much - if there were five of you, there were ten of them. If a driver jumped out of his cab to help matey in front, his own cab was likely to be broken into, or he might simply get a bar across his head for his trouble.

Four and a half k's… Five… Three days.

One of the biggest problems, work-wise, was the amount of trucks – and loads, of course – that were being dumped. And not just in Romania. A lot of 'new' drivers suddenly decided that because Eastern Europe wasn't communist any more they'd like to 'have a go'; like to get a few stamps on their passports, etc., thought that the 'Commie Bloc' was now a safe bet (though why none of them ventured east when 'the wall' was up is beyond me).

So, every man and his dog quickly loaded up, saddled up, swaggered around a lot, then abandoned their charges halfway down and went home again.

There were trucks, trailers and cargoes dumped all over Europe, which left a lot of cleaning up for everyone else. These guys would get off the boat, do a couple of days' driving, pick up some news on the grapevine – and then lose their 'bottle'. That grapevine news was readily available in the UK – before they loaded! They could have learnt everything they needed to know back home - about the borders, the lack of any form of security or secure parking, of the stress, lack of sleep, of the baseball bats and c.s. gas, *before* taking out an expensive truck, and equally valuable loads.

And the aggro wasn't just at the borders. It's nearly seven hundred k's from any Hungarian border to cross Romania to Giurgiu. The state of Romanian roads at the time beggared belief, so it was more than could be expected of anyone to transit that distance (at an average speed of just 50 kph – 30mph) and then spend days in a queue without rest.

Stop in a lay-by and you may as well put both hands up in surrender.

Five and a half k's… Six…

The worst border of all was Giurgiu. There was no lighting, no police protection (they were either scared off – or paid off) and no movement.

Six and a half k's… Seven…

A driver simply joined the back of the queue, exhausted, and stopped. The handbrake went on and that was it for hours. Come nightfall or daybreak there might be a bit of a move. Just a few truck lengths maybe – assuming someone up front hadn't fallen asleep over the wheel – then the handbrake went on again.

In the meantime gangs of kids – mostly gypsies – of all ages appeared, brandishing sponges, squeegees, or just a plastic bottle full of water and a rock, *demanding* to wash your windscreen for payment, juggling the rock from hand to hand. A lot of the time they were 'politely' refused, whereupon the windscreen wouldn't need washing anymore, or, more often than not, the heavies would arrive by car soon after and demand money with slightly more menace.

Seven and a half k's… Eight…

These 'heavies' (they wouldn't have been so heavy in 'The Forest') mostly dark-skinned gypsies, as opposed to the fair-skinned English-Irish version, were always armed with knives and firearms, and, predictably, mob-handed. Brave bastards.

Most of them, dressed like '50s spivs with crombies, long greasy hair and trilbies, looked like George Cole (Arthur Daley) in his 'St. Trinians' role… but they weren't half as funny. And they wanted their penny's worth. A lot of the time they got it, though fights frequently broke out (running battles sometimes) and stab wounds were a regular thing. There was more than one killing too.

Eight and a half k's… Nine…

I won't listen to all the 'heroes' who say, 'I just told 'em to fuck off, didn't I?' because the people who come out with that shit either weren't there, or have very short memories. Like not forgetting the Pole who jumped out for a piss and had his throat cut.

We were alone, left to our own devices, and I don't mind admitting that, at the time, it was scary stuff. Our lives, not to mention the truck, trailer and load, were under constant threat. A lot of responsibility for underpaid, soft-skinned humans.

Nine k's… Ten… Eleven…

The Embassies, ours in particular, bless their red, white and blue taxpayer's socks, did absolutely *fuck all!* They just shrugged their shoulders, hung up the phone, or simply refused to acknowledge us, hoping we, and the 'problem' would go away.

And the queues stretched…

And the casualty list grew…

To top it all loads of 'do-gooders' began to arrive on Romania's doorstep with trailer-loads of free gifts! 'Aid to Romania' to help feed and clothe the bastards! They arrived sporting red crosses on the front of their donated trucks (advertising), official letters stating that they were carrying humanitarian aid, etc. They were then (illegally) charged an arm and a leg for entry visas!

We met these people *en route*, told them to go back home, warned them that they were likely to get beaten up and/or robbed, that a red cross and an ego actually meant fuck all, that they'd do a greater service distributing the goodies to needy children back home… but they were all deaf and blind to us… As were the French, the Swiss, the Paddies…

They were all on an ego trip, playing god to the poor and needy. Bless their honourable intentions and all that, but they wouldn't have it that most of the goodies they brought in ended up on the black market as soon as their backs were turned; that the only people who benefited from this 'humanitarian aid' were, in reality, *everyone* involved – *bar the children*!

And still they came.

And the queues stretched.

Twelve k's… Thirteen… Three days and nights… No sleep… Hassle…

It was like a bad dream, but we were all 'expected' to put up with it - without back-up and without complaint. The harassment was constant, as was the fear – the dread of the next loud drum-roll of fists on the cab door, the next bevvy of grinning faces to appear at the window at 3 a.m. – of the next battle.

TIR drivers must have the cleanest windscreens of any truck between Moscow and Muscat, but the strain soon began to tell.

A lot of guys said enough was enough and decided to become 'boat people' and cut their losses. A lot more decided to chuck it in altogether, and I can't say I blame them.

Before too long the numbers of British TIR 'Overlanders' began to dwindle, and when I heard on the grapevine that the queue at Giurgiu had passed the 20 km marker one trip, I decided to try the Calafat ferry instead – and spent nearly four days and nights trying to cross the Danube to Bulgaria.

I then decided enough was enough. In August 1990 I rolled into Zeebrugge Docks, set fire to all my mickey permits, went back to England and threw the towel in. Jan and I then hopped a tube train to Heathrow, boarded one of Aeroflot's finest, spent a month in Thailand – then buggered off to Australia.

Fuck the queues.

At the end of a scorching February in 1991, on return from a one-month tour of the Australian outback, I pulled up outside her mother's house in our overheating VW Golf, knackered.

As Jan struggled with the luggage I happened to notice that the television was on, a rare daytime event, and that, so too, was the Gulf War.

In the cool of the air-conditioned front room I stood rooted to the spot, watching allied aircraft bomb the shit out of drainholes and chimney-pots, while a massive force of combined troops assembled for the forthcoming ground assault into Kuwait.

I was fascinated, but horrified. I may have had friends there! Drivers – mates – that regularly drove to both Iraq and Kuwait. Were they okay? Had any of them been caught up in all this mayhem?

For their sakes I hoped not.

I was wrong.

A few days later I could stand the tension no longer. I had to speak to someone. The Australian public, though fully aware of the facts via NBC News, seemed 'distanced', uninterested, as if it was someone else's problem 'over there'. So I phoned 'home'.

Kate answered.

'John!' She almost accused (how do women do that?) 'where are you?'

'What? What did I do now? I only rang to say hello!'

'Where are you?' she yelled again.

'Er, I'm in Australia.'

'No, not good enough. Oi need you over 'ere, John, roit now.'

'Bit awkward, luv. I'm 12,000 miles away. What's up?'

'What's up? The war! The Kuwait war!'

'Sorry Kate – I'm only 5'7" and I haven't got a gun.'

'Oh, shut up you silly sod. The war's over. It's you oi need, an' your passport – *yesterday*!'

'Why do you want my passport?'

'Oh what're you loik? For visas, you silly bugger – you're going to Kuwait!'

THE END

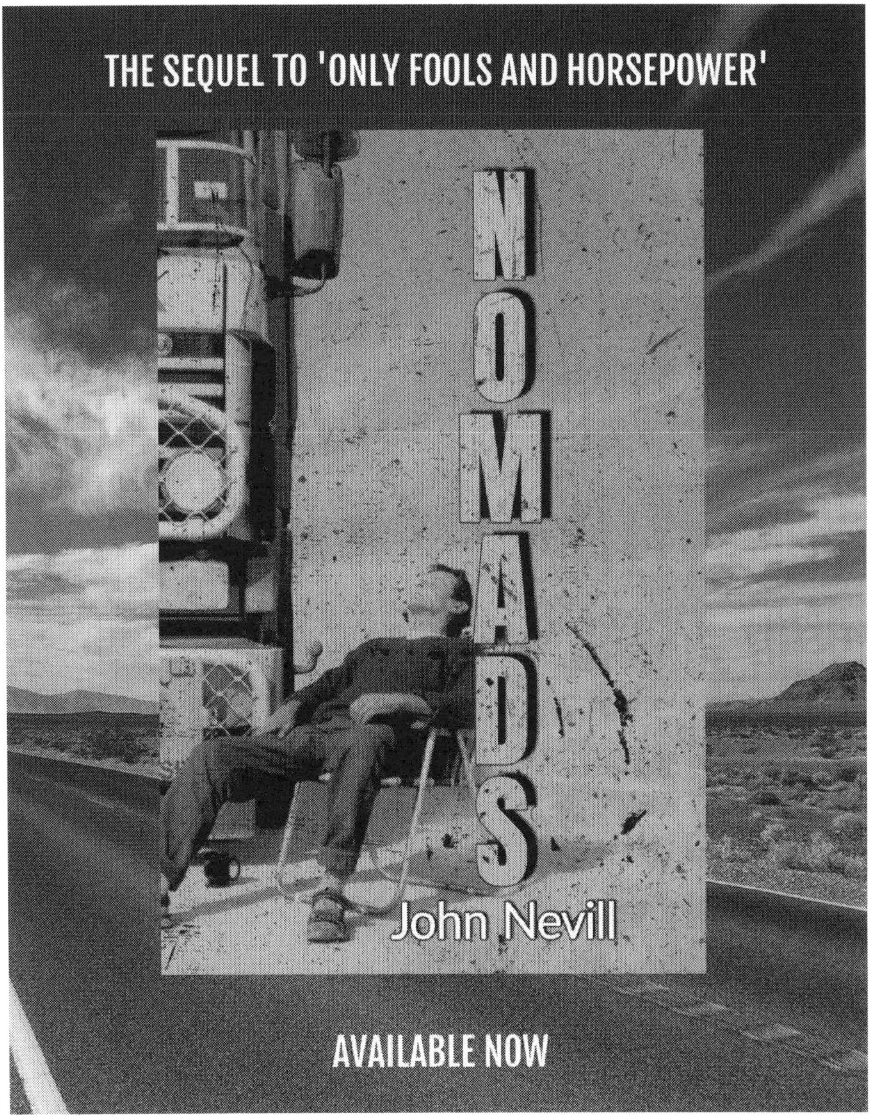
THE SEQUEL TO 'ONLY FOOLS AND HORSEPOWER'
NOMADS
John Nevill
AVAILABLE NOW

With Special Thanks
(in alphabetical order)

Alex 'Al The German'

Alex Clarke Smith and Sarah Clarke Smith

Bernie McGawley

Carl Strangeway

Charlotte Nevill

Darren Eiffert

David Pryce

Diane Berridge

Edward Higgins

Ellis Evans

Emma Wilson

Graham Ball

Jack Duckworth

John Cooper

Paul Coleman

Paul Hawkins and Tracey Hawkins

Pete Matthew

Phil McEveley

Richard Thorne and Tracy Thorne

Roger Haywood

Steve Neale

Stuart Jeffries

Printed in Great Britain
by Amazon

85303552R00131